D1358960

DECEIT

Enjoy!
Diane Sheehan Shovak

Diane Sheehan Shovak

Spilled Ink Press

Dedication

To my family

My husband Rich, my children Kristen and Michael,

And my grandchildren Jack and Finn

"The cruelest lies are often told in silence."

Robert Louis Stevenson

1

July

Dangling one foot in the cool water, Kate Rourke found relief from the stifling heat, so rare for a summer night in Vermont. She had come down to the dock to escape the intolerable closeness of the bedroom after yet another scorching argument with Jack.

Pulling the soft T-shirt away from her sweat-soaked body, Kate rested her head against the wooden post. There was no moon. The stars were duller than usual, their light filtered through the wet blanket of humidity. Kate smiled when she located the Big Dipper, the first constellation her dad had shown her when she was a little girl. Closing her eyes, she allowed herself to sink into the blackness.

The roar of a motorboat approaching at full torque ripped apart the stillness of the lake. Kate's eyes snapped open. She jumped to her feet and scanned the black expanse. Nothing. She couldn't differentiate the boat from the water or the shore. There were no running lights. *Jesus!* Boating at this time of night could be dangerous. Not having lights was insane.

A low idling replaced the full throttle of the engine. Kate heard yelling. A female voice carried across the water. "Can't take it ... stupid ... jealous."

Holding the post, Kate leaned out over the water and strained her eyes, trying to penetrate the darkness. Words, louder, almost hysterical, struck her like hailstones. "Sick ... this shit ... you!"

She heard a loud crash, then another, and another. Like things were being thrown around. Then random splashes. Was someone hurling objects overboard? "Messed up ... nothing happened ... drunk." It sounded more like a young girl than a woman.

Underlying all this was a muffled lower pitched tone that was swallowed up by the sound of the motor. A man?

"Fuck you!" It was the girl again.

Then a splash—different and deep sounding.

Kate recognized the sound of someone jumping, diving, or being pushed into the water. She'd spent enough summers on the lake with her children when they were younger to know. Usually it was in fun. But the memory of Tim falling off the back of the boat when he was six reverberated through her and she shivered. Despite the years, it's a sound a mother never forgets.

She listened. Silence. Someone had cut the motor.

Kate jumped from the dock into the family boat and grabbed the Maglite from the emergency box. "Damn it!" She shook the light, banged it, and threw it down in frustration. Back on the dock, she took the first few steps up to the house two at a time.

"Are you crazy?" The male voice, clear for the first time, paralyzed her.

Kate grabbed the railing with both hands. Rough splinters dug into her palms. She jerked as loud repetitive whacks echoed off the mountains. Her insides twisted with each crack of something being hit.

"Quit playing games." He sounded angry, frustrated.

Kate forced herself to turn toward that solitary voice.

No!

Pushing down her fears, she vaulted the last few steps as something else hit the water. She threw the switch for the spotlight. It bathed only the dock and boat in light. The surrounding water remained black. Kate focused on the middle of the lake. Dead silence hung in the moist air.

The motor started up. Stunned, she listened as the boat took off. Still with no lights.

2

Sweat-matted hair sticking to her forehead, Kate charged into the house and turned on all the lights. She raced up to the loft bedroom. The sight of her husband's inert form angered her, just as his earlier drinking had. "Jack, wake up." She shook his shoulder.

Lifting his head an inch from its prone position, he squinted through bloodshot eyes. "What the…? Have you lost your mind?"

"I think someone went overboard and is still in the water." She turned on the bedside lamp. "I heard a boat, then yelling, things being thrown around and into the water. Then one big splash." The words tumbled out in a breathless stream.

Jack rubbed his face and leaned on one elbow. "Slow down. What are you talking about? Where were you?"

"On the dock."

"What were you doing on the dock? Never mind." He glanced out the window. "What time is it?"

"I don't know." She looked at the bedside clock.

"Three-thirty."

"You're waking me up at three-thirty in the morning?" He rolled back onto his stomach and pulled the pillow over his head. "I've had enough drama for one night. I'm going back to sleep."

She grabbed the pillow. "Did you hear what I said? Someone's in trouble." She was in his face.

"Yeah, we are," he mumbled into the mattress. "Unless you found some money floating by on the weeds."

"Listen to me, Jack." She pulled the sheet off him. "It sounded like a young girl. There was an argument and she's in the water. I know it. I didn't hear her again after the big splash. Maybe she jumped or was pushed, I don't know. But the boat left. Just took off and left her! We have to do something."

"Like what?" He groaned and reached for the pillow but she still had it. "Sounds to me like kids out for a good time, probably drinking—underage. Happens all the time."

"There was a fight." It came out strained with desperation. "Somebody throwing things."

"Dumping the empties, my guess."

"I couldn't see. I tried to shine the flashlight but the batteries were dead. And the spotlight didn't reach far enough."

He grabbed the pillow, punched it and folded it under his head. "Let it go, and shut off the damn light. Come back to bed."

"No. We have to go out there and look for her. A 911 call will get routed through God knows where. It's not like at home. It will be too late."

Jack struggled to a sitting position, his bare chest glistening with sweat. "I'm too tired for this, Kate." He pushed fingers through his dark hair. "You want to track down a bunch of locals? Count me out."

"Fine. I'll do it myself." She grabbed her cell and headed for the door.

"You can't go out there alone."

"Watch me."

"Dammit, Kate. Where the hell are my shorts?"

She heard him stumbling around as she slammed the bedroom door. Kate ran downstairs and grabbed the large flashlight kept in the kitchen for emergencies.

She was down at the boat untying the bowline when Jack jumped in. Releasing the stern, he turned on the running lights and eased the Bayliner out. Without speaking, he kept the engine to a low rumble as Kate navigated them to the place she thought she'd heard the fight. There wasn't a breath of air and with Jack's imposing silence, she felt as if she were suffocating.

Despite the heat, Kate shivered. Underwater a swimmer ran the risk of getting tangled in weeds. In the shallow areas, there were water snakes. She imagined being abandoned in this inky water and prayed they were in the right place. The male voice she'd heard intruded into her thoughts. She pushed it away.

They trolled slowly, without speaking to each other. Kate shone the light into the water, attracting every bug in the area. Swatting blood-thirsty mosquitoes, they called out and searched, going back and forth until they reached the opposite shore. The light glowed in the shallow water and on the bank. Nothing.

Humid air hung heavy, intensifying the rank smell of weeds.

Jack cursed the tangle of native pondweed and invasive milfoil that hampered their vision. "I can't see a damn thing in this crap. I'm done." He rubbed his eyes and started to turn the boat around.

"Wait. I see something." Kate leaned over the bow.

Groaning, he maneuvered the boat toward where she pointed.

"Yeah, empty beer cans and some full ones. What did I tell you?"

"No, there's something else. There." She pointed off the port side.

The bow of the boat tapped something. Jack grabbed the light and leaned over to retrieve an oar. The surface was newly gouged and the side splintered, exposing fresh wood.

Kate remembered the whacking sound she'd heard. "Now do you believe me that something happened out here?"

"Yeah, somebody had a party. And we've got the beer cans and a busted oar to prove it!" He gunned the engine and headed back across the lake toward home.

"I'm going with my gut on this," she yelled over the roar of the engine. "I'm calling the constable." She checked her cell. "No service. I'll call from home."

"And tell him what? You think somebody's in the middle of the lake even though you can't see your hand in front of your face and we found nothing?"

Once at the dock, Kate left Jack to secure the boat, ran up to the house and made the call. She put a robe on over her thin T-shirt and boxers and made a fresh pot of coffee. Ignoring the unmarked canister of decaf on the counter, she reached on tiptoes into the back of the cabinet. This morning they needed caffeine.

Jack came into the kitchen. "Getting out the high test, I see. Did you think I didn't know you've been substituting decaf since my last check-up?"

Kate didn't answer. There was a time when a comment like that would have ended with a flash of Jack's famous smile—the smile he used to end every argument, the smile that undid her every time. But no more.

She moved away before he could touch her. "The constable will be here shortly."

He shook his head. "I'm surprised he's even coming. How'd you reach him? There are no blue pages in the phone book for Willow Bend and you don't know his name, do you?"

"I cut out the list of town officials and their phone numbers from the last town report. I put it on the bulletin board."

"Of course you did. Perfect Kate. It must be nice to be you." The heat of anger emanating from him seared her. "I'm going to put on a shirt."

3

Constable Norm Johnson filled the doorway. Just under six feet, he must have weighed at least 250 pounds. Dressed in a rumpled shirt and jeans, he did not look happy to be called out of bed before dawn. He removed his baseball cap and brushed a hand over short graying hair, cut regulation military style.

Accepting a mug of black coffee, Johnson sat down in one of the dark brown leather chairs flanking the fieldstone fireplace. Kate sat opposite him on the couch. He took out a small notebook and a pencil and leaned forward. "You see something out on the lake last night, Mrs. Rourke?" He glanced out the two-story floor-to-ceiling windows facing the lake. "It was pretty dark."

Kate shook her head. "No, it was what I *heard*. It was early this morning around three. I was on the dock."

"Why was that?" Eyes narrowing, he looked up from his notebook.

"It was very hot in our bedroom, Constable. I needed to cool off."

Johnson looked at Jack who shrugged. "And what was it you heard, Mrs. Rourke, while you were cooling off?"

His tone was condescending but Kate continued. "A boat going at full throttle with no running lights. Then an argument between a male and a female, a young girl maybe."

"Could you hear what they were saying?" He settled back into the chair.

"A few words here and there from the woman or girl like 'can't take it, stupid, sick of you.' Things like that. And there was some swearing."

"Like what?"

"Like 'shit' and the f-word." Kate shifted in her chair. "Then things crashing and splashing, like someone throwing things around and into the water."

He rested an ankle on one knee. "You said there were two people. Did you hear the male?"

Kate hesitated, feeling the knot in her stomach tighten. "His voice was pretty much drowned out by the motor. I did hear him say, 'Quit playing games.'"

"Sounds like kids, probably liquored up, out for a good time." He sighed.

"We did find beer cans—some full, some empty— when we went out on the boat." Jack, standing off to the side, spoke for the first time.

The constable nodded to him. "Goes on all the time." He uncrossed his legs and stood.

"Constable, wait." She saw his eyes narrowed in frustration. "I know what I heard, and it wasn't a party. The argument intensified, then I heard one last splash, loud and deep like a person going in."

"But you didn't actually *see* any of this." His voice was clipped. "Hard to tell what a splash might be when you can't see anything. Did you hear anyone thrashing about? Calling for help?"

"No, but I know what it sounds like when someone goes overboard. My son fell out of our boat when he was six." She saw Jack roll his eyes. "We were slowing down, getting ready to put out the anchor to swim. He was on the back of the boat and lost his balance. He had his life jacket on, but it's not a sound I will ever forget." She looked to Jack who said nothing.

Johnson shrugged. "That may be, Mrs. Rourke, but I don't have much to go on here. As for someone in the water tonight, could be they were skinny-dippin'. Hot night like this." Johnson wiped his brow and smiled at Jack. "That might explain the lack of lights."

"But I never heard the girl again!" Her voice quaking, she leaned into the constable.

"Could be she got back in the boat and passed out. You did say the boat took off shortly after that."

"Yes, but before that I heard loud banging like someone hitting something. Hitting it hard. And we found an oar that was all gouged up." She knew she was talking fast.

Without a word, Johnson put his back to Kate and turned to Jack. "Where'd you find the oar, Mr. Rourke?"

Stunned into silence, she watched Jack motion with his head toward the windows.

"Over by the far shore across from here," Jack said.

"Well, it may or may not have anything to do with the rest of it. Hard to tell. I'll include it when I file your statement." The constable returned the small notebook to his back pocket and shook Jack's hand. "My guess, just some kids messin' around. I wouldn't worry about it."

"Wait! Someone could still be in the water." Kate

stood, her fists clenched at her sides. Johnson was already at the door but turned to face Kate. "You and your husband didn't find any signs of that. And you really didn't *see* anything. I'm sure everything's fine. I'll be in touch if we need anything else."

"That's it? Aren't you going to investigate or something?"

"Mrs. Rourke." His voice deepened. "I know how to do my job, and that's what I'm doing. I'll take a ride around the lake on my way home, see if I see anything."

Kate looked at Jack. "Say something!"

"Uh, Constable Johnson, thank you for coming," Jack pointed at the oar leaning against the deck door. "What about the oar? Do you want it?"

"Yeah, sure." The constable took it and looked it over. "It's been damaged that's for sure, but we don't know how or even when. And we can't get fingerprints off wet wood." He shrugged then turned back to Kate. "Thanks for the coffee."

Kate exploded when the door closed. "The guy's an incompetent jerk. He just totally blew us off!" She stood in front of Jack and glared at him. "God, Jack. Thanks for coming? What about the oar? That's the best you could do?"

"What's with you, Kate? Let it go. You called. He came. The guy didn't think there was any foul play. *I* told you that but you wouldn't listen." He started up the stairs. "I'm going back to bed."

"I can't let it go," Kate said to the empty room. Her body was taut, a violin string ready to snap.

She walked to the French doors that opened onto the deck and stared at the lake. Was someone still out there? For an instant it wasn't Willow Lake Kate was seeing. It was another lake and another young girl. She shuddered at the

12

memory.

The black shroud was lifting now. Early morning fog would give way to sunlight. But the lake would still hide whatever secrets lay beneath.

Kate's thoughts turned to the other voice in the boat. She hugged her arms to her chest. *It couldn't have been him; he wouldn't do that, just leave her.* She checked her watch. It was too early. She'd call his cell in an hour or so.

A raw sense of dread settled low in her belly. She was a mother. In her gut, she knew.

4

Hannah Ward stirred her cold coffee, the chipped Formica tabletop littered with empty Sweet 'n Low packets. She rubbed her forehead. The aspirin hadn't touched the pounding headache.

Daylight seeped in through the cracks in the trailer walls. It was five o'clock. She had woken about two a.m. and checked Mel's room. Her bed hadn't been slept in. Curfews meant nothing to her daughter no matter what Hannah did. She'd tried grounding her, taking away her cell phone, demanding passwords to de-activate social media accounts— nothing worked. Mel would stay out until two or three in the morning, but never all night.

Hannah's hand shook as she dialed Mel's cell. She'd lost count of the number of times she had called. Again, it went straight to voicemail. Tears filled Hannah's eyes as terrifying images ran through her mind. She fingered the dull brown braid that hung heavily over one shoulder.

She was tired, so tired of everything—the waiting and

worrying every night, the struggling to make ends meet. Once Kmart had closed along with most of the other businesses in the area, jobs were hard to come by. The few days a week she cleaned houses up at the lake weren't enough. Hannah ground out her cigarette in the overflowing ashtray. Leaning on the table, she pushed her considerable bulk up off the chair.

She tied the belt on the threadbare cotton robe and scuffed across the worn linoleum to the counter. Grabbing the phone book, she glanced again at the faded plastic wall clock in the shape of a teapot. It was early but she didn't care. She'd wake them all.

One by one she called the homes of Mel's friends and woke their parents. Hannah waited as the teenagers were roused.

No one had seen her. At least that's what they said.

Taking a deep breath, she dialed the one number she dreaded calling. He answered on the first ring.

"Johnson here." A pause. "Hello? Is anyone there?"

"It's Hannah." She heard him sigh.

"What can I do for you, Hannah?"

"It's Mel. She didn't come home last night."

"And this surprises you, why?"

"Norm," she pleaded in a small voice.

"You knew it was just a matter of time. I'm sure she'll come home when she's good and ready."

"Wait, Norm. Don't hang up. It feels different this time. She's never stayed out all night before and she won't answer her cell or texts." There was no response. "Are you still there?"

"I'm here." His voice sounded tight, strained. "When did you see her last?"

"Dinner last night, around six."

"Then where'd she go?"

"I don't know." She swallowed.

"What do you mean you don't know? The kid's fifteen! You have absolutely no control over that girl, Hannah."

"About as much as my mother had over me at fifteen." She locked her lips letting it sink in.

Norm cleared his throat. "I'm guessing she's out partying and answering a call from her mother isn't big on her list. Probably crashed in some college boy's dorm room. You do know she's been hanging out up at the college, right? Guess she's too good for the kids in town. That was good enough for you and me."

"First of all, there is no you and me. Hasn't been for a long time. Second, I've *told* her to stay away from the college. She doesn't listen to me. She's not the only one going there." She clenched her jaw. Why did she let him do this to her?

"Don't make it right, Hannah. If she was my daughter, she'd damn well be home and I'd know where she'd been."

"Norm, stop. The important thing is, she's *not* home." She took a deep breath. "Mel's a good kid no matter what you think. And she's smart, smarter than me. She's got the brains to make it out of this town. Something I could never do."

"Hanging around with college boys doesn't seem so smart to me. She's asking for trouble and you know it."

"Forget it. I don't know why I bothered to call. I'll find her myself."

Hannah hung up on him and it felt good. At eighteen, he was the handsomest boy she'd ever known. She was fifteen when she fell in love with him—and he had broken her heart.

She wouldn't let herself think about Norm. She got dressed and grabbed her car keys and cell. Driving the winding road that hugged the lake, Hannah checked out all the local haunts: the meadow, the fairgrounds behind the elementary school, the abandoned girls' camp near the state park. She saw no one. She looked at the dashboard clock. It was doubtful anyone would be up this early on a Saturday morning but she had to try. She continued north and drove the few miles to Ethan Allen College.

Approaching the imposing iron gates, Hannah sat up tall. Cold sweat formed on the back of her neck. She drove the deserted campus, eerie in the early morning light, and tried several of the buildings including dorms. Everything was locked.

Seeing a lone runner on the track, she got out and approached him. "Do you know Melody Ward?" He shook his head and continued his run, never slowing his pace.

Back in the car, Hannah grabbed the steering wheel with both hands and lay her head against it. Tears soaked her face and neck.

What if she'd come home? Hannah called the landline and waited, imagining the loud rings banging against the trailer walls. She wiped her eyes and dialed her best friend.

"Carrie, it's me. I know it's early but I need your help. Mel didn't come home. I'm out looking for her. Can you go to my house in case she shows up?"

"Sure. What else can I do?"

"Nothing. Just please, call me if she comes home."

Hannah thought hard. There was one more place. A place she never went anymore. After calling and texting Mel again, Hannah headed for the old quarry.

~~

17

Norm stared at the phone with his mouth open. Who was she to hang up on him?

How many times had he tried to tell her that Mel was headed down the wrong road? He'd tried to tell Mel too. But did they listen? No. Now he was supposed to solve the problem?

He ground his teeth and fumed. With an election coming up, contested for the first time, he didn't need her bringing this to him right now. People in this town had memories like elephants. They remembered all his mistakes and many considered Hannah one of them.

The phone rang again. "Constable Johnson."

"Constable, this is Kate Rourke on West View Road."

"Yes, Mrs. Rourke." Norm tipped his chair back and swallowed the irritation in his voice.

"Did you see anything when you rode around the lake this morning when you left our home?"

Had he told her he was going to do that? "Uh, nope. Nothing out of the ordinary."

"Did anyone else hear anything or report someone missing?"

Norm hesitated and felt the first pangs of uncertainty creep into his gut. "I follow up on all leads, Mrs. Rourke. That's my job. Enjoy the weekend with your family now." He hung up before she could ask more questions.

He leaned forward and chewed on a fingernail. Could Mel be in trouble? Was it different this time or just the usual partying? Hannah had annoyed him with her intrusion, but worry had crept in that she might be right.

He fingered the white marble rock that served as a paperweight on his desk. He remembered the day he'd gotten it. It was the summer he turned eighteen.

A vision of a young, pretty Hannah flashed in his mind. He could see the sun glinting off the red highlights in her hair. She was tiny and fit perfectly against him. They were at the quarry with a group of his friends.

The beer came out and games of "chicken" began—how high they would climb before jumping into ice cold water of unknown depth, just to prove their manhood. Norm shook his head. "God, adolescent boys are so stupid!"

He smiled. Hannah could hold her own with the boys. She was fearless, jumping from the highest ledge. Later she spread her towel on one of the rock outcroppings and lay down in the sun. She wore a modest navy and white two-piece bathing suit, nothing like those skimpy things the girls wear now. Norm sat down beside her and offered her a beer. Her bright blue eyes sparkled with mischief all the time, even when she was trying to be serious. Her laugh could bring him back from dark places, and back then his life was a black hole.

They went for a walk through the woods to the more secluded "back quarry." But they never made it to the rope swing. They made love for the first time that day on a bed of pine needles at the edge of the quarry, high above the deep pool of blue black water. He knew he was playing with fire; she was only fifteen. Hannah found two pieces of white quarry marble and gave him one. Did she still have hers?

He put the white rock back on the pile of papers needing his attention. He had to try, for Hannah. He called Travis Cunningham at home. The second constable was in his twenties and probably not up yet.

"Yeah, Norm, what's up?" He sounded groggy.

"Mel Ward didn't come home last night. I'm gonna take a ride and look around, maybe head out to the quarry. The college crowd is drinking there now too, not just the usual suspects from town. If I don't find anything, I want you to ask around, talk to some of the kids. See if any of them were at that party we got the complaint about last night. Find out if they've seen Mel. They like you. Somebody has to know something. In the meantime, come on in and cover the office."

"You got it. I'll be there as soon as I can."

Traffic was backed up on the state road by Hager farm. With lights flashing, Norm went around the cars to the intersection of Quail Ridge Road where a hay truck had smashed into an SUV. Norm assessed the scene and called the paramedics and the state police.

A woman and two children were still in the SUV. The rear door on the driver's side was pushed in beside the younger child's car seat. The children were crying but didn't appear to be injured. The mother was holding her left arm at an awkward angle but was able to answer his questions. Norm told them to stay put until the paramedics arrived. The truck had rolled over into a ditch. The driver was unresponsive, his pulse thready and weak.

Norm heard the sirens and called Travis, who answered on the first ring.

"There's been an accident where Route 30 intersects Quail Ridge by Hager's farm. EMTs and the state police are on the way. I need you to get over here to divert traffic and help with witness statements while we clean up this mess."

"Did you make it to the quarry?"

"That'll have to wait. We could be looking at a fatality here."

5

Kate slammed her cell down on the granite counter. "That man is infuriating. I don't think he's done one thing to follow up on what we told him."

Jack looked up from the paperwork spread out on the kitchen table. "You're like a pit bull. These small town cops have their own way of doing things. What *we* need to do right now is discuss these bills. Calmly."

"We went through this last night." She was irritated and sleep deprived.

"No, we didn't. You didn't let me finish. If Tim doesn't get his act together, pass these summer classes and get the financial aid reinstated, we're screwed."

Tim. Kate sighed. The issues changed but the predictable choosing up of sides was always the same in this dance of theirs, well-choreographed after years of marriage and parenthood.

Jack took his reading glasses off. Bloodshot eyes

bored into hers. "We can't keep doing this."

"Doing what?" She frowned. "His college tuition?"

Jack nodded. "Things are tight."

"What about our investments, our stocks? I signed last year's tax return. The money's there."

"You're an educated woman, Kate. Don't you read the papers? Markets have crashed big time. Most of our stocks have tanked and tuition is way up."

"I know what I make after twenty years in the classroom, even with the time I stayed home with the kids. And I know what you make. Our savings balance was very comfortable the last time I looked."

"I withdrew some to put into a CD with a better return but it's locked in for five years. I told you."

"No, you didn't. How much? Don't you need two signatures to do that?"

"Don't worry about it." He waved his hand at her.

"Don't wave your hand at me. I *do* worry about it. How much?"

"I don't know." He shrugged. "A few thousand."

"How much is a few?" She walked around the island to the table.

He shuffled papers. "I don't have the numbers here."

"What aren't you telling me, Jack? A few thousand shouldn't break us." He didn't respond. "We have excellent credit. We could take out a home equity loan or a second mortgage if we have to."

"I already re-mortgaged the house and could still lose the business."

"Lose the business? And you re-mortgaged our home without even talking to me? What's going on?"

"I thought that would take care of things and you'd

never have to know."

"Never have to know! We *live* there, Jack. When were you going to tell me? When the bank came to foreclose and evict us? And what about this house?"

"I've looked at the numbers. I don't know what we're going to do."

"Oh, my God." Kate eased herself into the chair across from him. "How did this all get so bad? You're not...?"

"No, of course not. Jesus, Kate, give me some credit and a little trust here."

She shook her head. "I was so busy with the new job at school. When you offered to take over paying the household bills, I was actually glad. You were already handling our investments and the books for the business. I didn't think anything of it." She blinked back tears. "I stopped paying attention. My mistake, I guess."

Jack rubbed the pencil between his palms and said nothing.

"What are we going to do about Tim?" she asked.

He pushed his chair back and put the pencil down. "It's always about Tim. His tuition is the least of our problems."

"We put Sarah through college. Tim deserves the same."

"Jesus, Kate. Listen to yourself. The kid's not a student. All he does is party."

"Ah, the voice of experience."

"Let's not go down that road again." His voice was calm. "Tim might actually grow up if he drops out for awhile, gets a job, goes to community college. They're two totally different kids. Sarah's focused and responsible, always has been."

23

"And he's what?" She braced herself for the expected response.

"You have to let that kid grow up."

"Forget it." Her head was pounding. "I can't talk about this right now. I'm going for a run."

"It's not going away." He shoved at the pile of papers.

"I know that. And I know we have to talk. But I'm hearing this for the first time. Give me some time to digest it. We'll figure something out."

Already dressed in black running shorts and a blue tank top, Kate laced up her sneakers and stretched. After stuffing black curls under a Red Sox hat, she grabbed a bottle of water and her phone. "I'll be back in awhile." She got no response.

~~

She got her stride and took the first couple of hills with ease. Kate made the four-mile run to town and back at least three times a week. The rhythmic pounding of her running shoes on asphalt usually helped clear her mind, but not today.

Her conversation with Jack played in a continuous loop. She berated herself for her stupidity. How could she not have known how bad things were? And Jack. Transferring money without getting her signature, re-mortgaging the house without telling her. It didn't make sense.

And underlying it all were the sounds that haunted her: the girl's voice, the splash, that other voice. And Tim, always Tim.

Taking a deep breath, she tried to center herself. It was the only way she could face whatever came next. She forced herself to absorb the sights and smells around her—the deep greens of summer, the farms, animals grazing in the pastures, the pungent smell of fertilizer...

They'd first come here eighteen years ago when Sarah was five and Tim not quite two. They'd fallen in love with their little spot on the lake and couldn't wait to come every summer as soon as school let out. Jack commuted on weekends. A twitch of a smile played across her lips as she remembered the kids jumping off the dock into his arms. Theirs were "Huck Finn summers" of swimming, flashlight tag, scavenger hunts in the woods. As the kids got older they built a tree fort with a zip line, cannon balled off rope swings, learned to water ski and fish. Kate recalled one fishing adventure when Tim was eight that ended with a hook in his left cheek. He was so proud of those stitches.

They'd made life-long friends here. Ellen and her family were here from the beginning. The kids traveled as a pack. Wherever they were at lunchtime, that mom fed them. Kate loved the quiet evenings with Jack once the children were tucked into bed.

She missed those days. She missed her kids.

She missed Jack.

The rumble of an approaching dump truck on the narrow road broke her out of her reverie. She and Jack were alone now and navigated the empty nest as if it were a minefield. Everything was an argument. Not just their finances. They fought over Jack's drinking, his long hours at work, her increased responsibilities at school.

And Tim. They'd always fought about Tim.

Jack could never understand why Tim didn't share his fierce competitiveness. Sarah thrived on Jack's challenges academically and athletically. But Tim had a gentler nature. To Jack, Tim was never aggressive enough on the soccer field, daydreamed in little league, shied away from conflict. Jack's attempts to toughen him up had been a source of contention between him and Kate for years.

She couldn't deny that Tim did embrace the party atmosphere at Ethan Allen. Being placed on academic probation this past spring was just the latest. He'd been written up more than once by his freshman dorm RA for having beer in his room and had called again last week asking for money. She'd only heard Jack's end of the conversation and knew he was right. Tim did need to grow up and be more responsible. But even when she agreed with Jack, she somehow found herself in the position of defending her son.

Defending her son. The words jolted through her as she came into town. She was going to be sick. She sat down on the green and swallowed the last of her water. Wiping sweat from her forehead, she tried Tim's cell, which went straight to voicemail. "Tim, it's Mom. Call me."

She walked past the village library and school on the east side of the green and crossed to the general store, the focal point of Willow Bend. As Kate opened the heavy wooden door, she saw other early risers sipping coffee, their newspapers spread out on small wrought iron tables. The murmur of easy conversation and the soothing smell of fresh baked goods swirled around her, a contrast to the jumble of feelings and thoughts ricocheting around in her head.

She grabbed a bottle of water from the refrigerated case that filled one wall.

"Hi, Kate." She turned to see Jenny putting pies into the case beside the polished oak counter. "You're running in this heat?"

"Yeah, it's brutal out there, humid too. Will you hold one of the mixed berry? I'll be back for it later. Sarah's coming for the weekend."

"Sure. That's great. How are the wedding plans?" The owner tucked a strand of gray hair into the loosely knotted bun at the nape of her neck.

"Coming along. An exciting time," Kate said, trying to project enthusiasm.

"Tim coming home too?" Jenny asked.

"No, he's in Burlington this weekend. A project for his summer course." She bit her lower lip. Kate didn't want to chat, or answer questions about Tim. She glanced at the people behind her. "Looks like I'm holding up the line. I'm going to look around a bit, take a break before I head back. Thanks for holding the pie." She retreated to the back of the store.

The old cowbell over the outside door clanged. Excited voices of young girls, all talking at once, filled the store.

"My Mom was pissed when the phone rang at five. She woke me up but I told her I didn't know anything."

"My Mom made me talk to her myself. *I* didn't know where she was!"

"Yeah, she was like going ballistic. Calling everybody in town looking for her."

Kate moved so she could see the girls. Dressed in shorts and T-shirts, they looked about fourteen or fifteen.

"You girls are up bright and early," Jenny said.

The tall girl with the blonde ponytail walked around the waiting customers to the counter. "We need to see Mel. Is she here?"

"She's not due in 'til noon. Can I give her a message?" Jenny handed a woman her change.

"No, that's okay. Thanks." The blonde rejoined her friends as they took three Cokes out of the case.

"She was fine when we left her. Don't worry about it,"

the chunky redhead in the Go Green T-shirt said in a low voice to the third girl.

"She was *not* and you know it." Petite with a cap of short dark hair and glasses, the girl fisted her hands and didn't budge. "She was *wasted*. Who knows what happened to her after we left."

"Shut up, Molly." The blonde was looking around at the patrons, now quiet and watching. "Let's go." They paid for the sodas. "She would have texted us if there was a problem."

As they walked toward the door, Kate heard the one named Molly say, "I'm freaking out. We left her there with him and she didn't get home. I don't care what you say. It's our fault if something's happened to her."

Kate tossed a dollar on the counter for the water and headed out the door. She spotted the girls, still arguing, off to the side by the community bulletin board.

The redhead and the blonde had the third girl between them and were both talking at once. "What's wrong with you?" "It's not our fault. Stop saying that."

Kate stood behind a lattice screen of climbing clematis in front of Jenny's. The rest of the girls' conversation was drowned out by a black pick-up with a torn muffler. It careened behind the white steepled church and past the pristine clapboard houses on the green. It skidded to a brake grinding halt beside the girls.

"What's going on?" The driver seemed to be addressing the redhead. Kate noticed for the first time the sprinkling of freckles across her nose.

"Nothing. We were … umm … looking for Mel." The redhead lowered her voice and looked around. "She didn't come home."

"Didn't you all stay together?" he asked.

From what Kate could see, the young man looked older, eighteen or nineteen. The bill of a sweat-stained ball cap partially obscured his face. He held a cigarette cupped in his left hand against the side of the cab. The sleeve of his dark T-shirt was rolled up to expose a tanned muscled arm.

"What are you talking about?" the redhead said. "Of course we were together, at Molly's."

"Not unless Molly's parents bought a big house on the lake. Do you think I'm stupid? I knew something was up with you and checked Facebook. Big party."

"Did you tell Mom?" The words rushed out of the redhead.

"No. I drove by there a couple of times looking for you. If I had seen you, I'd have hauled your ass home. Becca, you and your friends are asking for trouble. I saw Mel. Looked like she was hooking up with that college boy I've seen her with. What's his name? JT? TJ?"

Kate's knees buckled. She grabbed the lattice-work almost knocking it down. She had to quiet the hammering of her heart so she could hear.

"TJ's a nice guy," Becca said.

"I'm a guy, Bec. There's only one thing he wants from a fifteen-year-old girl." He blew smoke out the window.

The blonde stepped up to the truck and put her hand on his arm. "And what's that?" She waited a beat and added, "You stalking Mel now? Or all of us?"

He gave the blonde a crooked smile. "I'll catch up with *you* later."

"In your dreams." She undid her ponytail and let it fall over one shoulder.

The driver flicked his cigarette butt onto the road and laughed. He waited until the girls started to move away then gunned the motor. With tires screeching, he turned left onto the main road out of town.

Kate stepped out from behind the flowers. The small dark-haired girl saw her and stopped.

"Molly? Is that your name?" Kate took a step toward her.

"Come on, Molly," the blonde called. Molly turned and ran after them.

"Wait!" Kate tried to make her jelly legs move, but the girls were gone.

The initials *TJ, TJ* screamed inside her head until she thought it would explode. She got inside the store somehow and pushed the restroom door closed behind her. Collapsing to her knees, she hung her head over the toilet. She retched until her throat was raw. Holding on to the sink, she pulled herself up. She splashed cold water on her face and rinsed out the foul, sour taste in her mouth. She should report this. She had the first name now of a girl who was missing and the names of two of her friends.

She also knew the initials, of the boy who was with the missing girl.

Kate walked outside and took out her cell phone. She looked at it as if she'd never seen it before. Making the decision, she shoved it back in the pouch. On the run home it pressed against her hip with each stride as if to remind her of the choice she had made. She cranked up the music and pushed herself into mindless exhaustion.

~~

Drenched in perspiration, Kate walked up the gravel driveway and onto the deck. She sank into a chair and bent over, her forearms on her knees.

"Did you think to pick up a paper"? Jack carried a cup of coffee onto the deck.

She looked up and wiped her flushed face with the hem of her top. Her breathing was deep, labored.

"You don't look so good. Are you okay?"

"I'm just hot." Sweat ran between her breasts. "I'm going to take a shower." She wouldn't tell him what she'd overheard. She wouldn't tell anyone.

"Sarah called. They should be here around one, depending on the traffic getting out of the city."

She pulled off the ball cap and pushed damp curls off her forehead. "Jenny's holding a pie for us and I have to pick up corn and tomatoes at the farm."

"Don't worry about it," Jack said. "I'm going to the marina to get a new ski rope. On my way back, I'll pick up the pie and the vegetables. Maybe there'll still be a copy of *The Times* or *The Globe*. These local papers never have any real news." Heading into the kitchen, he said, "Oh, Ellen called." He put his cup in the sink and grabbed his keys. "She and Gil invited us over later for drinks. She wants to hear all about the wedding plans. I told her you'd call her."

Minutes later, from the upstairs bedroom window, Kate watched as Jack backed the Tahoe down the driveway. That's the way it was with them now. Fight and argue then go on as if nothing had happened. They didn't even use sex anymore to resolve their differences, just let whatever was wrong fester between them.

Kate stood in the shower under the scalding spray. Salty tears mingled with the water pumping in rhythm *TJ, TJ, TJ*. She closed her eyes. "Oh, Timothy John. What have you done?"

6

Hannah sat in the rusted Dodge Dart and stared at Jenny's. If there were any other place to get cigarettes, she wouldn't be here. By now, everyone in town would have heard Mel didn't come home last night. Hannah hated this about Willow Bend, everyone in your business all the time. Weighing her need for nicotine against the whispers she'd have to endure, Hannah got out of the car. She noticed a good-looking man carrying a newspaper under one arm and balancing a pie.

His face was tanned and he had thick dark hair. Trim khaki shorts and a yellow golf shirt screamed "flatlander." Hannah was surprised when the man called to Norm who was getting out of his truck.

"Constable Johnson, any developments with that incident on the lake last night?"

"Nothing yet, Mr. Rourke. We're checking on a couple of leads."

"Let us know if we can help." He was already walking

to his car.

"Will do," Norm said to the man's retreating back.

Hannah watched the stranger get into an SUV and head toward the lake, apparently unconcerned with the reduced speed limit in town. She wondered who he was.

"What was that all about?" She hurried over to Norm. "What incident on the lake? What leads?"

"It's nothing, Hannah. He lives up on the east side. His wife thought she heard something last night."

"What did she hear? When?" Hannah's heart beat faster.

"It's *nothing*. A boat, an argument. It doesn't concern you." Norm tried to step past her. "All I want is a cup of coffee, just left the scene of a big accident. Travis is still there."

She blocked his way. "It damn well *does* concern me if it has anything to do with Mel." She was powerless to curb the rising volume of her voice.

"I doubt it has anything to do with Mel. Trust me. She know anyone with a boat?" Norm was at the door. "Don't get yourself all worked up."

"Don't tell me what I can get worked up about, Norm Johnson. My daughter's missing!" She leaned into his face, drawing out the next words. "And don't you *dare* tell me to trust you."

Several patrons coming out of the store stopped to stare.

"Hannah, you're making a scene," Norm said in a hushed voice.

"I don't care! I've been all over this damn town and to the college too. She's nowhere! What if she's lying hurt somewhere?" She fought back threatening tears.

"All right, Hannah." Norm looked around and took her arm. "Let's sit in my truck. We can talk there without the whole town gawking."

Hannah pulled herself up into the passenger seat and faced Norm. She felt slightly winded. *Damn cigarettes.*

Norm looked at her. "You called her friends?"

"Everyone I could think of—Becca, Molly, Courtney Chandler. Those four are always together but no one's seen her. They said they didn't know anything. Somebody must!"

"You looked around the places where the kids hang out? The meadow, the state park—"

"Yes. Yes. Everywhere but the quarry. I'm on my way there now." She averted her eyes and pictured all the things that could have happened to her daughter.

"Hannah, I'll need those friends' names and addresses. I'm sure she's all right but I'll have Travis follow up. He's better with the kids."

She gave him the girls' names again and the street names. "I'm not sure of the house numbers."

"Not a problem. Travis can get them easy enough. I'm concerned that she's not home yet. I was actually out looking for her when I came upon the accident."

"Then come with me to the quarry right now." The quarry was ancient history. All that mattered was finding Mel.

Norm punched in Travis' cell number. "The rest of that accident scene cleaned up? Okay. Don't go back to the office. Leave the paperwork. I want you to go see three of Melody Ward's friends who might have been with her last night. I'll text you their names and addresses. Find out what you can about where they were, what went on and what they know. I'm on my way to the quarry now with Hannah."

They drove the short distance in silence and found the

quarry deserted. As they walked the perimeter of the deep rock gorge, Hannah trembled and felt dizzy as she looked down. It would be so easy to slip off these rocks, to hit your head. She rubbed her eyes to dispel the image.

They searched the surrounding area. "There's nothing here," Norm said. "Let's check the back quarry."

Single file, they walked deeper into the woods where the forest floor was damp with humidity and decay, the sunlight touching only the highest branches of the trees. Beer cans, an abandoned bong, used condoms, and an empty bottle of Captain Morgan littered the clearing. It was hot, the air fetid. Hannah's head spun. She'd had nothing but coffee since supper last night. Feeling as if she might faint, she took a step back.

Norm put his hand on the small of her back. "Let's get you out of here. You don't need to be looking at this."

Hannah let herself be led back to the truck and was grateful for the bottle of water he handed her.

"I'm going to take another look around. Stay here," Norm said.

She wiped her mouth. "Why? Did you see something? Do you think she was here?" Fear congealed into a stone that lodged in her throat. She rubbed at the tears tracking furrows down her face.

"I don't have any reason to believe that, Hannah. If I did, I'd call the state police. I just don't want to miss anything." His voice trailed off.

"Wait." She touched his arm to stop him. "What are you looking for?" Her heart raced.

"Honestly? I don't know."

Hannah crossed her arms in front of her chest and leaned against the truck. She watched him disappear into the woods. Restless, she began to pace.

When she saw him re-emerge, she ran to him. "Did you find anything?"

He shook his head.

"Then let's keep looking. I didn't go to the cemetery. The kids hang out there sometimes. But on the way, you're going to tell me about that guy at Jenny's. Just what happened on the lake last night?" She waited for Norm to answer.

"Okay. Come on. I'll tell you everything I know."

As they rode the back roads of Willow Bend, Hannah tried Mel's cell again. She let it ring and ring. A disembodied but familiar voice told her—again—the voice mailbox was full.

Norm took a deep breath and kept his eyes on the road. "I got a call early this morning from the guy's wife. They live on West View Road. Seems she was down on her dock around three, couldn't sleep. Said she heard someone arguing in a boat, some swearing, a splash, and then the boat took off. She was afraid someone was in the water, maybe fell or jumped in, so she woke her husband. They went out in their boat but all they found were some beer cans and an oar. That's when they called me."

"Could she see them? Was it kids? Guys, girls?"

"It was too dark. She thinks she heard at least one male and a female."

"What were they arguing about?"

Norm shrugged. "Don't know."

"Who did she think fell in?" She studied his profile, saw his eyes flick her way for just an instant. "Norm?"

"She couldn't tell, Hannah. It was pitch dark."

"You're not telling me everything." Her words were measured. "I need to know."

He stared at the road, as if the answer were there. "She said she didn't hear the female's voice again after the splash."

"My God, Norm! And you never put two and two together? Did you go out there to look yourself?"

"I figured it was kids drinking and raising hell, maybe skinny dipping." The words rushed out of him. "The only complaint that came in last night was about a party at one of the big houses at the north end of the lake. Rich summer kids, you know? It was only a noise complaint, no big deal. And why would I think Mel was hanging out with flatlanders?" He paused and looked at Hannah. "There was no connection that I could see. Plus, the lady and her husband found nothing, Hannah. Nothing. Just some empty beer cans."

She narrowed her eyes and looked at him hard. She spoke in a calm, deliberate voice. "You didn't answer my question. *Did* you go out on the lake yourself?" She waited. "You didn't, did you? You dismissed that woman just like you dismissed me."

"Hannah."

"No. I don't want to hear it. I want you to take me to that spot on the lake. Get a boat, call Travis, do whatever you have to do. But take me *now*."

7

Norm made a quick call to the game warden and then to Travis. "I'm on my way to the boat ramp with Hannah. I just talked to Will Parker. We're taking his boat to check something out. "You talk to any of those girls yet?" He paused. "Call me as soon as you do. Use the radio. My cell's crap out on the lake."

He swung by the town hall to get the game warden's boat key and admitted to himself that Hannah was right. He hadn't taken her seriously when she reported Mel missing.

Back in the truck, he put it in gear and drove to the lake without a word. Hannah perched on the edge of the passenger seat. Norm tried to imagine what she was feeling. Dressed in a loose, shapeless dress and old Birkenstocks, she barely resembled the beautiful young girl he'd once know.

"I know you think I'm a total asshole, Hannah, but hear me out. I was tied up all morning with that accident. There were serious injuries. I had to call the state police helicopter–"

Eyes flashing, she cut him off. "I don't care about any of

that. That's your job. But what about earlier this morning? I asked you for help and you did nothing. I've never been able to count on you."

"That's not true." Norm struggled to keep his eyes on the road.

"It is. But this isn't about you or me. It's about Mel, no matter what you think of her." Hannah twisted her fingers in the folds of her dress. "I can't lose another child. I can't do it."

That tore at his guts, like it always did. He wasn't there for her when her parents made her give up their baby, a son. "I'm so sorry, Hannah," he whispered.

She turned on him. "Sorry? For what? For getting in that damn pick-up and never looking back? For not writing? Not calling? Do you have any idea what it's like to give up a child?" She stopped yelling and stared at the road.

"You know how bad things were between me and my dad back then. I would have killed him." His eyes met hers. "I *had* to go."

"And you did. My problem was I believed you when you said you'd come back."

"I asked you to come with me. I begged you."

"I was fifteen for God's sake! How could I go?" Her voice reverberated around the cab.

"I tried to—" He started as they pulled into the boat launch area.

"No." She put up her hand to stop him. "No more lies. I don't care anymore. All I want from you now is help in finding my daughter." She was out the door and moving toward the boat slips before Norm turned off the engine.

Once onboard the boat, Hannah sat in stony silence. Norm said nothing. He consulted the property map and located the Rourke camp, 176 West View Road, on the east shore. The sizable log home, hardly a camp, was directly across the lake from the old Walker farm. The Rourkes' view of those fields stretched from the top of the hill to the water's edge.

He stopped in the middle of the lake directly in front of the log house, close to where the Rourke woman said she'd heard the commotion. "We'll start from here and fan out to the far shore like spokes of a wheel."

"Is that the best way to do this?" He heard criticism in the clipped tone of her voice.

"Look, Hannah, I'm trying here. The most I've ever done is give a speeding ticket or break up a disturbance at somebody's house. If we don't find anything, I'll call the state."

She was quiet, then said," Mel's a good swimmer. If that was her who fell out of that boat, she could make it to shore. The lake's not too wide right here."

Norm didn't respond. Mel might be a good swimmer—but not if she was drunk. And if she'd made it to shore, where was she now?

"We should search the shore over by the Walker place too," Hannah said with a catch in her voice, like trying to hold back tears. "I have cell service here. I'm trying Mel again."

Tears gathered in her eyes, pale blue now as if the light had drained out of them. He knew Mel had not picked up.

They continued searching, drifting south with the current.

"Hannah." His voice was gentle. "I'm going to check with Travis and see if he's been able to track down those friends of Mel's. Then I'm calling the state police." Hannah stared at him with a blank expression. *Had she heard him?*

Norm unclipped the radio from his belt. "Where are you? Were you able to speak with any of the girls?"

"Yeah." Travis' voice came through with some interference. "I figured I'd start with Becca McVeigh and talk to her brother too."

"Shane McVeigh—minor scrapes, nothing major—he should know if anybody had a party on Daddy's bass boat last night. What'd you find out?"

"As I was leaving the office, Molly Townsend came in with her mother. The kid was pretty upset. Said she was at a party on the lake last night with Mel, Becca McVeigh, and Courtney Chandler. Molly was crying. She said they left Mel there."

"Was this the party up at the north end on Steed Hill?"

"Yeah, they were invited by some college boys they know."

"She give you any names?"

"Molly said Mel was with the 'cute guy'—her words, not mine—that she's been seeing. He's a student at Ethan Allen."

"Jesus, Travis. How old is this guy?"

"Maybe nineteen. He's a freshman."

"You got a name?"

"Everyone calls him TJ. She said he's got this 'cute'— again, her word—little scar on his left cheek."

He looked over at Hannah. "Mel ever mention this TJ?"

Hannah shook her head.

"Anything else?"

"With some coaxing she named two others, Mike and Brandon. No last names. She also said Shane McVeigh drove his truck by the house a few times during the party like he was looking for someone. Molly said he had a thing for Mel but he creeped her out, made Mel nervous." Travis paused. "She wasn't sure of the time but thinks they left Mel there around two. Mel was pretty drunk. Molly's been calling her but just gets her voicemail."

Norm ran his hand over his face. One look at Hannah told him she had heard every word. *Damn radios.* "Text me those boys' names, then get over to the McVeighs'. Shane's got some explaining to do. I'm coming in and calling the state police as soon as I get service."

"You got it."

Hannah's eyes blazed. Her hands fisted in her lap. "You can't give up!"

"I'm not giving up, Hannah. Just getting help." Norm felt useless as he docked the boat. "Do you want me to drop you off at your car, at home?"

"No. I'm staying with you."

"Okay. Then let's go." They headed back to the truck.

As Norm took out his cell to call the state police, the radio crackled. Travis' voice intruded again. "Norm, I'm at the old dam at the south channel. You better get here. Fast. Some fishermen flagged me down. They found the body of a female partially submerged and tangled in the weeds. I called the rescue squad but I don't think—"

"NO!" Hannah grabbed her hair with both fists and doubled over in the passenger seat.

Norm attached the flashing blue light to the roof and sped to Travis' location. He jammed on the brakes fifty feet from the scene. Hannah gripped the door handle.

"Hannah, please. Stay here until we know."

"No, I'm going with you." Her knuckles whitened as she tightened her grasp.

He put his hand on her arm and waited until she faced him. "Let me do this." He spoke just above a whisper.

42

Alone, Norm plowed through the high wet grass to the old concrete dam, partially submerged beneath the surface of the water. The lake narrowed there into a shallow, silt-filled channel that emptied into Willow Creek. The murky water brimmed with weeds, cattails, and choking lily pads. A heavy canopy of willow trees added to the seclusion of the area.

Travis waited on shore beside the dam. Two men in fishing gear stood off to the side.

Norm approached, careful not to disturb anything. A young girl's body was wedged up against the base of the cracked dam. Norm knelt on the soggy bank and leaned in closer. Her legs were bent and covered in muck and weeds from the knees down, as if she'd been there for a while. Long brown hair, tangled in broken branches and other debris, floated on the surface of the shallow water. Her bruised face was partially turned and submerged, one vacant brown eye staring up through the muddy water. Her lips were dark blue. The purple T-shirt was ripped down the front exposing small pale breasts. Norm looked away, exhaling sharply. Forcing himself to refocus, he saw that her underwear was also torn, the elastic band in place only around one thigh.

He rested his head in his hand. "Christ," he whispered and closed his eyes. Clearing his throat, he stood and hitched his belt up. "Travis, close off this whole area. Don't let anyone near here, not even first responders. We can't disturb anything. Call the resident trooper—it's a new guy—and tell him what we've got. Then call the regional medical examiner. Get Doc Braddock over here to meet the EMTs." Norm paused. "You know this is Melody Ward, right?"

Travis nodded and got out his cell phone. "Where are you going?" he asked Norm.

"I've got Hannah in the car. I'm taking her to Carrie

43

Ryan's. I'll be right back. Start taking statements from those two guys." He nodded toward the fisherman. "Be sure you get their addresses and phone numbers. And for God's sake, don't touch anything!"

He turned to walk back to the car and saw Hannah running toward him. He grabbed her upper arms and tried to block her way.

"I'm so sorry." He willed his voice not to crack.

Tight fists pummeled his chest as great sobs heaved her body. Norm put his arms around her trying to absorb the shocks and the blows. Her tears drenched the front of his shirt.

"Let me go." She struggled against him. "Let me see her."

"Not like this, Hannah." He tried to hold onto her.

"No!" She ripped out of his grip, propelling herself to the edge of the water.

She sank to her knees, mindless of the grass and mud soaking through her dress. She bent in half, hugged her arms to her chest and let out a ferocious keening sound that came from deep within.

Norm had never heard a human being make that sound. He rushed to her side. She tried to reach into the water but he put his arms around her again. "No, Hannah, you can't touch her." He tried to pull her away.

Hannah lay prone in the mud. "My baby," she sobbed. "My baby." Her face was streaked with tears and dirt. Norm pulled her off the ground like a rag doll, the filth of her dress staining his uniform.

Supporting most of her weight, he was able to lead her, weeping, back to the truck. He placed her in the passenger seat and covered her with a tattered blanket from the back. Shivering, she stared vacantly as sobs continued to rack her body.

He picked up her phone from the floor and scrolled down to find Carrie's cell number.

She answered on the first ring. "Hannah, did you find her?"

"It's Norm. I need to bring Hannah to your house."

"I'll meet you there in ten minutes. What's happened?"

"Hannah needs you. Mel is dead."

During the brief drive to Carrie's, Hannah rocked back and forth, hugging herself, as tears streamed down her face. The siren of the approaching rescue squad couldn't drown out Hannah's wrenching cries, each one striking a blow to Norm's heart.

The truck kicked up dust as it fishtailed into Carrie Ryan's driveway. The once imposing farmhouse showed signs of wear with peeling white paint and sagging steps. The wicker chairs on the wrap-around porch listed to one side, the floral cushions mildewed and faded.

Carrie, Hannah's best friend since childhood, hadn't spoken to Norm in years.

An old VW Bug stopped beside them and Carrie jumped out. "I got here as soon as I could. I was at Hannah's when you called, waiting in case Mel came home."

"Can you help me?" Norm said as he got Hannah out of the truck.

Carrie folded Hannah into an embrace. "I've got her."

Norm watched her murmur into Hannah's ear as they climbed the porch steps. He called to Carrie. "I'll send Doc Braddock over to take a look at her. I'll be back as soon as I can."

Neither woman responded. They seemed to have

forgotten him.

~~

Several people were standing near the dam when Norm returned. What is it about police tape that draws people like flypaper? Assuming his most authoritative bearing, he started moving them back. The state police would be there any minute. He didn't want to look completely incompetent.

Dr. Glenn Braddock parked his black Cadillac in the grass beside the tape. He had opened a practice in town a few years ago, but Norm didn't know him well. "What have you got, Constable?" He took out a pair of latex gloves.

"It's Melody Ward, Doc. No one's touched a thing. The trooper's on his way."

They walked together down the embankment to the edge of the water. Braddock's dress shoes sank into the mud. "I don't know how long it will take the ME to get here," Norm said. "Can you check the body and pronounce her?"

The doctor knelt down and did a visual exam of the body. He placed two gloved fingers against her carotid artery and looked up at Norm.

"She's dead. We can't disturb anything until the ME gets here." He stashed the gloves into his back pocket. "Does Hannah know? Where is she?"

"Yes." Norm heard again the unearthly sound that had erupted from Hannah. "I took her to Carrie Ryan's over at 269 Poplar. Can you check on her when you're done here?"

"Sure, I'll just wait for the medical examiner. Then I'll go and give her something so she can rest. This is going to be tough on her. Melody's her whole life."

Norm didn't need to be reminded of that.

.8

A state police cruiser, sirens blaring, pulled onto the grass by the dam. A tall lean trooper all spit and polish—hat squared just right, sharp creases in his green uniform—stepped out.

"Trooper Clayton Storrow." He didn't extend a hand to Norm. "What can you tell me, Constable?"

Norm introduced himself and strained to see past the aviator sunglasses. He liked to see a man's eyes when he spoke to him.

"The victim's name is Melody Ward. She's a fifteen-year-old resident of Willow Bend, lives with her mother at 29 Swamp Hollow Road. Some fishermen found her. They gave their statements to Travis Cunningham, the second constable. Nothing's been moved or touched. Our local doctor, Glenn Braddock, has pronounced her."

"All right. Good. Anything else?"

"There was a party last night on the lake. We got a complaint from a neighbor around ten about noise and parking on the grass. I drove out there. Told them to keep it down and move their cars. I checked a couple of IDs. They were legal. I didn't see any locals but have learned since that some underage girls from town were there, including Mel, uh, I mean the victim. One of her friends, Molly Townsend, told Travis that they were invited by some students from Ethan Allen and that they left Mel there around two this morning."

"Do you have the students' names?"

"First names."

"We'll need those, Constable, as well as the girls who were with the vic. Was that the party on Steed Hill?"

"Yeah. You know about that?"

"We also got a noise complaint from that location at three this morning. When the trooper got there, kids scattered in all directions. Some jumped in cars, others ran into the woods behind the house. Probably underage. The few that were apprehended were students at the college. Their parents have been called. The homeowners returned this morning and reported considerable property damage. I was on my way to Ethan Allen now to meet with the Dean when I got this call."

"The girls with Mel were Molly Townsend, Becca McVeigh, and Courtney Chandler. All good kids from town." He checked the text message from Travis. "The boys, according to Molly, were TJ, Mike, and Brandon. No last names. TJ, reportedly a freshman, is the one they left Mel with. Molly also mentioned a local kid, Shane McVeigh. Said he liked Mel, but she didn't return the feelings. Molly saw him drive his truck by the house a few times during the party."

"Good. I'll see what I can find out about these students from the Dean and have one of my men question McVeigh. Know anything about him?"

"Kind of a wise ass. A few incidents, nothing serious. I'll see that you get our reports.

"Thanks, we'll bring him in if he's not co-operative. He and this TJ are the only ones so far we can definitively tie to the victim."

Norm was thinking about his own casual response to the complaint about the party. He didn't see any kids from town there but then he didn't look around all that much either. What if Mel was there then? His heart pounded.

"Anything else, Constable?" Norm could hear the impatience in Storrow's voice.

"Yes, sorry." Norm reiterated the statement from Kate Rourke, such as it was.

"You don't have any more details about what this Mrs. Rourke saw or heard?"

"No," Norm said.

"Did you check out her story? Go out on the lake yourself when you left there?"

"No." What could he offer as an excuse? That he was tired? Didn't think it was important enough to pursue? Disregarded her and her story?

Storrow jotted something down. "You said you took the oar the Rourkes found. Where is it now?"

"It's in my office. I'll have Travis get it for you," Norm said.

"Is it locked up? It could be evidence." The trooper looked at him from behind the dark sunglasses.

Norm honestly couldn't remember if he'd locked his office door. "The building's locked. It's Saturday. Nobody's there." He tried to sound more confident than he was.

"I don't suppose you used a glove when you removed it from the Rourke premises?" When Norm hesitated, Storrow said, "Forget it. I'll send one of my guys. One of you go with him to unlock the building."

Norm called Travis over. As Storrow stepped away, Norm overheard some of the trooper's conversation: "oar ... possible evidence ... compromised chain of custody."

"Shit," Norm said under his breath as his face grew hot.

He realized Storrow was talking to him again.

"My men will keep this area cordoned off. I've called my supervisor and the major crime squad in Rutland. We're closing down this dirt access road immediately and the main road in both directions."

"For how long?" Norm asked.

"For as long as it takes." There was no doubt who was in charge. Storrow turned his back and made another quick call.

Norm knew he was in over his head and was sweating. He'd dealt with traffic violations, process serving, the occasional disorderly conduct, petty thefts. He hadn't even completed the state's basic criminal justice training course. It wasn't required when he took the job, and he'd been grandfathered in. He had absolutely no experience with violent crime. Norm couldn't remember a bona-fide homicide in Willow Bend. Ever.

Storrow was walking away. "What do you want us to do?" Norm called to him.

"Next of kin's been notified?"

Norm nodded, thinking of Hannah's utter devastation.

"Then we're all set. Thank you, Constable. Once the forensics guys get what they need, I'm going to pay a visit to your Mrs. Rourke. See if she can remember anything else."

Before Norm could respond, the crime squad descended on them. It was just like TV. Norm stood by his truck and watched. With gloved hands they combed the area, took photos, set up numbered markers, and put samples of whatever into evidence bags. It looked to him like they were picking up debris but they cataloged and bagged it all. Travis and a trooper returned with the oar in a large plastic bag.

The ME arrived and approached Storrow. "Dr. Howard Gray. You in charge?"

"Yes, Trooper Clayton Storrow." They shook hands.

"Do you have a positive ID on the victim?"

"Yes, Melody Ward, fifteen years old."

"We'll be working this scene for some time before we can move the body. Nothing's been touched?" the doctor asked.

"Affirmative. Let me know if you need anything."

Norm saw Dr. Gray take an expensive looking camera and a black case out of the van and put on latex gloves. He began taking pictures of Mel from all angles. He then took a sample of Mel's hair and what must be skin from under her fingernails. He placed clear plastic bags over her hands and tied them at her wrists. Bile rose in the back of Norm's throat and he had to turn away when the doctor manipulated Mel's body to examine it further and snap additional images.

He knew he could leave; his presence was not required or expected. But he had to bear witness—for Hannah. After what seemed like hours, Norm watched transfixed as Mel's body was zipped into a black body bag and loaded into the medical examiner's van.

Fighting the impulse to vomit, he went to find Storrow, who was conferring with another trooper over a laptop.

"Excuse me." Norm stopped and stared. "Is that a mug shot of Shane McVeigh?"

Storrow closed the computer, nodded to the trooper

and turned to Norm. "Can I help you, Constable? I thought you'd left."

Norm caught the dismissive tone. "Is that McVeigh?"

Storrow hesitated. "Yes. Charges of sexual harassment and attempted sexual assault were brought against him by a young lady in Tinmouth several months ago. She later recanted and withdrew the charges. She was of legal age and there was no physical evidence so we had to let him go. His fingerprints are on file. Could be she was just ticked at him or maybe he doesn't understand that no means no. At any rate, he's of interest to us since your eyewitness places him at the party where our victim was last seen. Now, what can I do for you, Constable?"

"I'd like to be involved in this case in any capacity."

"That's impossible. It belongs to us now." He had taken off the glasses.

"I understand. But I know the victim's family. I know this town and its people. I know Mel's friends. They'll talk to me and to Travis." *And I need to do this—for myself and for Hannah.*

He'd been so wrong about everything. He'd felt like a fool when Storrow questioned him about the damn oar. The forensic guys were all over that. Turns out you *can* get prints off wet objects after all. Who knew? He had to find a way to make up for screwing up big time.

He could almost hear Storrow weighing the pros and cons in his head. This was not a man who bent the rules easily.

The state trooper finally responded. "You can go with me to the Rourke home since you made the initial contact. It's on the way to Ethan Allen. I'll call the Dean to let him know we'll be delayed. But Johnson," Storrow leaned in. "You are *only* along as an observer, this one time. You say and do *nothing.* Got it?"

Norm nodded and walked around to the passenger side of the shiny green state car. "I'll get the son-of-a-bitch if it's the last thing I do," he said to himself before getting in.

·9

Wiping her hands on a dish towel, Kate glanced at the slate wall clock. Everything was ready. She had a few minutes before Sarah and Joe got there.

Upstairs she called Tim again. *Pick up!* A canned voice advised her that the voice mailbox for this customer was full. She groaned. He hadn't answered her earlier text either.

Kate scrolled through account numbers and passwords stored in her phone. She entered the appropriate ones and pulled up the most recent savings account statement. Squinting at the numbers, she frowned and entered the same information into her laptop.

There it was—the same balance, just on a bigger screen.

She sat at her desk and scanned statements from the last several months. No large lump sum withdrawal was made that might have been deposited in a CD. Instead, a pattern of regular withdrawals of varying amounts emerged: $1000, $700, $10,000, sometimes weekly. She gasped as she noted two withdrawals of $30,000 each and another for $50,560 a week ago. The digits on the screen seemed to mock her as she leaned in closer.

"He lied to me." The precipice she'd been clinging to crumbled a bit more. "He's gambling again."

She tried to open the account for the business but was locked out. *He must have changed the password!* She heard a car in the driveway.

Jack called up to her, "They're here."

Kate closed the laptop. In the adjoining bathroom, she applied a little concealer under her eyes and some blush. She ran a brush through her hair and went downstairs.

Sarah was standing by the passenger side of a dark blue coupe. Kate hugged her, then leaned back to look at her daughter. Slender and fair-skinned, Sarah had Jack's blue eyes and Kate's dark curly hair. "I've missed you. You look great. Fieldwork agrees with you. Not too much with grad courses?"

She shook her head. "I love it, Mom. Monday I start shadowing a caseworker in Child Services."

"You're doing what you've always wanted." Kate smiled.

"Yep," Sarah said. "But I'm ready for a weekend at the lake. Is Tim here? I tried calling his cell."

"No, he's in Burlington for the weekend. His intro psych class went to UVM for a three-day seminar. Some visiting professor." Kate checked her watch. "He's probably in class now but we can call him later."

"In class?" Jack said. "Sleeping it off more likely." He gave Sarah a big hug. "How's my girl?"

"Hi, Dad." She circled his waist with her arm.

Jack shook hands with Sarah's fiancé, who had taken the suitcases out of the trunk. Joe Parelli was tall like Jack with broad shoulders.

"How's the job?" Jack asked.

"Good. Busy. The way I like it."

"Still looking to make detective?"

"You bet." He smiled.

"Welcome." Kate hugged him.

"Hi, Kate, it's great to see you and get out of the city for a few days. Thanks."

Joe never hugged her back, never seemed to let his guard down. After eight years on the NYPD, he probably saw people at their worst every day. Kate felt the familiar stab of concern that it had hardened him emotionally as well as physically. She wondered again about this match but resolved to say nothing more. He was good to Sarah and that's what mattered. Kate had seen how her daughter looked at this man. Sarah loved him.

Kate turned to her. "Ellen called while I was out for a run. She wants us to stop over later, wants to hear all about the wedding plans." She put her arm around Sarah's shoulders and pressed her head against her daughter's. "It's been hard but I haven't divulged any details. I'll call her once we get you settled in."

Jack picked up the second suitcase. He and Joe followed Kate and Sarah into the house. In the kitchen, Sarah unwrapped cheeses she had brought from the city while Jack took drink orders.

"So how are things in the city?" Jack asked as he handed Joe a beer.

"Lots of action. Speaking of action, what's going on here today? Traffic's backed up in both directions as you approach town. There's an area cordoned off by the old dam and several state vehicles are parked there."

"Yeah, Dad," Sarah said. "Do you know anything about it? We stopped at Jenny's to get some wine for dinner. A woman there said she heard someone had drowned."

Kate dropped the knife she was holding and grabbed the counter. "Oh God."

"What's the matter, Mom? You look awful."

"Take it easy, Kate," Jack said. "We don't know if it has anything to do with that."

"With what?" Sarah looked from one parent to the other.

"Let's take our drinks out to the deck and we'll fill you in," Jack said.

Sarah and Joe listened as Jack summarized the events of early that morning with Kate adding details.

Joe listened intently, stopping them periodically for additional information and clarification. His voice was calm, his comments focused on the facts. Kate had never seen this professional side of Joe. He was thorough and patient.

When they finished relating the visit from Constable Johnson, Joe looked at them. "That was it? He didn't press you for further details?"

"Nope. That was it." Jack took a pull on his beer.

"You said you heard some of what the woman or girl said, Kate. Did you hear the man say anything?" Joe asked.

Kate paused before she answered. "His voice was drowned out by the motor."

"What about when the motor was shut off?"

"I think he said something like 'Quit playing games.' It was hard to hear him."

Joe frowned. Kate held her breath. She thought he was going to ask more but he didn't.

"Mom, do you think the person who fell in is the one

who drowned?"

"Hold on, Sarah." Jack raised his hand, palm out. "You're just like your mother, jumping to conclusions. First of all, we don't know for sure that it was a *person* who went into the water. I'm with the constable on this, probably a case of empties being chucked by underage kids who then beat it out of there. The boat left, remember? And second, we don't know that anyone actually drowned. Jenny's is a gossip mill, you know that."

The phone rang and Jack went inside. He picked up on the second ring.

"What's with Dad?" Sarah looked at her mother.

Kate shrugged. "He didn't listen to me when I first told him what I'd heard. Maybe now he realizes we should have done more, sooner."

"Don't beat yourself up, Kate," Joe said. "Sounds like you did what you could. And you were right to call the constable."

"That was State Trooper Clayton Storrow," Jack said coming back onto the deck. "There's been a development. He and Constable Johnson are coming back to ask us more questions." He glanced at Kate. "Here's your chance to be Nancy Drew. I'm getting another drink. Anyone else?"

An uneasy silence settled over the group. Sarah and Joe shook their heads. "We're fine."

When Jack returned, he had moved on from beer to bourbon, straight up. Never good. Kate watched him swirl the amber liquid. "You know the police will be here soon."

"I'm fine, Kate. Just stop." He took a big swig and went back inside.

"I'll make a fresh pot of coffee," Sarah said.

Kate sat where she was. *Had the girls talked to the*

police? Given them a name?

Joe moved to sit next to her. "Is something else bothering you, Kate?"

"What?" Kate licked her lips. "No, no, I'm fine. Just didn't get much sleep last night." She stood and picked up the discarded napkins and the cheese that was left. Her cell rang. "It's Ellen. I have to take this. I'll be right in."

Sarah came to the French doors. "Coffee's ready. Do you want some, Mom? Joe?"

"I'll get it," Joe said and walked into the kitchen.

Kate waited a second. She had to pull it together. "Hi, Ellen. I'm sorry I haven't gotten back to you. We're kind of in the middle of something here. I'm not sure we're going to be able to come over."

"Is it Jack?" Her friend asked.

"For once, no," Kate said. "I'll call you as soon as I can." She hung up and went inside.

Jack scowled at Kate as he poured the coffee. A car came up the gravel driveway. "What's the matter with you? You were so hot to help solve the case. Now's your big chance."

Jack opened the door before they could knock. "Officers, come in. This is my daughter Sarah and her fiancé, Joe Parelli, one of New York's finest. What can we do for you?"

Trooper Storrow introduced himself and Constable Johnson and got down to business without preamble. Neither of them accepted coffee.

"Mr. and Mrs. Rourke, we need to go over your statement to Constable Johnson earlier today and see if you can remember anything else."

Kate squared her shoulders and came toward them.

"Whatever we can do to help."

Trooper Storrow removed his hat. He was an imposing figure in his impeccable uniform and polished shoes. He sat in one of the leather chairs beside the fireplace. The constable sat in the other. His stomach, tightly cinched with a dark brown belt, pressed against the small buttons of his shirt and threatened to break free.

Storrow took out his notebook and addressed Jack, who stood by the French doors. "How long have you lived at this address?"

"This is our eighteenth summer. Our son wasn't quite two when we bought. Our permanent home is in Connecticut."

"You have another child?" Storrow looked up.

"Yes, Tim," Kate said.

"Is he here now?" The trooper looked around.

"No, he's in Burlington," Jack said.

"We've recovered the body of a young girl from the lower end of the lake south of your property," Storrow said.

Kate's breath caught. "Do you know who she is?"

"She's a fifteen-year-old girl from town. Her name is Melody Ward."

Melody. Mel? Kate felt the blood drain from her face. "Fifteen?"

"What happened?" Jack asked.

"That's what we're trying to find out." Storrow turned his attention to Kate, who sat opposite him. "We need your help, Mrs. Rourke. Please take us through the events of last night and early this morning. No detail is too small, even if you think it's insignificant."

"I went to bed around ten. I don't know what time Jack came up but I woke up around two-thirty maybe. I'm not sure."

"Was your husband in bed with you?"

"Yes, of course." She frowned. *Why would that be important?*

"What did you do next?"

"I couldn't fall back to sleep. It was very warm so I decided to go down to the dock."

"Is that something you do regularly, Mrs. Rourke?"

"No. I thought there might be a breeze by the lake. Why is this important, Trooper Storrow?"

"Just trying to get a complete picture, ma'am. What time did you go down to the lake?"

"I don't know, maybe it was around three?"

"And what happened next?"

Kate rubbed her hands together. They were clammy. "I heard a boat approaching very fast with no lights." She looked at the constable. "I already told all of this to Constable Johnson."

"Sometimes when you retell something, you remember details you may have forgotten the first time. Did you think it was unusual that there were no lights?" Storrow asked.

"Of course. I've been boating on this lake for years. You could see nothing out there last night." She gestured in the direction of the lake. "I only know what I heard."

He nodded. "Please continue."

Kate reiterated what she'd heard of the argument as it escalated, stopping and backing up each time Storrow interrupted her to press for more or to ask her to repeat verbatim what she'd heard. All the while, she thought about the girls at Jenny's looking for their friend Mel.

"How many people do you think were in the boat?" Storrow's pencil poised over the page.

"I think two, a woman or a girl and a man. She sounded young. It was mostly the girl's words I heard. The man's voice was unclear, muffled by the sound of the motor."

Kate shifted in her chair. How was he able to take such copious notes and yet his eyes never left hers?

"Did you hear anything else, Mrs. Rourke?"

"Yes, I told Constable Johnson I heard things being thrown around the boat and into the water, and loud banging sounds later. Trooper Storrow, I'm sure someone went into the water!" Kate felt her composure slipping. She knew now that a girl was dead. "The girl yelled 'Fuck you!' and then there was a deep sounding splash. I don't know how else to describe it but it was different from the other sounds." Kate squeezed her hands together to keep them from shaking. "Trooper Storrow, I never heard her again."

"No screams? No calls for help?" Storrow paused in his note taking.

Kate shook her head.

"Is that when the engine was cut?"

"Yes."

"Did you hear the other voice then?"

She felt five pairs of eyes on her but didn't respond for a few seconds. Beads of sweat formed above her upper lip. "It wasn't clear but he said something like Are you crazy? Quit playing games."

"He didn't call out to anyone by name?"

"No." She whispered.

"Please speak up, Mrs. Rourke. I'm sure this incident was very upsetting to you, but I need you to answer a couple more questions. What happened next?"

"The boat left." Her voice was quiet. She shut her eyes, remembering. "He left her there."

Sarah sat beside her mother and took her hand.

"Can you estimate the total time of the incident, Mrs. Rourke?"

Kate took a deep breath and looked at the trooper. "It was probably no more than a few minutes, but in the dark it seemed like an eternity."

"Thank you, Mrs. Rourke."

She was relieved when he turned to Jack. "Tell me about the search you and your wife conducted by boat."

Kate listened to Jack's calm, factual responses as he described their search pattern and finding the beer cans and the oar.

"What time did you get back to the house?"

"About four-thirty, five o'clock?" He looked to Kate who nodded.

"And that's when you called Constable Johnson?"

"Yes," Kate and Jack answered together.

Kate hoped he would have no more questions for her. She'd told him all she could—nothing more about that voice, nothing about what she'd overheard outside Jenny's. The police already knew the identity of the girl and could find out her friends' names. The painful, gripping feeling in her belly tightened.

"Mrs. Rourke." Storrow stood. "Just one last question. Are you absolutely sure you heard the striking sounds *after* the splash?"

She knew this was important and was definite. "Yes. I'm sure."

He put out his hand. "Mr. and Mrs. Rourke, thank you both for your co-operation. We'll get back to you if there's anything else we need." He nodded to Sarah and Joe. "Ms. Rourke, Officer Parelli."

Joe had kept quiet during the questioning and now shook the officers' hands. "Let me know if there's anything I can do, assist in any way."

"We may not be the NYPD," Constable Johnson said, "but I think we've got it covered. Thanks."

"What do you think happened?" Jack asked as he walked them to the door.

"We don't deal in conjecture, Mr. Rourke." Storrow eyed Jack. "We examine all the facts and the evidence and only then come up with a conclusion. I can't tell you anymore than that." He and Norm left and closed the door behind them.

10

Clayton Storrow slipped easily behind the wheel and buckled his seatbelt. Norm sucked in his gut to fasten his own.

"Did it seem to you Rourke was drinking before we got there?" Norm asked.

"Yeah, the coffee did little to conceal it. These summer people like their cocktails in the afternoon, on their boats too. Between our state boat and the game warden you'd be surprised how many we nab on a weekend."

"And what's with the big city cop fiancé? I don't think we need him sniffing around."

"I wouldn't worry about him, but we'll be damn sure we play this one by the book." Storrow put the key in the ignition and backed down the driveway. "What's your take on the wife?"

"Typical flatlander. But she seems like a nice lady. She was pretty torn up about what she heard when I was there this morning. She's the one who called, not him."

Storrow was quiet for a few minutes. "I don't know. Just a gut feeling, but I think she's holding something back."

They passed one car as they headed north out of West View Road. Norm glanced in the rear view mirror, saw the black Toyota slow and put on his blinker before turning in. He smiled. Nothing like a cop car to make people slow down and signal.

He punched in Carrie Ryan's number. Hannah was still sleeping.

Twenty minutes later, the state cruiser drove through the wrought iron gates of Ethan Allen College, twelve miles north of town. Norm took in the lush manicured lawns and the imposing red brick buildings, some with white columns. Huge oaks and maples provided shade for the clusters of summer students in shorts and T's sprawled on the grass. Others played Frisbee or walked the well-worn paths with backpacks.

"Impressive, just like those glossy pictures in the college catalog," Norm said.

"Yeah." Storrow looked around. "The perfect New England setting."

Norm detected an edge to the trooper's voice. "Not so perfect, huh?"

"There's a lot of crap goes on in these schools. We get called all the time. Underage and binge drinking are just the surface symptoms. There's drugs, rape, sexual harassment, gay bashing, you name it."

Norm smiled. "Now you sound like me—cynical."

"College campuses are just microcosms of society, Constable. Whatever you find outside you'll find here only magnified. You put all these kids and their raging hormones together with little or no adult supervision and you've got big problems. These campuses aren't the idyllic ivory towers people think they are, especially the parents who pay the bills."

"You got any kids, Storrow?"

"Yeah, two boys in high school. We'll be doing the whole college thing soon enough. How about you?"

"Nope, no kids." Norm thought about his son, out there somewhere. He'd be about twenty, maybe even in college.

They were approaching the administration building with its floor-to-ceiling pane-glass windows. The staircase of Vermont marble formed a semicircle around the entrance to the building.

Storrow parked in front and both men got out. The trooper extended his hand as a security guard, a man in his fifties, approached. "Hey, Dan, how're you doing? This is Constable Johnson from Willow Bend."

"Good to see you again, Trooper Storrow." Dan shook both men's hands.

"Dean Albright's expecting us," Storrow said. "Do you know if he's in his office?"

"He was earlier. Go on in, the building's open."

"You hear anything about a party on the lake last night?" Storrow asked.

Dan snorted and shook his head. "With these kids there's always a party somewhere."

"Thanks, Dan."

Norm followed Storrow into the reception area of the administration building and made a low whistle as he looked around. "Jeez, no wonder the tuition's out of sight. The inside's as pricey as the outside."

Storrow knocked on a door to the left that was ajar. A man in is late forties came out from behind the desk. "Come in, Trooper Storrow." They shook hands and Storrow introduced Norm.

Dean Albright ushered them into his air-conditioned office. He leaned one hip against the highly polished mahogany desk, the top of which was completely clear except for a computer.

"How can I help you, officers?" He crossed his arms in front of his chest.

"Sorry for the delay, Dean," Storrow said. "I was called to the scene of a young girl's suspicious death at the lake. That took priority."

"Of course." The dean walked around and sat at his desk. "You're here to follow up on the students who were at that party. The parents of those you apprehended have already called me. I've stressed the seriousness of the situation, but I'm sure many of them are on their way here with their lawyers."

"We're investigating whether the two incidents are related," Storrow said.

"The party and the girl's death? Is that what you're saying?" The dean's composure appeared to slip.

"The victim, a fifteen-year-old girl from town, was last seen at that party with an EA student, possibly a freshman."

"Fifteen years old? What happened?" The dean seemed to pale.

Norm watched and listened as the two men discussed Mel in factual, almost clinical terms. He fought hard to keep quiet.

"You think one of our students was involved? Do you have a name?" The dean bent forward. Norm imagined he was seeing the repercussions—financial, legal, PR.

Storrow checked his notes. "We have the first names

of two of the boys we believe invited this girl and two friends to the party. Mike and Brandon. The third is a kid they call TJ, but we don't know if the J is a middle or last initial. That's the one that was last seen with the victim."

Norm's fist tightened, as did his voice. "Her name is Melody Ward. Could we please give her the respect of calling her by name?"

The men looked at him as if remembering he was still there. "You're absolutely right, Constable Johnson," the dean said.

Storrow said nothing.

Dean Albright went to his computer and called up the freshman class males. "As you can imagine, there are several Michaels and two Brandons. As for a TJ..." The dean shook his head. "We'll need more information."

Norm sat forward in his chair and wiped his palms on his thighs. Here they were farting around with a computer when they should be out looking for the asshole that did this to Mel. He opened his mouth to say something but Storrow cut him off.

"Dean, we have the full names of several more students who were reportedly at the party in addition to those we've already apprehended. Sometimes we get lucky when kids get scared. We need to talk to them. Before the lawyers get involved."

Norm thought the dean was about to object when Storrow continued. "We have a suspicious death on our hands. These students may have valuable information." He handed the list to the dean.

Dean Albright thought for a minute and then opened another database. He cross-checked the new names with dorm assignments. "Here they are. Trooper Storrow, I'm responsible for ensuring that students' rights are protected here on campus. I insist on being present when you question these students."

Norm had had it. "A girl is dead. We only want to talk to these kids. What do you think we're gonna do?"

"Constable Johnson, Dean Albright is certainly welcome to accompany me to these students' rooms. Why don't you go to the Student Center and wait for me there."

Norm felt as if he'd been stung. He left the office without another word. From the top of the marble steps, he looked out over the campus. He'd go check things out for himself, damn it!

He made his way to the center of the main quadrangle where he found a map painted on a large wooden sign. Norm got his bearings and made the rounds of the dining hall, the student lounge and the fitness center. There were plenty of kids hanging out. He tried engaging them in conversation, but didn't get far. He wasn't good at this and the uniform definitely didn't help.

An hour and a half later he was sitting in the Student Center. A third cup of coffee had him wired. He was up and down like a yo-yo watching for Storrow. When Norm thought he couldn't wait one more minute, the trooper came in. "Where have you been?"

Storrow ignored the question and sat down. "We got lucky. These kids are tough but they're still kids—they come clean once they hear there's been a death. Partying in an empty house is one thing. Being implicated in a death is something else."

He opened his pocket notebook. "It appears the party was instigated by a junior named Bud Foley. His parents are friends of the homeowners. Foley knew they wouldn't be up this weekend. Somebody posts it on Facebook and Twitter and whatever else. Next thing more than a hundred kids show up, some that nobody knows."

He watched Norm. "Some of them thought they remembered seeing Melody Ward there. They'd seen her at other parties."

Norm didn't like that. Just how much time was she spending here? He cleared his throat. "Anybody know this TJ character?"

Storrow nodded and almost smiled. "He just finished his freshman year and is taking summer classes. He's sublet an apartment with some friends off campus."

"Where?" Norm was on his feet. "Let's get over there right now."

"Hold on. The house is at 1402 Church. And guess who else is subletting? A Mike O'Malley and a kid named Brandon. No last name."

"Yes." Norm punched his left palm with his fist. "Did you lose the dean?"

Storrow smiled for the first time since Norm had met him. "He had to leave, said he had a prior commitment tonight." Storrow glanced at his watch. "It's almost six o'clock, much later than I thought. He gave me his cell number. I assured him we were done on campus for now, but I don't see why we can't pay a visit to a private home off-campus without the dean."

"Well, let's go then." Norm tossed his coffee cups in the trash. "I'm glad you got something. I got zilch."

Storrow frowned at Norm, who also smiled for the first time and said, "What? You thought I was just hanging out at the Student Union all this time?"

11

Tim Rourke slowed when he saw the cruiser. What's with all the cops? He had enough problems. He heard kids had gotten arrested at the party after he'd left. Were these guys heading to campus now to round up the rest? It was a good thing he'd left and didn't tell anyone where he was going.

He turned onto the secondary town road that led to the lake house. He'd traveled this road countless times since before he was two. Looking in the rear view mirror, he rubbed his bloodshot eyes and replaced his sunglasses. He felt like crap, and looked like it too. He reached for the two-liter bottle of water next to him and downed two Tylenol. *They'll take one look at me and know I'm hung over and that I was in a fight.*

Tim tried to smooth out the khaki shorts and T-shirt as he got out of the black Toyota but gave up. He looked like he'd slept in them and he had. What the hell time was it, anyway? He checked his phone. After 3:30. They were going to be all over him about not going to Burlington but it beat waiting around campus for the cops to pick him up.

He opened the door to the lake house and kicked off his flip-flops. Sarah was the first to spot him. "Hey, little brother." She hugged him. "You look like shit," she said an inch from his ear.

"Yeah, thanks. You, too."

"Tim, what are you doing here?" His mom looked tired and kind of pale. "What happened to you?" She inspected the bruises on his face and the gash across his knuckles.

"I'm fine, Mom. Don't worry about it, okay?" Towering over her, Tim put an arm around her shoulders. She seemed smaller, fragile almost.

She looked up at him. "Why aren't you in Burlington?"

"I decided not to go."

His dad's voice boomed as he came around the corner from the kitchen. "You what? You blew it off? You're on probation, Tim. These summer classes aren't for fun."

"I know, Dad. Hello to you, too." He raised his water bottle and took a big gulp.

"Water, huh?" His dad studied him. "Too much partying last night? How's the other guy look?"

"Jack, not now." His mom was always trying to run interference. She stepped between him and his dad. "Let's get some ice on your eye and cheek, and clean up that cut."

"I had a good time in college too, Kate, but not *all* the time." He turned back to Tim. "So now you're fighting too? How much are you drinking these days?"

"Said the man with the bourbon," Sarah said to no one in particular. "Joe, let's take a walk. I've seen this before."

"Hey, good to see you, man." Joe slapped Tim's back and left with Sarah.

"Answer me." His dad got in his face. "You're

underage. The cops don't fool around with this stuff anymore. And fighting could get you bounced out of school on your ass."

"Jeez, Dad, I get it. We all know you're perfect—the brilliant student, the perfect husband, the successful businessman. And I'm the fuck-up."

"Watch your language in front of your mother."

"Sorry, Mom." He sat at the table while she applied ice to his face and dressed his knuckles with an antibiotic and gauze. "Thanks."

Tim stood then and faced his father toe to toe. He'd wanted to do this for a long time. "You're never satisfied with anything I do. You want me to major in business, be like you. But that's not what *I* want. I don't have any idea what I want."

"A business degree will open doors for you. Believe me, Tim." His dad seemed to be calming down.

"I don't care about that. I don't care about school." Tim took a deep breath. "I want to go to Colorado, for a year maybe. I could get a job at a ski resort, snowboard every day. Mike's thinking of going too."

"Colorado? Nothing but hippies and druggies out there. Is that what you want? Well, you'd *better* get a job because I'm not financing a year of finding yourself. I'm not financing *anything* if you don't shape up. Do you hear me?" He banged his glass of bourbon down, sloshing some onto the table.

"Take it easy," his mom said. "No one's going anywhere right now." His mother, the peacemaker. It didn't matter whether he was last at bat and lost the game or blew an algebra test; she was always there, deflecting criticism, smoothing things over.

She brushed his hair off his forehead. "Your Dad and I

love you, and we want the best for you. You're nineteen. We don't expect you to know what you want to do for the rest of your life. And we want you to enjoy college but we want you to be responsible too, and safe. Underage drinking puts you at great risk, Tim. Not just your own safety but legally as well. We're worried about you."

"What did you do last night?" His dad asked.

Tim didn't answer.

"This is important," his mother said. "Where were you?"

"I'm not a little kid anymore, Mom." He wanted to get away from this scrutiny. His head ached.

"But I am still your mother. Answer me."

"I went to a party. Who cares?" He rolled his eyes and looked up at the ceiling.

"Where was this party?" His mother's voice sounded kind of shaky.

"What's with the third degree?" He looked from one parent to the other. "I don't know, somewhere up at the other end of the lake."

"Whose house?" His father hadn't bothered to refill his glass.

"I don't know. This guy knows them. They're friends of his parents, I think. They were away. What difference does it make?"

"Did this guy have a key or are we talking breaking and entering now too?"

"Jeez, Dad, what's the big deal? It was a *party!*"

"Were there a lot of people at this party?" his mom asked.

"Sure. Word gets out and kids just show up."

"Were there kids from town there?" Her eyes

narrowed.

Why would she ask him that? And why was his dad looking at her and frowning? "How would I know?" He shrugged. "There were probably a hundred kids there."

His mom sat down and motioned for him to join her. "Listen to me, Tim. Did you leave the party at any point?" She was looking at him like she could see right through him.

He didn't answer.

"You know if you left the damn house or not," his father said.

"Were you in a boat?" His mother looked like she was going to cry. "Tell me the truth."

"What are you talking about?" *What the hell was going on? How could she know?*

"Are you kidding me, Kate?" His father looked like someone had punched him in the gut. "When were you going to tell me?"

Something was going on between his parents, but what?

When she didn't answer, his dad loomed over him. "Was that you? Were you so drunk that you didn't know you were right across from here?" He pointed toward the lake. "Yeah, that's right. Your mother was on the dock early this morning. She heard people arguing, someone fall in the water, and a boat leave. Who was with you?"

"You guys are crazy. It wasn't me!" Tim stood up and paced.

"Tim." His mother's voice sounded like she was talking through a tunnel or from very far away. "I heard two people arguing in a boat. The girl was much clearer, louder. At first, I couldn't hear the man at all. His voice was muffled, lost in the sound of the motor. After she fell or jumped in, I finally heard him. His voice—it screamed in my head. I refused to believe it. I kept telling myself it couldn't be. You weren't even here this weekend. But deep down…" Tears ran down her face. She didn't wipe them away.

"In town this morning I heard some girls talking about their friend. She hadn't come home and they were worried about her. They'd left her at a party last night with a guy named TJ. I know that's what they call you at school."

"What the hell? You couldn't mention this?" His dad pivoted toward his mom.

She was still crying. "When I saw you, I knew for sure."

His father grabbed his arm and turned him around. "What the hell were you thinking? Joy riding in the pitch black, no lights, drinking, fighting. Jesus, Tim! And the girl— did you stop to think what happened to her? Your mother heard the boat leave. She was frantic, sure that someone was still in the water. We went out in the boat but found no one. When we came back in, we called the constable."

"You called the constable, Mom?" He was yelling and holding his head with both hands. "I can't believe this!"

"*You* can't believe it? I had to! Someone was still out there. You left her there, Tim. How could you do that?"

He'd never seen his mom look at him like this, like he was a stranger. Her tears were ripping him apart. He felt like he would dissolve into the floor.

"Do you know a girl named Melody Ward?" his father asked.

Tim tried to decipher his father's words. It was like someone had thrown a scrabble board up in the air and the letters were falling all around him in random patterns.

"Do you know her?" His dad's voice was slow,

measured—like before he explodes.

"I'm not having this conversation with you." Tim watched as his dad's face turned from dark crimson to almost purple.

"The girl's fifteen years old! What the hell's wrong with you? There are laws against this! But that's the least of your problems now."

Tim had no idea what *that* meant but he wasn't going to hang around and find out. He needed to get away from here. From them. "I'm done."

He ran out and left the door wide open behind him.

~~

Kate walked to the door, quietly closed it, and lay her head against it.

"So you knew? You knew it was him all the time?" Jack was behind her.

She turned to face him. "I didn't want to. I tried to convince myself it wasn't." She shook her head. "But, that voice ... that voice ..." Her words trailed off.

"I have to hand it to you, Kate. You gave a stellar performance for the constable and again for the trooper. Didn't think you had it in you to conceal evidence from the authorities."

"Cut the sarcasm, Jack. This is our son. What are we going to do?"

12

It was a short ride from campus to the house on Church Street. Norm punched in Carrie Ryan's number. "How is she?"

"She's asleep. Glenn, Dr. Braddock, gave her something a little while ago."

"When she wakes up, tell her I'll be over as soon as I can. I'm following up on something with the trooper."

"Yeah, well, you do your thing, Norm. We can take care of Hannah." She hung up.

Norm put his phone away.

"Problem?" Storrow looked over.

Norm shook his head. "There's 1402 right there."

They pulled up in front of a run-down white colonial. The paint was peeling and there were no curtains at the windows. They crossed the front yard, knee high with weeds, walked up the broken front steps and rang the bell.

A thin, freckle-faced kid in a T-shirt and boxers answered the door.

"I'm Trooper Clayton Storrow and this is Constable

Norm Johnson. Do you live here?"

"Yeah. I mean yes, sir."

Norm watched the kid's Adam's apple bulge as he swallowed. Probably still hung over and never expected to see the cops at his door.

"What's your name?" Storrow took the lead.

"Mike O'Malley."

"Anyone else at home, Mike?"

"I don't think so. I just got up." He rubbed his red hair, which was sticking up on end.

Norm glanced at his watch. After six. *What time did this kid get to bed?*

"We'd like to ask you a few questions," Storrow said. "May we come in?"

"Umm, what's this all about?"

"Do you know anything about a party last night on Steed Hill?

Mike hesitated and looked around.

"Right now, we're not interested in the underage drinking. The owners may decide to sue for property damages, but there'll be time enough for that later. We already have a list of the kids who were there. It would be in your best interest to talk to us, Mike."

"Okay. I guess." He opened the door wider.

Stepping over a pile of discarded sneakers, Storrow and Norm stood in the front hall. The adjoining living room smelled like a combination of a corner bar and a locker room with clothes and empty beer cans strewn about the stained carpet and torn mismatched furniture.

"There's been an accident, Mike. That's our main concern right now. We need to know if you were at the party," Storrow said.

Mike looked at the trooper stunned. "What kind of accident?"

"Were you there?"

"Umm. Maybe for a little while." He shifted his weight from one foot to the other.

Norm couldn't stay quiet any longer. "Do you know a girl named Melody Ward? Did you see her at the party?"

"I'm not sure." He looked around again. "There were a lot of people there. Why?"

"Melody Ward is dead." Norm emphasized each word.

"What the fuck? Sorry. What happened to her?" He rubbed his face as though to dislodge what he'd just heard. He looked at Storrow. "Is she really—dead?"

"So you do know Melody Ward?" Storrow said.

"Yeah, I guess." He spoke now in just above a whisper.

"How well do you know her?" The trooper studied Mike's face.

"I just know who she is. She hangs out here with her friends sometimes."

"At this house?" Norm wanted details.

"No. No. On campus, at parties and stuff."

"Did you see her last night?" Storrow's demeanor was controlled.

"I'm not sure." His eyes darted from one cop to the other.

"Listen, kid." Norm's patience was ready to snap. "Just answer the question. Did you see her or not?"

"Yeah, I guess. But I wasn't with her. What happened?"

They heard the back door slam.

"That's what we're trying to find out," Storrow said.

"Do you know a guy called TJ? We have a witness who puts them together at the party."

Before Mike could answer, a tall, preppy-looking guy holding car keys came in from what must be the kitchen.

"Hello, officers. I know TJ. He lives here."

"And you are?" Norm asked.

"I'm Todd Anderson. This is my apartment. Mike and TJ are subletting a couple of rooms for the summer along with Brandon Weiss."

"Are you a student at the college?" Storrow asked.

"Yes, I'll be a senior in September. What's this all about?"

"We're investigating a party last night on Steed Hill. Would you know anything about that?"

"Yes, I was there. But I'm of age. There's no law against having a good time as far as I know." He smiled.

Storrow ignored the remark. "There's been an accident involving a girl named Melody Ward. Do you know her?"

Todd frowned. "Melody Ward ... Melody Ward. Young girl? From town?" He looked over at Mike. "Isn't she TJ's girlfriend?"

Mike was silent, his face red and blotchy as he looked from Todd to the cops. His hands were fisted at his sides.

"Yes, that's right. I remember now." Todd snapped his fingers. "He was with her at the party. I think they had words. He started a fight with my buddy Buck Sweeney, messed him up pretty good. The last time I saw Melody Ward, she was getting into a boat with TJ."

"Boat? What are you talking about? I didn't see any boat." The words exploded in rapid fire from Mike's mouth.

"You were probably passed out with the other amateurs, O'Malley." Todd laughed.

"Do either of you know where we might find this TJ?" Norm had had enough of these college boys.

"I don't know," Mike blurted before Todd could answer. "I haven't seen him since last night."

"How about you?" Norm looked at Todd who shrugged.

"Well, if either of you hears from him, tell him to get in touch with me." Storrow handed each of them a card with his number. "We'd like to talk to Buck Sweeney too. Where would we find him?"

"I think he went home, to New Jersey," Todd said. "He'll be back tomorrow. He lives at 1429 down the street."

Norm glared at Mike who hadn't moved. "Tell this TJ if we don't hear from him, we'll be back. You got that?"

Mike nodded.

"What's TJ's full name?" Storrow asked. Mike shook his head back and forth.

"Tim Rourke." Todd Anderson smiled.

Bingo! "Does he drive a black Toyota?" Norm's heart rate accelerated.

"He sure does." Anderson drew out the words.

Norm looked at Storrow. "I think I know where he is."

13

Barefoot, Tim took the stairs two at a time. Gravel bit into the soles of his feet as he ran down the driveway. He bolted across the road and into the woods where he had played as a child. Not slowing, he plowed through the underbrush, sidestepping roots and jumping over rocks and downed logs. When he found the remnants of the old tree fort, he stopped. Bending over with his hands on his knees, he took several deep breaths.

He tried Mel's number. It went directly to voicemail. Again. "Shit." She hadn't answered all day. Was she still that pissed?

He climbed the tree and ducked into the plywood shelter, smaller than he remembered. Leaning his back against the rough wooden walls, Tim sank to the floor and shut his eyes. He rested his elbows on bent knees. His feet and legs were bleeding but he didn't care.

An image of that fat slob Buck Sweeney with his hands all over Mel flashed in Tim's mind. If he had another chance, he'd hit him again.

And he didn't need his father to remind him about the law. He knew how old she was but it didn't matter. Mel was different from any girl he'd ever known. Tim scrubbed at his face.

And Mom! Calling the cops! What the hell was that all about?

He tried Mel's cell again. Voicemail.

Tim crossed his arms on his raised knees and lay his forehead on them. He tried to remember what had happened after he convinced Mel to get in the boat with him. He only wanted to get her alone, talk to her. He didn't remember driving the boat or where they went. He'd been on this lake practically his whole life. Wouldn't he know if he were in front of his own house? They fought. He remembered that. She was yelling and throwing stuff around.

In a sudden flash, he saw her hit the water.

"Oh, God!" He bolted upright, eyes wide, and stared at the scarred wall in front of him.

His cell vibrated. "Mel! I've been calling you all day. Are you all right?"

"It's Mike. Where are you, man? You okay?"

"Leave me alone." He started to disconnect.

"Don't hang up. I need to tell you something. The cops were here."

"About the party?"

"Yeah, that too. When the cops got there, most of the kids ran but they caught some of them. The owners of the house are probably going to press charges. But listen, there's something else. Something bad. I wanted you to hear it from me."

Air rushed out of Tim's lungs as he waited in silence

for his best friend since high school to say something.

"Mel's dead."

He shook his head back and forth as his insides turned to liquid and blood drained from his head. "NO!" The word ripped out of him and echoed off the empty tree house walls. When he was able to speak, a weak and raspy voice asked, "What … happened?"

"I don't know. Someone told the cops she was with you last night and they're looking for you. They didn't know your real name, just that everyone calls you TJ. That asshole Anderson told them. He's had it in for you since the day we moved in. He's such a dick."

Tim swallowed and forced himself to keep listening. "He told them about the fight with Buck Sweeney too and that he saw Mel get in a boat with you. I said I never saw a boat. Hey, are you still there?"

"Yeah."

"Anyway, I said I didn't know where you went even though I figured you were at your parents' lake house. Tim, this is serious. These cops are on a fuckin' mission. If I were you, I'd come clean with your parents before the cops get there. Your Dad must know a lawyer."

"A lawyer?" The word jumped out at him from the jumble of sounds he was trying to make sense of.

"Yeah, man, this is bad."

"I gotta go, Mike. Thanks."

Tim didn't move as the walls and the surrounding woods closed in on him. Shafts of sunlight through the gaps in the plywood roof made slashes on his legs and the stained floor. His own strangled voice ripped the silence. "Mel!" He began to cry and to puke until there was nothing left in his stomach.

Images and words bombarded his brain in no sane order: their kisses, the argument, her silky skin, her anger. Then he saw her again—in the water. How did she get there? Did she jump? Lose her balance?

He punched the wall until he bled through the bandage his mom had applied. "I can't remember shit!"

He tried again to picture the last time he saw Mel in the boat. His brain hurt from trying to dredge up memories mired in a drunken haze. With painstaking effort, he dug until he finally saw her—standing on the back of the boat. Yes, now he remembered. She said something about swimming in. She wanted to go home.

Did he try to talk her out of it?

He saw himself grabbing her arm, felt his fingers digging into soft flesh. Had she pulled away? Jumped? Fallen? He started to cry again. "I can't remember!" He kicked a hole in the plywood wall. *Did I let her go?*

Mom said she heard the boat start up again. *Did I leave her there?*

Mike had told him he didn't know what happened to her. Did she drown?

Tim sobbed. "I never meant to hurt you … I never meant to hurt you…" The mantra continued until he had no more tears.

~~

The angle of the sun through the roof had shifted. It was much lower in the sky. Tim had no idea how long he'd been there. He rubbed his face. Grainy tears had dried on his cheeks.

How long before the cops found him? He'd have to tell his parents everything, at least as much as he remembered.

Tim looked around the neglected tree fort. A rotted

piece of wire cable, once part of a zip line, hung from the open doorway. A rusted fishing lure lay in the corner with dried butts from old pilfered cigarettes. Echoes of Truth or Dare games and the ghosts of stolen first kisses and beers hung in the air.

Knowing what he had to do, he climbed down— leaving behind the last vestiges of childhood.

14

Unable to warm the hollow place within her, Kate sat on the deck with her eyes closed, absorbing the early evening sun as it crept toward the horizon. She was still reeling from the certain knowledge of Tim's involvement, however indirect, in the death of Melody Ward. The truth had slammed into her the instant she'd seen him.

He still wasn't back. It must be close to two hours by now. Kate opened her eyes to check her watch and he was in front of her, backlit by the rays.

Shielding her eyes, she looked up at him. "Are you all right? Where have you been?"

"I'm in serious trouble, Mom. I need to talk to you and Dad."

She got up and put her arm around his waist, pulling him tight. They walked inside together.

Jack shut off the game when he saw them. He'd been holed up in front of the TV, not speaking to Kate again after she told him what she knew.

"I have to tell you something," Tim said. "It *was* me in the boat last night. Mike just called. The cops are looking for me. Someone told them Mel was with me." He paused. "She's … she's … dead." He swiped at his red-rimmed eyes.

"Just start from the beginning," Jack said in a controlled voice.

"Do you want Joe and me to leave?" Sarah asked.

"No. You're gonna find out anyway. You might as well hear it from me." Tim sat on the couch beside his mother.

Kate looked at her son's man-sized hand in her own, fresh blood on the bandage across his knuckles. The rest of him was tall and lanky, as if his body hadn't yet grown into its frame. Closing her eyes for just a moment, she saw a towheaded toddler laughing and running loose-limbed through high grass. She braced herself for what was coming.

~~

Tim sat before his family, feeling like a child making his confession to the priest. He took a deep breath. He'd have to make sense of the random sensations and images in his brain— the noise, the kids, kissing Mel, the drinking, playing beer pong, kissing Mel, the argument, the bonfire, *her in the water!* God, he still couldn't remember how she got there.

"I went to a party on the lake last night. I'm having a hard time remembering a lot of what happened but I'm trying. Mel and her friends showed up. We were drinking a lot.

"She's been quiet lately. Like something's bothering her. We went into one of the other rooms. I tried talking to her but she wouldn't tell me what was wrong."

"You just talked?" His dad raised an eyebrow.

Tim shrugged and looked away. "She wanted to go

back to the party. I told her I'd meet her outside. I found her down by the fire." Tim rubbed his forehead. "It gets fuzzy here but I remember this guy Buck Sweeney was all over her. He had his arms around her, tickling her maybe. I'm not sure. I think she was laughing. I told him to get his hands off her. Maybe I took a swing at him, I don't know. But Mel was yelling.

"The next thing I knew, Buck was on me. He's a big guy. Somehow, I got in a lucky punch. I remember blood. It could have been mine but I think his nose was bleeding. This girl, a blonde … no, wait a minute. Somebody got him off me and then I think the girl came. Maybe she was a redhead. Anyway, she grabbed his arm and started kissing him. I think they staggered off together but I'm not sure."

"You'd better start remembering. 'I don't know' and 'I'm not sure' isn't gonna cut it with the cops," his dad said.

Tim ignored him and wanted to get it all out before anyone else interrupted. "The music was blaring. Everyone was pretty wasted. I kind of remember karaoke and maybe some kids skinny-dipping. I figured the cops would be coming any minute."

"Good guess," His dad said in his sarcastic tone.

"Mel and I walked toward the dock at the far end of the property. There was a boat there. I think the key was in the ignition."

"So you decided to take it? Steal it?" His dad leaned forward.

"Let me finish, Dad. I just wanted to be alone with her, that's all." He felt his mom squeeze his hand. "I didn't think anybody would notice if we took it. Mel didn't want to go. She yelled something like 'I'm not going anywhere with you.' I asked her if she wanted to be there when the cops came and saw all the booze. That got her in the boat."

"Did anyone see you get in?" His dad was still leaning forward with his arms on his knees.

"I didn't think so, but Mike said Todd did and told the cops."

His dad swore and sat back.

"After that I don't remember much at all. I drove around. I don't know for how long. I know we argued. Mel was yelling about the fight with Buck. She said I couldn't tell her what to do, that she didn't belong to anybody.

"I was furious. I thought we had something special." He sniffed. He would *not* cry in front of his father. "I stopped and put the boat in neutral. I had no idea where we were. She started throwing things around." He shrugged. "Stuff that was in the boat, I guess."

"This is about where your mother came in." His dad picked up the glass of bourbon and glared at Tim. "How could you not know you were right out here?"

"I don't know! I couldn't see anything." He pulled away from his mom and stood.

"What happened next?" His mother's voice encouraged him to go on.

"I think she climbed up onto the back of the boat." Tim closed his eyes and tilted his head back. *Remember, damn it.* "I can almost see her standing there, saying she was going to swim in. I think I grabbed her arm but that's it. I don't know if she yanked it away from me, lost her balance, or jumped." He squeezed his head with both hands as if to force the answers to the surface. He looked at his family. "She was in the boat—then she wasn't. What if I let go and she drowned?" He pushed down the tears.

"We don't know what happened to her." His mom

stood and rubbed his back. "Did you hear anyone swimming? Any splashing or kicking?"

Tim wiped his nose on the sleeve of his T-shirt. "I don't know!"

"Did you call her; try to get her back in the boat?" Sarah looked at her brother.

"I don't remember." He shook his head.

"What about a flashlight? Was there one in the boat?" Sarah asked.

"I don't know. I don't know! It was dark. I couldn't see anything."

"Didn't you think she could have hit her head or passed out?" His dad drained the last of the bourbon and walked over to him. "Look at me, Tim."

"I don't know! I keep telling you. I … don't … remember!"

"Well, you'd better. Get yourself out of that drunken stupor you're in. Think!"

Tim sifted through the images in his brain but found no answers. He looked at his mom. "You heard the boat leave. I guess I took off." His voice was low, his arms down by his side.

"You just left her there?" Tears ran down Sarah's cheeks.

"Maybe I thought if I went back to the house, I could get someone to help me look for her." Face flushed, he was screaming and crying at the same time. "I didn't think anything happened to her!"

His dad waved toward the bank of windows looking out on the lake. "Jesus, Tim. You were right here! *We* could have helped you. Now a girl is dead."

"How could you just leave her there? I don't

understand." His mom was crying.

It tore at him. "I wasn't thinking, Mom. I was drunk."

"That's no excuse." She spoke in barely a whisper.

Joe spoke for the first time. "What's the next thing you do remember?"

"Umm … I woke up at the house where the party was. Covered in puke."

"Do you know what time that was?"

"No, but it was light out. The place was trashed and no one was around."

"So what did you do?" His father stood in front of him, close to his face.

"I found my car and drove home." He felt hollow inside, empty.

"Did you ask anyone for help when you got there?" His dad studied him.

Tim shook his head. "Nobody was around."

"So no one saw you go back to the party or to your house?" Joe said.

"I guess not." Tim sat again and put his head in his hands.

"Did you call the girl's house?" His father loomed over him.

"No. It was morning. I figured she was home by then." He looked up. "Mel's a really good swimmer." He heard the desperation in his own voice. "Then I … I guess I fell asleep." Tears rolled off his chin and pooled in the neck of his T-shirt.

"You mean you passed out—again—while this girl who's so *special* to you never made it home! I can't stand to look at you right now." Anger raging in his face, his dad turned his back on him and walked to the French doors. Leaning against the frame, he rested his head on his arm.

"How could you not get help, call her house, nothing?" His mom was still crying.

Tim sobbed. "I've called her cell like a million times since I woke up. I thought she was still pissed and wouldn't pick up."

"You said the cops know who you are." His back still to him, his dad's voice was flat.

"Yeah, I think they might come here to question me."

"Oh, they'll come. And it won't be long."

"You need to call them before that happens, Jack," Joe said.

"Screw the cops. I'm calling Hutch." His dad left the room without another word.

15

"He's at his parents' house, I'm telling you." Norm struggled to fasten his seatbelt. He and Storrow were leaving the house on Church Street. "That was his car, the black Toyota, turning in when we left."

They'd finally gotten the break they needed and Storrow was dragging his heels. He was freakin' driving the speed limit!

"What the hell are we waiting for, Storrow? We need to get back to the Rourke house ASAP and grab him. That O'Malley kid's his friend. You know he's gonna call him."

"Take it easy, Constable. We're not barging in there unprepared. We need to verify that Tim Rourke is in fact their son, and that he is the same Tim Rourke who was with the victim."

"How many Tim Rourkes do you think there are?" Norm was ready to go to the house himself if that's what it took.

Storrow ignored the question. "We need to check the

college records to verify Tim Rourke's permanent address, parents' names, etc. If we can get the dean to access the records from home, it will save us getting a court order and a hell of a lot of time." He looked over at Norm. "Can you take care of that?"

Norm nodded and took the dean's business card. He didn't want to deal with him again but anything to move this along.

"I'll call the ME when we get to your office," Storrow said. "He may have a preliminary cause of death by now. I'll relay the information to my supervisor. He may want me to hand everything over right now to the detective from BCI."

Damn. The Bureau of Criminal Investigation. If that happened, Norm would be out of the loop.

It was after 7 o'clock when they pulled into the town hall parking lot. Norm unlocked the building and his office. He took two Cokes out of the fridge and remembered he hadn't eaten anything since breakfast. He handed one to the trooper and dialed the dean's cell number.

"Dean Albright, this is Constable Norm Johnson from Willow Bend." He explained what he needed and thrummed his blunt fingers on the desktop while he waited. He was smiling when he hung up.

"Be right back," he said to Storrow. "I'm going to check the tax records in the town clerk's office."

Clayton Storrow was off the phone and writing in his notebook when Norm returned. He looked up. "What have you got?"

Norm read from a torn piece of paper. "Timothy Rourke, presently on academic probation, is enrolled in two summer courses at Ethan Allen. He should be a sophomore in the fall. Home address is 6 Fales Drive in Fairfield, CT, son of

John and Kathleen Rourke. Town records show this same couple owns a home at 176 West View Road, Willow Bend. He locked eyes with the trooper and grinned.

"Okay. Same kid. Good work."

"So why do you look so bad?" Norm cocked his head and squinted.

Storrow cleared his throat. "The medical examiner's preliminary finding is that Melody Ward did not drown. Asphyxiation and blunt force trauma to the head are the likely cause of death, sometime between two and five this morning. The back of her skull was cracked."

Norm sat down. "What else?"

Petichial hemorrhaging in the eyes, consistent with strangulation. Some bruising, like finger imprints, on her neck and upper right arm. Skin cells under her fingernails indicate she likely struggled with her attacker. I'm sorry, Constable." He paused. "It also looks like she was raped, definitive results pending."

Anger ripped through every muscle. Norm kicked the bottom drawer of his desk and crushed the empty soda can in his fist. "This will kill Hannah. We've got to nail this son of a bitch. I'm going back to the Rourkes' with you."

Storrow shook his head. "Can't do it. The BCI detective is going to meet me there and he's not going to want to see you. Those guys don't bend the rules. He said we got an anonymous call on the state tip-line that Tim Rourke is at his parents' house and could be planning to run."

"I told you that an hour ago! Where did this tip come from?"

"Traced to a pay phone behind the Rite Aid on Church Street. Didn't know there was a working one there."

"If he doesn't bolt, you know he's gonna lawyer up

fast." Norm grabbed his hat. "I have to go with you—please."

Storrow's cell rang. Norm paced from his desk to the office door and back.

The trooper disconnected. "The detective's delayed. I'm going there now. No heads up this time. I'm going to question the son if he's there. But we don't have enough to arrest him."

"What do you mean? We have witnesses that put them together at the party, and the Anderson kid saw them getting into a boat." Norm's palms were sweating.

"Yes, and all that means is he was with her, not that he raped and killed her. You're too close to this, Constable. I'm going alone."

Norm put his hands up and took two deep breaths. "Okay. I get it. I do. I'm the observer." He squared his posture and looked Storrow in the eye. "I swear I won't say a word. But I *have* to go, for Hannah."

Storrow said nothing for several seconds and arched an eyebrow. "We play this strictly by the book. Not a word."

"Fine. Fine. Let's just go." Norm was already at the door. "Thanks."

16

"Criminally negligent homicide." Pocketing his cell phone, his dad walked over to Tim, who was back on the couch. "Best case scenario if they can prove your leaving her caused or contributed to her death. In Connecticut, it's a misdemeanor carrying a fine and/or a year in jail. Hutch isn't sure about the Vermont statute."

Tim was digesting that when his mom asked, "How can you say that's a *best* case scenario?"

"Because that's assuming there's no evidence that something else directly caused her death." His dad's voice was monotone.

"What are you talking about? I told you. I didn't *do* anything! She fell or jumped in. All I did was try to grab her so she *wouldn't* go in." They had to believe him.

"I didn't say you did." His dad's voice stayed level, calm. "But you said yourself you can't remember. I'm only relating what Hutch told me." He paused. "He also said that's assuming there's no evidence of sexual intercourse. Then they could go for sexual assault because of her age."

"Man, this is a nightmare." Tim shook his head. "Evidence of sexual intercourse? You sound like the cops, Dad." He tried to swallow but his saliva had dried up.

"This could be your *worst* nightmare. There is no consensual sex when the girl is fifteen."

"Did I ever say we did anything? Did I?"

"I'm giving you the facts, Tim. That's all. And if I were you, I'd fill in those gaps in your memory—fast."

"This is getting us nowhere, Jack," his mom said. "When will Hutch be here?"

"He's at a conference in Greenwich. He'll leave early tomorrow morning. A law school buddy who practices in Vermont will meet us here at nine."

Tim trusted Hutch and hoped he could make sense of everything. He wiped sweaty palms on his pants. "So what do we do until he gets here?" Tim asked.

"Just sit tight. If the cops come back, we say we'll talk to them with our lawyers present."

"Won't that just piss them off, Dad? What do you think, Joe?"

Joe looked from Tim to his future father-in-law. "It's always a good idea to cooperate with the police, Tim. And I'd like to know what they've got and where they're going with this. But your Dad's right too. You have the right to have an attorney present during questioning even if you haven't been charged."

"But I don't have anything to hide! I'll tell them anything they want to know. I'm the one who left her there. She's dead because of me." His eyes filled.

"That kind of talk will get you in a lot of trouble." His dad's eyes cut into him.

"I'm already in a lot of trouble. It can't get any worse."

"It can get a lot worse. Trust me," his dad said under his breath.

A look passed between his parents that Tim didn't understand. "Now what?"

No one answered. Tim looked at his mother who shook her head as if to say "Let it go."

Sarah turned to Joe. "What do you think?"

"It's hard to know at this point. Criminally negligent homicide is one way they could go. Everything depends on the ME's findings. I've learned not to assume anything and to be prepared for everything."

"What do you mean?" Tim's stomach roiled.

"Something just seems off. There was too much activity, too many state crime scene vehicles at the site. My gut tells me there's more to this. I hope I'm wrong."

"What else could it be? She fell out of the boat!" Tim was yelling and gesturing wildly with his hands. "Doesn't anybody listen to me?"

"Do you really think there's a chance she could have made it to shore?" Joe said.

Tim stopped. "Yeah. She's a really good swimmer."

Joe frowned and nodded toward the farm across the lake. "Sarah, do you know that shoreline? Is it rocky or muddy?"

"We used to row over there in our bare feet and play hide and seek in the hay. I remember the bank as muddy. Don't you, Tim?"

Tim's head rested on the back of the couch, his face looking up at the exposed beams. He grunted in agreement.

"If it's muddy, there should be footprints or drag

marks if she pulled herself onto the bank. Jack, Kate, do either of you know if anyone checked for that?" Joe asked.

Tim heard his mom. "When Constable Johnson left here this morning, he said he was going to drive along the lake and look around."

"Do you know if he did?" Joe asked.

"How would we know that?" His dad answered. "He didn't seem too concerned about anything. But you'd think if it's important, *someone* would have. What are you getting at?"

"Nothing, I'm sorry. Just thinking out loud, getting ahead of myself. We'll have a better idea what's going on if and when the police get here."

Tim didn't follow Joe's line of reasoning but it didn't sound good. Out of the corner of his eye, he saw the reflection of car headlights coming up the driveway. He sat up straight.

His mother pulled aside the curtain. "I think we're about to find out."

The loud knock at the door plunged them into silence even though they were expecting it. Tim's gut plummeted as his dad opened the door.

"Officers, come in." He seemed to know them.

A state trooper, whose name tag read Clayton Storrow, entered and surveyed the room and its occupants. A heavier man in a khaki uniform followed. Neither man sat down. The trooper crossed his hands in front, one hand holding the other wrist.

"Mr. Rourke," the trooper said. "We'd like to speak with your son Tim. Is he here?"

"I'm Tim." Tim got up on unsteady legs. His mother moved to stand beside him.

"We'd like to ask you a few questions, Tim. I'm Trooper Storrow and this is Constable Johnson."

His dad stepped between him and the officers. "My son has nothing to say."

"Dad, don't." Tim drew himself up to his full six feet.

"Mr. Rourke," the trooper began again. "We need to question your son about the events of last evening. How old are you, Tim?"

"Nineteen."

"He's not a minor, Mr. Rourke. We don't need your permission to speak with him."

"But you *are* in my home, Trooper Storrow. My son will say nothing without our attorney present. He'll be arriving in the morning. Surely this can wait until then."

Tim took a step forward. "I'll talk to you now."

"No, Tim. You say nothing." His dad extended an arm as if to stop him.

Storrow turned and looked directly at Tim. "This won't take long. I'd like to keep this informal but if you prefer to have your attorney present, that is certainly your right."

"I'd rather just do it now." Sweat pooled in Tim's armpits at the same time a chill went through him.

"Use your head." His dad's voice was getting louder. "You do not want to do this. Wait for Hutch. He knows how this works."

"Dad, I'm going to tell the truth whether Hutch is here or not." He faced his father. "I just want to get it over with."

His father's face burned red with anger. He spoke in a low measured cadence. "Think about this."

"I have thought about it. I want to answer their questions." Tim glanced at Joe whose face gave nothing away.

Storrow directed Tim to sit. He sat beside him and took out a small notepad like the cops do on TV. "Do you know a girl named Melody Ward?"

That first question drove all thoughts of TV from Tim's mind. "Yes. We're friends." The full weight of Mel's loss filled him.

"Did you see her last night?"

"Yes, sir. At a party."

He felt his mom position herself behind him and place a hand on his shoulder. Tim focused on the questions and his answers. The trooper already knew about the fight with Buck Sweeney and about the boat. *Who had he been talking to?*

"Tell me about Melody Ward." The trooper stopped writing. His voice held no emotion.

Tim took a deep breath and tried to be consistent, telling everything as he remembered it.

He hoped it was the truth.

He had no idea how long he talked. He just wanted it done.

His father's voice cut in now and then. "Don't answer that, Tim."

But Tim wasn't listening.

"Had you been drinking?" The trooper's eyes narrowed.

"Yes. At the party." He couldn't stop.

"Your parents found beer cans in the lake."

They told him that? "I don't know, man. Not mine. I wasn't drinking in the boat. Maybe kids were drinking there earlier. Mel threw a bunch of stuff out. Maybe it was beer."

"You said she didn't want to get into the boat with you." The trooper inched closer. "Did you force her?"

"What? No!" Tim raised his voice, shook his head. "I just wanted to talk to her." He put his head in his hands.

Trooper Storrow sat back. "So, did you two talk?"

"Argued mostly. She was really pissed at me."

His mother tightened her grip on his shoulder and spoke. "I think the rest can wait until our lawyer arrives tomorrow."

Tim knew it sounded bad—his jealousy, the fight with Buck, stealing the boat, taking Mel away from the party and her friends, their argument. He rubbed his temples. *How had she ended up in the water? God, why can't I remember?*

Storrow pushed on. "Did that make you angry?"

"Did you hit her?" The question came from the corner of the room and jolted Tim. "An oar was found with gashes on the side."

"Wait just a minute, Constable." His dad stepped forward. "My son has nothing further to say."

"Constable, that's enough," Storrow said.

"What? NO!" Panicked, Tim looked from Johnson to Storrow. "I would never hurt Mel. All I did was grab her arm when she was standing on the back of the boat. Then she fell in the water, or jumped in. I don't know. I don't remember!" Tim shouted through his tears.

"What did you do then?" It was Storrow's voice, calm and relentless.

"I can't remember! Did she drown?"

Joe stood. "I agree with Jack. I think you've got what you came for, Trooper Storrow."

"She didn't drown!" Constable Johnson blurted out. "Melody Ward was brutally raped and murdered."

The air went out of Tim as if he'd been pummeled by a linebacker. He tried to speak. "How? What are you talking about?"

His mom dug her nails into his shoulders. "No!' She screamed.

He heard Storrow's voice as if from far away.

"Constable, wait for me in the car. Now." The constable left, fuming but silent.

"Stop." It was his dad. "Tim, not another word. Are you accusing my son of rape and murder? This interview is over."

Storrow stood. "We're not accusing anybody of anything, Mr. Rourke. Your son may be the last person who saw Melody Ward alive."

The words and the accusations were swirling around him. The force propelled Tim to his feet. Shaking, he looked the trooper in the eye. "I'm not saying another word without my lawyer."

"Then we'll continue this at the state police barracks in Castleton tomorrow at ten. Be there." He headed for the door.

"Trooper Storrow, just a minute before you go." Joe walked over to him. "Melody Ward was supposedly a very good swimmer. Did you find any indication that she did, in fact, make it to shore? Footprints on the bank, drag marks, anything?"

Storrow's face hardened. "I have nothing further to add to this conversation, Officer Parelli. Tim, I'll see you tomorrow at ten."

Tim stood gaping at the closed door. The policeman's departure left everyone speaking and shouting at once.

"What's happening?" "Why the hell would he say that?" "Tim's innocent!" "What kind of evidence can the police have?" "What are we going to do?"

"Stop. Just stop!" Tim shouted. "I'm right here. Don't talk about me like I'm not."

"Tim's right," Joe said. "Sorry. We have to calm down, think this through logically. We need to give the lawyers as much information as possible. And we need you, Tim, to do that."

They sat at the table and made lists of everything: who was at the party, Mel's friends who were with her, who might have seen Tim come back to the house or to his own place, where Mel lived, what Tim knew about her family.

"Did you ever see her with another guy, Tim?" Joe asked. "Or talk about anyone who made her uneasy? Think."

"Yeah. There was this guy who kept calling and texting her. Following her too. I think she used to go out with him. He gave her the creeps."

"Did you ever see him?" Sarah asked.

"I think so. We were walking on campus a couple of weeks ago and this guy in a black pick-up drove by real slow. He was around my age, wore a ball cap. He didn't stop or say anything, but Mel yelled, 'Leave me alone.' I asked her about him but she wouldn't say anything."

"You get a name?" Joe asked.

"Shane." Tim's shoulders relaxed just saying the name.

"Do you have a last name?"

Tim shook his head.

"Wait!" his mom said. "That sounds like the guy I saw this morning at Jenny's when I followed the girls out."

"What are you talking about?" Joe looked confused.

"Oh, Kate has secrets. She doesn't tell us everything," His dad said. "Like that she knew it was Tim in the boat the whole time. And that she did her own undercover work this morning, listening in on some teenage girls in town. She even knew they had left their friend at a party last night and the girl hadn't come home." He looked around the room. "None of which she told the police. That's withholding evidence."

"Jack, stop. Let me explain," His mom began.

"I have a call to make." His dad walked onto the deck without looking at her.

"Is that true, Mom?" Sarah turned to her. "And you didn't say anything? Why?"

"Because they said they left her with TJ." His mom's voice was barely a whisper. She began to shake and turned to him. "I couldn't tell *anyone,* not even Dad!"

Tim wrapped his arms around her. "Mom, I'm so sorry about everything. But you gotta believe me. I didn't do this."

"I know that, Tim." She hugged him, her head against his chest.

Joe waited and touched Kate's arm. "You did the right thing, reporting the incident and looking for the girl yourself. When you heard the girls mention TJ, I'm sure you were scared and you did what you thought you had to do. The police know now anyway. So, you can help by telling us about the guy in the black pick-up. That's what's important. He could be a person of interest."

She described the encounter and added, "I think he was one of the girls' brothers. He told the redhead … he called her Becca … that he drove by the party and saw her but didn't tell their parents."

"That's Becca McVeigh!" Tim said. "If it's her brother, he's Shane McVeigh."

"Good, Tim," Joe said. "That gives us a good place to start."

"What's going to happen?" Tim kept his eyes on Joe.

"This is serious. You are the last person the police know who saw Mel alive. We'll give the attorneys Shane McVeigh's name, the girls' names, and anything else you can think of. They'll do their own investigation too."

"Could they arrest me?" Tim's voice trembled.

"I don't think they have proof. If they did, they would have come with a warrant tonight."

Tears flowed as Tim surveyed the pained faces around the room. "I didn't do this!"

"We know that." Sarah crossed to him and put an arm around his waist.

"I don't think you did either," Joe said. "We just need to find a way to prove it."

His dad came inside. "I just talked to Hutch. As soon as he's packed, he'll check out of the hotel. He'll be here after midnight. The other lawyer will be here by seven."

"I'm sorry," Tim said. "This time I messed up big time." He looked at his father—waiting for something, anything.

"It'll be all right. Hutch will straighten it out." His dad put an arm around his shoulders and dropped it just as quickly.

Why can't you just say you believe me?

His mom brushed the hair off his forehead like she used to do when he was little. "I love you, Tim."

"Love you too, Mom. I'm going to bed." Tears welled up as he walked away, and everything shifted beneath him.

17

"What the hell were you thinking?" Clayton Storrow peeled out of the Rourkes' driveway, spewing gravel in all directions. "I had him. He was talking. Then you all but accuse him of rape and murder. We'll be lucky if he says anything now. And he's our best lead—the last person we know of who saw the victim alive." He glanced at Norm. "That was our last chance to talk to him without a lawyer. You know that, right?"

"I couldn't help it. The kid's a rich prick. Thinks he can get away with anything. All I need is five minutes alone with him and I'll get the truth." Norm's fists clenched.

"What truth is that, Johnson? All we know for sure is that he took a girl for a ride in a boat that wasn't his."

"Bullshit. Not when that girl turns up dead."

Storrow hit the steering wheel with the heel of his hand. "I *never* should have let you come. *Never* should have let you get involved. My ass is on the line now and it's my own fault."

Norm made an effort to slow his breathing. How many

times could he screw up? "So what happens now?"

"The detectives will interview everyone who was at the party, follow up again with anyone who showed an interest in Melody Ward, like Shane McVeigh. Find out why Todd Anderson was so quick to implicate Rourke. Start back at square one and connect the dots."

"I know the town people. I could…" Norm heard the desperation in his own voice. He had to be involved somehow!

"No." Storrow put up his hand. "You're done, off the case. And so am I. BCI will take over and they won't be happy with tonight's turn of events."

The two men rode in silence for the next five minutes.

"Right before I left the house, the fiancé asked if anyone had checked the far shoreline for footprints or drag marks in case the victim made it to shore." An oncoming car lit Storrow's face. "Do you know anything about that, Constable? Our guys have been concentrating on the area where the body was found."

Norm's sense of guilt reared up. He never checked the lakeshore like he'd told Mrs. Rourke he would, but couldn't admit it. "How could she swim to shore—in the dark—drunk?"

Storrow took his eyes off the road. "You didn't answer my question. Did you or anyone else check it out?"

"No." Another failure he'd live with.

The trooper pulled up to the cordoned off area by the dam. "Get your truck, Constable. Take care."

In his truck, Norm checked the digital dashboard clock—nine forty-seven. It was late and he was beat. He'd been up since five. But he had to check on Hannah.

Ignoring all speed limits, he drove to Carrie Ryan's

house. The lights were still on in the old farmhouse. A black Cadillac with M.D. plates was parked out front. Norm ran up the stairs, ignoring his labored breathing and the pounding in his chest. He banged his fist on the door.

Carrie pulled it open almost immediately, then folded her arms across her chest. "Do you have any idea what time it is? She's sleeping." She nodded toward the living room.

"What's wrong? Why's the doc here?" As he fought to catch his breath, Norm vowed again to get in shape.

"Glenn came by to check on Hannah and gave her something else to help her sleep."

"I would think she'd be exhausted."

"So now you're a doctor?" She stepped back no more than a foot.

Norm entered the foyer. "Carrie, I won't disturb her. I just want to see her." He smelled fresh coffee and glanced left toward the kitchen. He could see a man's pressed pant leg and one brown dress shoe sticking out from under the table.

"I'm awake, Carrie. Who is it?"

Norm and Carrie turned toward the weak voice coming from under a pile of oversized faded quilts on the couch.

"It's me, Hannah." Norm approached her.

Hannah pulled herself up with some difficulty and leaned against the soft feather pillows piled at the end of the couch. "Come sit."

Norm pulled a chair close to her. He sat leaning forward, his hands clasped between his knees. She had aged in the last several hours. Her eyes were red and puffy. "I'm so very sorry, Hannah. I know nothing I say can make this better."

"I can't believe she's gone. I ache for her in every inch

of my body. It's like I've lost a part of myself."

Hannah closed her eyes. A single tear trickled down her cheek and into the folds of her neck. When she opened her eyes again, they focused on Norm. "What do you know?"

"We're still fitting the pieces together but we're close." He couldn't give her details now, not like this. "I promise you, we'll get whoever did this."

"I should have known where she was, who she was with." Hannah began to sob.

Norm slid onto the couch and gathered her close, surprised at how right it felt. He continued to hold her long after the wracking sobs ceased. When he laid her back against the pillows, she was asleep. He tucked the quilts around her. For the second time that day, his shirt was wet with Hannah's tears.

His attention was drawn to the front door. Glenn Braddock and Carrie were speaking, their heads together. Norm couldn't hear what they were saying.

Norm walked over. "I'll be going too, Carrie."

"Constable Johnson," Braddock said. "How's the investigation going?"

"The state's handling things at this point, but we've got a good lead." He turned to Carrie. "Thanks, Carrie. I'll stop back in the morning."

Satisfied that Hannah was safe and settled in for the night, Norm took his time driving home. He thought about Mel. He would never forget the image of her bruised and broken body. Every detail was imbedded in his soul.

She had been such a beautiful, happy little girl, always running and skipping—pigtails flying out behind her. She never walked anywhere. Her smile lit up her face. And melted his heart.

Hannah lived for her.

The road swam. He couldn't make out the center line. Pulling to the side of the road, Norm let the tears fall that he'd controlled all day.

18

The house was hushed at last. Everyone had gone to bed to catch a couple hours of sleep before Hutch arrived. Kate sat alone in the family room and tried to make sense of what had happened. Her son and the rape and murder of a fifteen-year-old girl—two pieces of a puzzle that didn't fit together. She'd stake her life on it.

Answering a need deep inside her, she knocked on Tim's door. "Tim," she whispered. "It's Mom. Can I come in?"

She waited, then heard a muffled, "Yeah. I'm awake."

Turning the knob, she waited for her eyes to adjust to the semi-darkness as light from the hallway seeped in. She saw her son's outline under the sheet on the bottom bunk. How many times over the years had she checked on him like this before going to bed?

"You should be in bed, Mom. I'm okay." The words were clear but contradicted the shakiness of his voice.

"Tim." She took a step into the room.

"No, Mom." That stopped her. "I can't. There's nothing more to say. I need to get to sleep and so do you." He turned to face the wall.

Kate walked to the bed, bent and kissed his head. "I love you, Tim. I believe you." She felt the almost imperceptible nod as fresh tears gathered in the corners of her eyes.

Upstairs, Kate changed in the light of the master bath nightlight and slipped into her side of the bed. "We have to talk, Jack."

No response.

"I know you're not asleep."

"I can't talk about it. I can't even process it. And I sure as hell can't fix this." He spoke into his pillow.

She propped herself on one elbow and stared at the back of his head, dark hair swirling around the stubborn cowlick. "You don't have to fix everything. Don't try to be your father. Just be here for him." When he didn't answer, she continued. "Tim needs to know you believe him."

Jack turned to face her, his features barely visible in the shadowy light. "I get going out in the boat with the girl. I do. He'd been drinking and it was stupid. What I don't understand is how he could leave her there." His eyes glistened. "How could he do that, Kate? We taught him better."

"What about the rest of it?" Kate held her breath and watched his face.

"The supposed rape and murder?" He shook his head. "No way he could ever do that."

"Tell him, Jack." She placed a tentative hand on his shoulder. "He needs to hear it from you."

Jack was quiet as he stared past her into the blackness of the large bay window. "You know how things were between me and my dad. Nothing I did was ever good enough for him, even when I was a kid. I started drinking and had mornings when I'd wake up with no memory of how I'd gotten home. I swear I did it just to piss him off. I had nothing to lose." He rolled onto his back and propped an arm behind his head. "He had a lot of political clout in Philly back then and got me out of a few minor brushes with the law in high school. Nothing serious. But I always wondered if he did it for me or for his own reputation.

"The summer before college I was charged with DUI, disorderly conduct and assault. It was a Friday night. I was drunk. I admit it. This guy cut me off and I went ballistic. We got out of our cars and started screaming at each other. He looked like he'd been in a fight—bruised knuckles, a black eye. When the cops came, he said I punched him." He turned his face toward her. "I never touched him, Kate. The cops didn't believe me and arrested me. There were no witnesses, just his word against mine.

"My father was furious. He refused to bail me out until Monday morning. Let me sit in jail all weekend. He said it was time I took responsibility for my actions. He didn't even come to see me. In the end, he called in some favors. The family lawyer had the charges dropped and my record expunged. But you know what?" Their eyes connected. "He never asked me if I did it, the assault. I never knew if he believed me. And I hated him for that."

Jack shook his head. "I've made a lot of mistakes, haven't always been the best dad. But I don't want him to hate me." He coughed to cover the catch in his voice.

"Then tell him." Kate squeezed his shoulder. "You are *not* your father." She leaned in to kiss him.

He turned away. "We'd better get some sleep.

Tomorrow's going to be tough." He was asleep in seconds.

An unexpected chill spread to her side of the bed and through her. Shut out again. What had happened to them? Her attempts at sleep, as well as his snoring, taunted her.

She went downstairs and warmed her palms around a cup of herbal tea. The hands on the slate clock moved like columns of marching ants, methodical and relentless, toward Sunday morning and the police interrogation. Restless, Kate yanked open the French doors and walked to the railing. She looked out onto the blackness of the lake, the choking weeds beneath lying in wait like so many secrets. Melody Ward's fear and terror seemed to vibrate off the surface of the water.

She sat in the rocker and, tucking her bare feet under her, lay her head against the back. She easily located the Big and Little Dippers and zeroed in on the North Star. Her dad had taught her how to find this bright star and to follow her own true north in difficult times. It would take more than a star to lead them out of this—a star that was light years away and perhaps already burned out.

A shooting star shot across the sky. She allowed herself the childhood magic of making a wish. Just before drifting off, she acknowledged it was all an illusion.

Not unlike the pretense of the perfect family.

A car door and then footsteps on the deck roused her. "I thought I might find you out here. That North Star showing you the way?"

"Not tonight, I'm afraid." Kate pushed strands of hair off her face and stood. "Thanks for coming."

"Where else would I be, Katie." His eyes were serious despite the smile. He enveloped her in a bear hug.

She pulled back to look at him. Everett Hutchinson III was dressed in his signature uniform of jeans and an oxford button-down, sleeves rolled up over tanned forearms.

"What time is it? You must be exhausted."

Hutch checked his phone. "A little after one."

"Do you want something? Coffee? Water?"

"No. Thanks. How are *you*?"

"Me? I'm fine. It's Tim I'm worried about." She turned toward the lake. "And I can't stop thinking about that poor girl, what it must have been like for her."

"And you would have some idea about that, wouldn't you?" He leaned his elbows on the railing next to her, his hands clasped.

"That was a long time ago." In her mind's eye, she saw that homesick freshman walking alone at night beside the small lake on campus. She smelled the weeds clustered at the edge and heard the symphony of crickets and the distant hum of traffic. But she'd never heard *them* coming. A circle of drunken frat boys closed in on her and passed her from one to the other. Laughing and making lewd remarks, they ripped at her blouse and shorts. She was terrified and screamed as loud as she could. She heard running and shouting. Someone was coming. She got away and ran into the water. She felt again its coldness and shivered.

Her would be attackers had been scared off. She was paralyzed, her feet rooted in the mucky bottom. But it wasn't campus security who came. The tall blond upperclassman, assigned to help the freshmen move in that week, waded into the water and led her to the bank. In little more than her underwear, she couldn't stop shaking and crying. He put his sweater around her.

Kate rubbed her arms in an effort to warm them. "I was very lucky. Thanks to you."

Hutch looked like he was about to say something

when Jack stepped onto the deck.

"There you are! I thought I heard a car." Jack hugged his best friend and clapped him on the back. "Thanks, man. I really appreciate you coming."

~~

The next morning, Kate was showered and dressed by six. She started the coffee and called Tim. Needing to keep her hands busy, she set out the zucchini bread she'd thawed overnight and a bowl of cut-up fruit. She prayed. *Dear God, help us get through this day.*

"I smell coffee. I'm going to need it." Hutch, hair still damp and smelling of shampoo, came into the kitchen. Pressed black slacks had replaced the jeans.

Kate looked over her shoulder. "Help yourself. Jack will be down in a few minutes."

"Hey, Hutch. Thanks for coming."

They turned together to see Tim emerging from his room. He looked as if he hadn't slept. His face was blotchy. "I didn't do this. I swear."

Hutch hugged him, then held his shoulders and stepped back. "I know that. I've known you since you were born. And I know who you are now. You're very special to me, Tim."

"Thanks," he said and looked at the table. "I don't think I can eat, Mom."

"Tim…" She stopped herself. She wouldn't push.

Sarah and Joe passed him in the kitchen doorway. "You okay?" Sarah asked.

"Yeah." Tim pushed by them and sat on the couch in the adjoining room.

"Hey, Pumpkin." Hutch embraced his godchild. "You get prettier every time I see you. You are going to make one beautiful bride."

He turned to Joe and extended his hand. "Good to see you again. How's the job?"

While Joe filled Hutch in, they all sat down. They were eating and talking when Jack came into the dining area.

He glanced over at his son, but neither spoke. Kate's heart sank. She thought she had made a breakthrough with Jack the night before.

Hutch frowned at Jack, then got up and sat next to Tim. "I can imagine this is all pretty scary, Tim, but you've got a lot of people in your corner. People who know you and love you. And believe you. I'm here to help too, as a lawyer. The only way I can do that is if you tell me the truth. Okay?"

"Okay." Tim clutched his hands.

A sense of calm settled over Kate that she hadn't felt since the early hours of Saturday morning.

Someone knocked and Hutch rose. "That will be Andrew Grady. You'll like him. He's a criminal attorney out of Burlington and has a lot of trial experience. I trust him."

Hutch made the introductions. The lawyer was about Hutch's and Jack's age, but with a weathered face that spoke of extended time spent outdoors.

Tim stood as the lawyer shook his hand. "Nice to meet you, Tim. Hutch speaks highly of you. It's my job to protect your rights and ensure that you are treated fairly according to the law. I'm going to ask you some tough questions. My number one rule is that you tell me the truth. Whatever I ask. Are we clear on that?"

"Yes, sir."

"You can drop the sir. Grady's fine. If you want

privacy, we can take a ride in my car."

"No, that's all right, Mr. Grady." Tim looked at his family. "They already know everything."

"If you change your mind, you tell me."

"I will."

"Okay then. Let's start from the beginning." Grady accepted a mug of coffee and sat opposite Tim and Hutch.

Grady questioned Tim about his relationship with Melody Ward and about the events of the night she was killed.

Kate listened as Tim spoke, at first self-consciously and then with more animation, about the young girl. She wondered if every mother felt this tug on her heart the first time she heard her son talk about another woman this way.

"Do you know where the body was found?" Grady seemed to introduce the subject abruptly and out of context.

"No." Tim sat up straight.

Hutch scanned the room and the adjoining dining area where Sarah and Joe remained.

"No one's told us officially," Joe said moving closer. "There were several state cars and emergency vehicles in the vicinity of the old dam at the south end of the lake.

"Let's play devil's advocate," Grady said. "What's to preclude the prosecution from speculating that Melody Ward was dead when she hit the water? Doesn't this lake flow south toward that dam?"

"She wasn't!" Tim blurted.

Kate placed her hand on Tim's arm. "Actually, I heard the woman, girl I guess, yell f- you *before* the loud splash. I told this to the police."

"*You* told the police?" Grady looked from Kate to Jack.

"Yeah," Jack said. "We reported the incident and had

the constable and the state police here before we knew Tim was involved."

"Whoa, let's back it up." Grady turned to a clean sheet on his legal pad.

Kate and Jack recounted what Kate had heard, their boat search, finding the oar, the call to the constable and the later visits from Johnson and then Johnson and Trooper Storrow.

Kate's stomach writhed. No matter what happened, she'd live with the fact that she was the one who called the constable and set all this in motion.

"Where's the oar now?" Grady said.

"I don't know," Jack said. "Constable Johnson took it even though he didn't think it was of any use since it was wet."

Grady made a notation. "I'll check with BCI, the state Bureau of Criminal Investigation. Your constable doesn't know what he's talking about. Forensics can use zinc oxide powder in what's called a wet powdering technique to lift prints off wet objects."

He angled his body toward Tim.

Tim looked confused. "What? I don't know anything about an oar."

"Will this oar have your prints on it?"

"How could it? Didn't you hear what I just said?"

Why didn't we just leave the damn thing in the water? Kate crossed and uncrossed her legs.

"If it does, any idea how they could have gotten there?" Grady pushed on.

"No. I told you. I don't remember anything after Mel hit the water. If they say *I* made those banging sounds since I was the only person in the boat..." He shrugged. "I don't know."

Andrew Grady lowered his reading glasses. "Are you sure, Tim?"

"I don't know what you want me to say. I don't remember!"

"Could it be that you were really pissed, maybe wanted to smack her or smack the side of the boat?"

"Yeah, I was pissed! I knew I'd screwed up fighting with Sweeney. She hated when I got jealous. I told you what she said! I figured we were done, broken up. And I was angry, big time. But I would never hurt her! And I still don't know anything about an oar!"

Kate could see Tim's legs shaking. He wiped his hands on his pants and held onto his knees. Kate started to go to him but Hutch put an arm around her son. There was comfort in the gesture. She fought to get her own frayed nerves under control.

"Okay, Tim, take it easy," Grady said. "Remember rule number one? Always tell me the truth. Don't bullshit me."

"I'm not!" His face was flushed and streaked with red.

Grady looked over his half glasses and eyed Hutch. "If this girl has any contusions, before or after she hit the water, we'd better hope they're not from a blunt instrument."

Tim was on his feet. "What are you talking about? I didn't hit her—with anything! What happened to innocent until proven guilty? You're supposed to be my lawyer."

Kate reached for Tim's hand but he pulled away. She looked at the lawyer. "Mr. Grady, when the police were here, I was very clear that I heard the banging sounds *after* the splash."

"That's fine, Mrs. Rourke, but it's the evidence that will speak the loudest in court."

"Then I'll testify. I'll do anything." Out of the corner

of her eye, she saw Sarah start to come to her. Kate shook her head a fraction. Any gesture of kindness now would break her.

"I'm sorry," Hutch said. Kate could see the pain around his eyes. "We have to discuss something else, Tim, and it might be better if we do it in private."

"Just ask." Tim lifted both shoulders and waved a hand. He sat down.

"If they find semen during the autopsy, will it be yours?"

"Umm … I don't think so. How long does it … umm … last?" He lowered his eyes.

"Christ, Tim." Jack pounded his fist into the arm of the leather chair.

"Easy, Jack." Hutch's voice was calm when he addressed Tim again. "Do you want to go in another room?"

Tim shook his head.

"When did you last have sex with Melody?" Hutch asked in a quiet voice.

Trying to make herself invisible, Kate got up and retreated to the recesses of the room.

"Last weekend maybe. I haven't seen her in about a week." High color crept up his neck and face. "I always wear a condom, but I know they're not a hundred percent."

"It should be okay." Hutch patted Tim's knee.

"Will they want a DNA sample today?" Jack asked.

"If they have a court order," Grady said. "One step at a time."

Kate watched Grady, who never seemed to lose his cool, professional tone.

"Let's think about this," Hutch said. "About other possible scenarios. If Melody Ward was alive when she went overboard as Tim contends, what could have happened?" He looked around the room. "Ideas?"

"Tim told us Mel's a good swimmer," Joe said. "It's possible she made it to shore. We don't know if anyone's checked that area across the lake. We know the bank is muddy, so there should be drag marks or footprints if she came up that way. *If* they're still there."

"Sarah, what about the field? Is there a path or anything up to the road?" Hutch said.

"Not a path, but it's an easy walk up to the road. We did it all the time."

"Say she made it to the road." Joe walked to the French doors and stared out at the hill across the lake. "Someone could have seen her, either in the field or on the road. Maybe picked her up." He turned back to the room. "An unknown subject."

"Who'd be in that field in the middle of the night?" Tim heaved himself back against the couch and flung his arms out.

"Interesting theory, Officer Parelli." Grady made a note. "Miss Rourke, is there anything else over there?"

"There's an old abandoned shack near the road, hidden by trees and high grass."

"Show me where it is." Grady handed her the pad where he had sketched the location of the field and the road in relation to the lakeshore.

Sarah pointed to a spot about three-quarters of the way up the hill near the road.

Grady marked an X and asked, "How big is it?"

"I don't know, not too big. I think there were two small rooms. We used to play in there sometimes. Remember?" She looked at her brother who nodded.

Grady held up his sketch again. "What if you walked

down the road from the shack, south toward town?" He traced the route with his finger. "No, what if you walked through the field diagonally to the south from the shack? Where would you end up?"

"You'd be at the end of the lake, in the channel." Sarah's eyes widened and she smiled. "You'd be at the dam!"

"All right! That's good news. We'll need to check out the shoreline, the field up to the road, and that shack. Nice work." Grady gathered his papers. "Tim, can you think of anybody who might want to harm Melody? An old boyfriend, a friend?"

"Yeah, Shane McVeigh. She used to go out with him. I told my family."

"We made lists last night," Joe said. "People at the party, friends of Tim's and Melody Ward's including Shane, anyone who might have seen Tim come back to the party or to his apartment, Melody's family."

"That's great. I want to go over every name." Grady checked his watch. "You can tell me everything you know about Shane McVeigh in the car, Tim. Right now, we need to get you to Castleton. You ready?"

"I guess." Tim stood.

"Remember, you let me do the talking. I don't know what evidence they have or just where they're going with this. This is a good time to go over my other two rules. Number two. Don't volunteer information. Answer only what they ask. Number three. Don't answer anything I tell you not to. Got it? Because if you don't, we're done."

"I understand." Tim's voice was subdued, serious. "You have to believe me, Mr. Grady. I never hurt her. I didn't do this."

It was as if she were watching her son grow up before

her eyes. Kate put an arm around his waist. "We'll be right there with you."

"Ah, Kate, Tim isn't a minor. You won't be allowed in during the questioning," Hutch said.

"What? I'm his mother." She *had* to be there.

"The law doesn't care, Mrs. Rourke. Tim is of age," Grady said as he headed for the door. "You'll have to remain in the reception area when we get there."

"Jack?" Kate looked at her husband.

He squeezed Tim's shoulder. "Everything will be all right, Tim. We'll be waiting for you when you're done."

19

Early morning mist was rising off the fields as Norm drove
around the lake. He liked the peacefulness of Sunday mornings
but today his nerves were strung as tight as a new clothesline.
He'd checked and found out that Tim Rourke was being
questioned in Castleton at ten. A detective was interviewing
Hannah at Carrie's at nine. He wanted to be there.

Up since 3:40 that morning, he'd taken refuge in his
woodworking shop as he often did when he couldn't sleep.
Taking raw wood and planing, sanding, and shaping it into
something useful and beautiful brought him a sense of purpose
and pride. Unlike the failure he felt after last night's outburst at
the Rourkes'. And his uselessness in being barred from the
investigation.

It was still an hour before the detective was due at
Carrie's. He turned off the road at one of the higher elevations
and looked down on the smooth, glass-like surface of the lake.
He unscrewed the top of his travel mug and took a deep swig
of black coffee. He breathed deeply, letting his insides absorb

the heat and caffeine.

How had that happy little girl morphed into the sullen, troubled teenager—the one who now lay on a slab in the medical examiner's office?

He remembered the last time he'd followed Mel, weaving and walking unsteady along the side of the road several weeks ago. He planned to bring her home to Hannah like so many times before. But when he tried to get her into his truck, Mel had pulled away from him. "You're not my father," she screamed. "You can't tell me what to do. Go save someone else. I'm not worth it."

He chased after her but when she veered off into the woods, he'd lost her. He was ticked and stomped back to his truck.

What if he hadn't?

Hannah was defensive the next day when he tried to talk to her. She said she could take care of her daughter and didn't need him. He let pride keep him away and would have to live with that. That was the last time he'd talked to Hannah until she called him yesterday morning.

Norm drained the last of the coffee. Bouncing over ruts on the shoulder, he pulled his truck onto the road and headed for Carrie's.

Turning into the driveway, he saw the black Cadillac. *Doesn't that guy ever stay home?* Norm parked his mud-splattered pick-up next to the shiny sedan and got out.

Carrie opened the door as soon as Norm knocked. "What are you doing here? The state police investigator will be here in about ten minutes."

"I know. That's why I'm here."

Carrie didn't respond as she stepped back.

Glenn Braddock emerged from the kitchen, cup of

coffee in hand. "Hannah's doing much better today, Constable." He smiled.

Norm looked into the living room. "Where is she?"

"Upstairs taking a shower," Carrie said. "Glenn was kind enough to bring over some clean clothes for her.

"I'll take a cup of that coffee, Carrie." Norm followed them back into the kitchen and pocketed his keys.

Pale with dark circles under her eyes, Hannah came into the room. Her hair, still wet, was held loosely at the nape of her neck with a tortoise shell clip. Norm saw the pain in her eyes.

Braddock pulled out a chair for her at the table. Carrie set down another cup of coffee. Hannah stared into it. She didn't seem to notice that Glenn Braddock was stroking her arm.

Norm noticed. "You okay, Hannah?" He leaned toward her slightly.

She turned to him with a puzzled frown as if seeing him for the first time. "What are you doing here?"

"I wanted to be here when the detective talked to you."

"Oh," was all she said and stared straight ahead.

"I'm here, Constable Johnson," the doctor said, "if you have other things to tend to." He moved his chair closer to Hannah. "Unless, of course, you're here in an official capacity."

"I have no official jurisdiction. It's the state's case now." Norm sized up the other man who was about his height, but in better shape. "I'm here for Hannah, as her friend."

Carrie snorted and rolled her eyes. "Come on, Hannah. Let's get you settled comfortably in the living room before the police arrive." Looking back at the two men eyeing each other at the kitchen table, she added, "If you two want to have a pissing contest, do it on your own time. Hannah is our only concern right now."

Detective Mark Whitcomb from the Vermont Bureau of Criminal Investigation arrived right on time. After brief introductions, he got down to business. "I'm very sorry for your loss, Ms. Ward. I promise to make this as easy as possible."

"Thank you," Hannah said in an almost inaudible voice.

Norm studied Detective Whitcomb, a man in his early fifties with thick gray hair combed back from his forehead. His face was ruddy and Norm bet those clear blue eyes didn't miss a thing.

"When did you last see your daughter?" Whitcomb maintained eye contact with Hannah.

"Friday night at supper before she went out."

"Do you know where she went, Ma'am?"

Hannah looked down. "No."

Norm watched for signs of judgment on the detective's face but it was unreadable.

Whitcomb checked his notes. "I have here the names of the girls seen with Melody that night that Constable Johnson gave to the state police. Molly Townsend, Becca McVeigh, and Courtney Chandler. Do you know those girls, Ms. Ward?

"Yes, yes. They're her best friends. I called them. I called them all when she didn't come home. They said they didn't know anything!" Hannah sniffed and swiped at her cheek.

"What about male friends, Ms. Ward?"

Hannah sighed. "There were a few boys in town she seemed friendly with for awhile, but she seems … I mean seemed … to have lost interest in them."

"Why's that, do you think?" Those blue eyes didn't blink.

"She's been spending time at the college. Ethan Allen." Hannah glanced at Norm and then back to the detective. "I know it wasn't good but she went up there with her friends, never alone."

"Any of the guys in town have a problem with the girls going up to the college, as far as you know?"

Hannah shrugged her shoulders. "She went out a few times with her friend Becca's brother, Shane. I didn't like him. He was older than Mel, nineteen I think. He used to call her after they broke up. I could hear him yelling at her on the phone sometimes before she'd go into her room and shut the door." Hannah started to cry. "Do you think it was him? I told her to stay away from him, but she didn't always listen to me."

Detective Whitcomb leaned forward. "I don't know, Ms. Ward. Do you think he would want to hurt her?"

Hannah sobbed into her hands. "I don't know. I don't know." Glenn Braddock, who was next to her on the couch, put his arm around her.

Whitcomb turned to Norm. "Are you familiar with this individual, Constable?"

"Yes. Petty stuff here in town."

The detective checked his notes and nodded. "Yes, I have that information." He focused his attention back on Hannah. "About these trips to Ethan Allen, did your daughter attend parties there?"

"I think so."

"She was fifteen, right?" Detective Whitcomb leaned back in the chair.

There it was—the judgment. "We all know how old she was, Detective." Norm's voice was tight.

Hannah wiped her eyes. "I guess she did. Sometimes she got home pretty late, way past curfew. But until Friday night, she'd *never* stayed out all night."

"Can we take a short break, Detective?" Norm asked. "I'll get you some water, Hannah." He headed for the kitchen without waiting for a reply from the investigator.

Norm heard the detective continue and tightened his grip on the glass as he ran the tap.

"I'm sorry to ask you these questions, Ms. Ward, but I'm trying to get a better picture of Melody and who she may have been with. Can you remember any names in particular from the college that she may have mentioned?"

Hannah accepted the glass of water from Norm and shook her head. "No, but she used to talk to someone on the phone. She was very secretive. When I asked who it was, she said I didn't know him." She looked around the room. "I *know* the boys in town. He could have been from the school, I guess. I never should have added texting to our plan. Just more secrets." Hannah's hand shook as she sipped the water.

"Did your daughter own a computer?"

"Yes."

"Did she spend a lot of time online?"

"Yes. But she did almost everything on her phone. And I don't know where it is." Her eyes filled again. "I called her so many times Friday night and Saturday morning. Just went to voice mail." Braddock patted her shoulder.

"Did your daughter have a Facebook account, Ms. Ward?"

"Yes. I didn't like the idea of that. I wasn't sure it was safe."

"We can access that and emails from her computer. How about Twitter? Instagram?"

"I don't know what those are." Hannah frowned and turned to look at Carrie.

Detective Whitcomb glanced at Norm, then back to Hannah. "Would you be willing to let us take a look at Melody's computer?"

"Of course."

Norm hoped the phone had been recovered from the boat. The texts would be important.

"I'd like to take a look at her room too if you have no objection," Whitcomb said.

Hannah nodded. She leaned on the upholstered arm of the couch to stand.

"Thank you, Ms. Ward. I know this is difficult." Whitcomb glanced around the room. "Since you're obviously family friends, can any of you think of anyone who may have wanted to harm Melody? Constable Johnson?"

Before Norm could respond, Hannah said, "What about you, Glenn? You've been spending a lot of time with Mel. Has she mentioned anyone?"

"What do you mean spending a lot of time with Mel?" Norm asked. *Just how close was Hannah to the doctor?*

"Glenn and I are friends. He has horses and gave Mel a part-time job cleaning out the stalls and grooming the horses. It gives her some spending money and keeps her out of trouble."

No one acknowledged the irony of her statement or her use of the present tense.

"How come I haven't heard about this?" Norm looked at Hannah.

"You know, Johnson," Glenn Braddock said. "Being constable doesn't make you privy to everything that goes on in this town."

Detective Whitcomb cleared his throat. "So, Doctor, did Melody mention anyone?"

"Not really. She did her job, didn't talk to me much. Lately, she's been riding her bike out to the farm. She used to be dropped off by a young man in a black pick-up. She called him Shane. Must be the same guy. Some days she looked upset, like she'd been crying."

"She ever indicate why she was upset?" Whitcomb looked up from writing.

"No. Like I said, she didn't talk much."

"Anyone else?" Whitcomb looked around.

Norm was sure Whitcomb would have been briefed on Timothy Rourke so said nothing.

"Okay then," the detective said. "Are you ready, Ms. Ward?"

"Yes." She turned to Braddock. "I'll see you later?"

"I'll come by your place after I take care of a few things." He kissed her on the cheek.

Norm was rooted to his chair and stared. *Hannah and Braddock?* Was he the only one who didn't know what was going on?

The police detective watched this three-way interplay but said nothing. He handed out business cards. "If any of you thinks of something, please give me a call. Doctor Braddock, other than her reaction to Shane McVeigh, did Melody Ward mention anyone to you that she was worried about or who may have threatened her?"

"No one."

20

Tim sat in the backseat of Grady's black Ford Escort, parked behind Hutch's white Beamer. He buckled his seat belt. A model citizen—what a joke! Murder. Rape. *Jeez!*

During the thirty-minute ride to the State Police substation in Castleton, Grady grilled him about Shane McVeigh, Mel's friends, other guys he might know from town, which he didn't.

This was some serious shit. It felt like it must be happening to somebody else.

Hutch tried to make him feel better. He'd known Hutch all his life; he'd just met this other guy a couple of hours ago. How much experience did he have? How much crime could there be in Vermont?

They pulled into the small paved lot. His dad followed and parked next to them.

"Shit," Tim said under his breath as he got out of the car. This was it. Lagging behind, he followed the parade into the one-story white building.

He pretended not to notice when his mother waited and offered him her hand.

The air-conditioning pressed into him. The round black clock, like in a classroom, showed it was ten a.m. exactly.

Grady said something to the desk cop. Within seconds, a guy in his thirties wearing jeans and a dark T-shirt opened a door on the right. It shut behind him with a heavy clang. Tim imagined how many locks might be on that door.

"I'm Detective Chuck Cobb with the Vermont State Police Bureau of Criminal Investigation."

He shook hands with Hutch and Grady and came over to where Tim was standing with his parents. The guy was tall. His shaved head and beefy upper arms made him look like a biker. He didn't smile.

"You must be Tim."

"Yes, sir." Tim's voice croaked, betraying him.

"Let's go then."

As Tim followed his lawyers and the detective through the same side door, he didn't look left or right. He was glad his parents weren't allowed into the interrogation room. God only knew what this guy was going to ask him. Besides, he couldn't watch his mother cry again.

He walked down the empty corridor, each step echoing on the scuffed tiles, bringing him further away from everything he'd ever known.

Tim, Hutch, and Grady sat in folding chairs on one side of a scarred wooden table, Detective Cobb on the other. There were no windows, just a one-way mirror like on *Law and Order*. Who was on the other side? The gray tiled floor was chipped in places, the walls painted pea green that didn't cover the dirt. Is this what prison was like? A shudder went through him. He hoped no one noticed.

The detective placed a small tape recorder in the middle of the table over a weird shaped stain he didn't want to guess at. "This interrogation will be recorded." He glanced at Grady.

"I have no objection, Detective." Grady produced a similar device from his jeans pocket.

Tim looked from one to the other, and then to Hutch who gave him the faintest nod and smile of encouragement.

Detective Cobb stated for the record the date and time and who was in attendance. His alert eyes focused on Tim, who tried to swallow the rock-sized lump in his throat.

"Timothy Rourke, have you come here voluntarily to make a statement with your lawyer present?"

Tim nodded.

"Please answer out loud."

"Yes."

"I'm sure your lawyer has explained to you that you are not under arrest."

"Yes, sir."

Cobb nodded. "We're investigating the rape and murder of Melody Ward."

Tim felt the blood drain from his face. His hands began to sweat.

"I'd like you to tell me everything you know about the events of last Friday night, July tenth. Start from the beginning."

Tim glanced at Grady, who nodded. He'd told this story so many times, yet every time he relived it all again. He paused only when the detective asked for clarification. His head was pounding. There was a glass of water on the table but if he drank it, it might look like he was stalling—or guilty.

When he was done, Tim looked at the detective, who was playing with a paperclip. He didn't even look like he was listening!

Sweat soaked Tim's shirt and he couldn't keep his feet still. He really wanted that water.

"Tell me more about this argument between you and Melody Ward," the detective asked in a neutral tone. "Were you angry?"

"Yes."

"What did you argue about?"

Tim swallowed. "I didn't like other guys touching her."

"Do you think she encouraged that?"

"I don't know. She liked to flirt sometimes." He looked at Grady's face and knew he shouldn't have added that last sentence. If his father were here, he'd tell him to keep his head in the game.

"Like with Buck Sweeney?"

"Yes."

"Is that why you beat him up?"

"That hasn't been established," Andrew Grady said.

"Mr. Sweeney may not agree, Mr. Grady, since he ended up with a broken nose. But we'll let that go for now." Detective Cobb put the paperclip aside and lay both hands flat on the table. He leaned toward Tim. "Did you have sex with Melody Ward that evening?"

"No, sir."

"Had the two of you ever had sex?"

"Don't answer that, Tim," Grady said.

Cobb pulled himself back just a bit and turned his palms upward. "I'm just trying to establish if you and she were boyfriend and girlfriend. Did you consider her your girlfriend,

Tim?"

"Yes."

"Did it make you jealous when other guys came on to her?"

"Yes." He would keep his answers to the point. Rule number two.

"So you got her away from the party just to talk, to tell her how you felt?"

"That's right."

Detective Cobb laced his fingers behind his head and leaned back in his chair. "Okay. Tell me again how Melody Ward ended up in the water."

Tim repeated what he could remember. He tried to keep it calm and factual even though his insides were twisting. *Do they let you leave to go to the bathroom?*

Cobb looked up at the discolored ceiling tiles. "See, that's the part I don't understand. You admitted you were pretty angry with her and you'd been drinking. Are you sure you didn't push her in or hit her and knock her out?"

"Don't answer that, Tim," Grady cautioned.

Tim forged ahead, his voice getting louder. "No! I told you. She was standing on the back of the boat. She pulled away from me. Then she fell or jumped in. It was dark."

"And you didn't see Melody Ward again or have any further contact with her after she went into the water."

"No." Tim's knees were shaking under the table. *Why doesn't Grady say something?*

"I think my client has already established that, Detective."

"Okay, let me ask you this. What do you know about an oar that was recovered from the lake?"

"Nothing, sir." *God, the oar again!* He wiped his

hands on his pants.

"The gunwales of the boat you were driving were damaged. Know anything about that?"

"No, sir."

"Come on, Tim." Cobb sounded skeptical. "You were angry. Maybe angry enough to hit her and then smash that oar against the side of the boat hard enough to splinter it?" Cobb's dark eyes drilled into Tim's light ones. Neither of them blinked.

"My client denies any knowledge of either the oar or the damage to the boat," Grady said.

"Then how do you explain your fingerprints on that oar?" The detective's eyes hadn't left Tim's.

"Don't answer, Tim." Grady's voice was a warning.

"What? I don't know! I don't remember an oar!" Tim's voice was at least an octave higher. *Calm down.* He breathed deeply. Grady didn't look happy.

"Let's go back to what you *do* remember." Cobb made a show of checking his notes. "Melody Ward was standing on the back of the boat. Is that right?"

"Yes. She was there and then she wasn't." *How many times do I have to say this?*

"And you have no idea how she got in the water?"

"No, sir. *Just answer the questions, nothing extra.*

"Did you try to find her? Yell to her? Shine a flashlight?" Cobb was relentless.

"I called to her but she wouldn't answer."

"And you want us to believe you just drove away? Left her in the water? This girl you were so crazy about." Cobb paused. "Do I look stupid to you?"

"No, sir."

"You didn't maybe circle around, look for her on

shore and finish the job? You said she was a good swimmer."

"No. No." Tim shook his head hard. This guy was twisting his words. Looking to Grady, he willed his lawyer to say something. Now.

"My client has already stated that he left the scene." Grady wrote something on his pad.

Cobb shrugged. "All right. So where did you go?"

Tim didn't trust this shift in the line of questioning. Or Cobb. He answered with conviction. "I went back to the house where the party was."

"Did anyone see you?"

"No."

"What did you do?" Cobb was twirling the paperclip again.

Tim fought back tears. "I guess I passed out. When I woke up, it was morning and everyone was gone."

"Then what?"

Tim looked down at the table. He hated to admit this part. "I drove home."

The detective consulted a file. "Would that be at 1402 Church Street?"

"Yes."

"Anyone there see you come in?"

"No." Tim's mouth felt like a sand pile. He tried making saliva.

"Isn't it true that you were obsessed with Melody Ward? You couldn't stand the thought of anyone touching her or being with her but you." The detective's voice boomed. "You got her away from that party and into a boat alone so you could teach her a lesson."

"Detective Cobb, we're done here." Grady reached for his recorder.

Cobb leaned across the table and yelled, inches from Tim's face. "Isn't it true that you were so angry, you raped Melody Ward and killed her, then dumped her body into the lake?"

"NO. NO. I didn't!" Tim jumped up. He wanted out of this room, wanted to run away as far as he could. He caught a glimpse of himself in the one-way mirror. His hair was a mess from pulling his hands through it. His face was red and streaked with sweat. His eyes were full with tears he would *not* shed. Who was watching through that window?

They think I did this! His entire body shook. Grady was saying something.

Andrew Grady stood and grabbed Tim's arm. "That's it. We're out of here. Detective Cobb, my client and I came here voluntarily to make a statement. Unless you're prepared to arrest him right now, we're leaving." They were at the door when Cobb spoke.

"Just a minute, Counselor. I'd like to show you something."

Detective Cobb produced a clear plastic bag tagged as evidence. "The boat your client says he was driving Friday night was impounded and has been in police custody since then. This item was recovered, stuffed up under the front seat. Several students that we interviewed stated that your client was wearing a shirt that night that fits this description."

"He already told you he was in the boat. This is not new information. Come on, Tim."

The detective turned the bag over. Red brown streaks covered the front of the white T-shirt, almost obliterating the Fairfield Prep logo.

Tim felt like he would pass out. His clenched bowels threatened to betray him. "It's not what you think … it's my shirt but it's not what you think."

"Don't say another word." Andrew Grady grabbed Tim's arm.

The detective pushed the bag into Tim's face. "A sample of this substance is at the lab as we speak. If you know what this is and how it got on your shirt, it would be in your best interest to tell us now." Tim felt the heat of the detective's eyes burning into him. "My guess ... it's human blood."

"We have nothing further to say." Grady opened the door and pulled Tim through it before he could say another word.

"Don't leave the state, Mr. Rourke." Detective Cobb's voice echoed down the hall.

Barely able to put one foot in front of the other, Tim let himself be dragged. *How could I have forgotten about the shirt?*

"I need to use the men's room."

The three of them—Tim, Hutch, and Grady—came as one through the door into the waiting area.

"We'll stop at the first place we come to," Hutch said. "Right now, we have to get you out of here."

Grady still had him by the arm and hauled him down the steps and into his vehicle.

Through the back seat window, Tim saw his father striding to the car. "What the hell is going on?" he yelled.

"We need to get Tim out of here, Jack. We'll explain when we get back to the house." Hutch jumped into the passenger seat of Grady's Escort.

Grady put his turn signal on and pulled out of the parking lot slow and careful. Once he turned onto the state highway, he pounded his fist on the dashboard and glanced at Tim in the rearview mirror. "What the hell was that all about?

Was that your damn shirt?"

"Yes." Tim spoke in a whisper and hoped Grady remembered he still needed a restroom.

Grady banged the steering wheel. "Is that blood all over it?"

Tim nodded. Drenched in sweat, he shivered in the air conditioning.

Hutch turned around as far as his seatbelt would allow. "Whose blood is it, Tim?"

Tim shook his head and didn't answer.

"Tim?" Hutch repeated.

"It's Mel's." Tim's voice was barely audible.

"When were you planning to tell me this?" Grady yelled. "One thing you need to know about me—I *hate* surprises. And I *really hate* hearing them from the cops." Grady's eyes darted from Tim to the road and back again. "If I'm going to be your lawyer, kid, you need to be straight with me."

"I wasn't trying to hide anything, honest." Tim leaned forward, his hand on the back of the front seat. "I really need a bathroom."

"How the hell could you forget something like that?" Grady pulled into the parking lot of a Stewart's convenience store and turned off the engine. "Go."

After washing his hands, Tim splashed water on his face. This lawyer's gonna bail. Then what?

Grady made no move to restart the car when Tim settled into the back seat. "We're not going anywhere until you talk. So talk."

Both men turned to look at him. "How did Mel's blood get on your shirt?" Hutch's voice was as calm as if he were asking Tim what classes he was taking.

"When we were walking to the dock, Mel cut her foot on a broken beer bottle. It was bleeding pretty bad, so I took my shirt off and wrapped it around her foot. She kept it on in the boat until the bleeding stopped. When she started throwing stuff around, she rolled it up and flung it at me. I kicked it under the seat and never thought of it again. When I woke up and didn't have my shirt, I had no idea what happened to it." He paused. "I was pretty drunk. When I saw it today ... I remembered."

Grady's eyes locked with Tim's. "This isn't good. The cops have witnesses that saw you arguing with Melody Ward and getting into a boat with her, which was the last time anyone saw her. No one saw you come back to the party or to your apartment. Now they have her blood on your shirt and probably in the boat too. It's all circumstantial, but it's not good. If your fingerprints *are* on the oar, that's one more thing. Cobb could have been bluffing to break you. I don't know. I think he was hoping you'd just blurt out a confession today." Grady glanced over at Hutch who nodded in agreement.

"But I didn't do anything!" Tim pulled at his hair.

"I don't think they believe that." Grady started the car and put it in drive, his eyes riveted on Tim's in the rear view mirror.

"Do you believe it?" Tim waited and held his breath.

Grady looked both ways and pulled onto the road. "It doesn't matter what I believe. My job is to make sure your rights are protected."

"Bullshit!" Tim spat out. "I don't want a lawyer who doesn't believe me. How many times do I have to say this? I ... didn't ... do ... it!"

Hutch reached over the seat back and touched Tim's knee. "I believe you, Tim, and we'll do our best for you." Tim thought about the anger in his father's face when he told him what happened. He wished it were his dad saying this.

No one said anything for the next few miles.

"What will happen now?" Tim wasn't sure he wanted to hear the answer.

"I think Detective Cobb will push for those blood results today if possible. He'll review the ME's report and the cause of death, go over all the evidence and probably seek a warrant for your arrest." Grady said it like he was giving the weather report.

"What?" Tim's voice cracked like he was in the fifth grade. This was moving way too fast. "They're not looking at anyone else for this? What about that Shane guy? Anybody talking to him?"

"We can find that out, Tim. Ask if the police have taken a statement from him, do a little checking on our own," Hutch said. "But we need to be prepared."

"This sucks," Tim mumbled. "Could they get a warrant today, Mr. Grady?"

"They could arrest you without a warrant if they have enough evidence, but these guys are going by the book. They don't want to make a mistake." Grady's attention was on the winding road. "I'll go over everything in detail with you and your parents as soon as we get you home. But, yeah, they could."

Tim felt as if he'd been sucker punched and said nothing the rest of the way home. His mom had taught him to pray when he was a little boy. He hadn't been to church in a while and couldn't remember the last time he had prayed.

Now would be a good time.

21

Norm paced back and forth in his office. Tim Rourke was
supposed to be questioned in Castleton at ten. He checked his
watch again. It was almost noon. Did they arrest him? Calls to
the state police substation had given him no information.
Storrow wouldn't be any help even if he were able to reach
him. He'd burned that bridge.

Not knowing was driving him crazy and he was never
good at sitting around. He should have gone home with
Hannah when she went with Detective Whitcomb—but it was
clear she didn't want him. She had done well during the
questioning, holding it together although he knew she was
breaking apart inside. He should tell her that. He could check
on her at the same time, even if he risked seeing Braddock
again. What was the story with him and Hannah, anyway?

He didn't need more caffeine but reached for the pot.
It was empty and scorched on the bottom. *Damn!* He
unplugged it.

As much as he wanted no part of the gossip at Jenny's,

he could get a quick cup there on his way to Hannah's. He grabbed his keys and was in his truck in under a minute. He didn't know he could still move that fast.

After waiting for a green pickup to back out, Norm pulled into the last available spot in front of Jenny's. "Looks like the whole freakin' town's here," he said to himself as he got out.

The sound of the bell above the door was lost in the din of competing conversations that swirled around him as he entered the store. He went straight to the coffee machine and stood with his back to the crowd at the tables. He had no trouble hearing them.

"I heard she was naked when they found her." It was an older man's voice.

"They say she was raped," a woman said in a stage whisper.

"My sister's kid's on the rescue squad. He said she was dead before they got there."

"I heard it was a kid from the college," a man said in a loud sure voice.

"What's she doing with a college kid? Wasn't she only about fifteen?"

"Likes the older guys. Just like her mother," said an older man, not looking up from his newspaper.

Norm stepped into view.

Silence descended as one by one they noticed him. Norm approached the counter and paid for the large black coffee without a word.

"Didn't see you there, Norm," a well-known town contractor said from the corner table.

"Yeah, that's obvious." Norm scanned the room. "You people have nothing better to do? I bet some of you just came from church. A young girl, one of *us*, has been murdered. Show some respect."

"Sorry, Norm." Jenny handed him his change. "How's Hannah?"

"Not good." He turned to go.

Muriel Proctor, a sixty-something teacher at the village school, stopped him. "You're right, Norm. I've known Melody Ward her whole life, taught her in third grade. This is a horrible tragedy. Is it true the police are about to make an arrest?"

"I can't comment on that, Miss Proctor. The state police are handling the case. Excuse me."

Norm let the door slam behind him and yanked open the truck door. What was wrong with people? What if it had been Hannah who'd walked in there instead of him?

He called the Castleton substation again. This time he got some answers, although there wasn't much to tell. No arrest yet. Waiting on lab work. The officer didn't give the name of the suspect but Norm knew. Jesus, he wished he could be there to see the Rourke kid's face when they went for him. He hoped they'd bring the SWAT team. Scare the crap out of him, just like he did Mel.

Norm thrust the truck into gear. Hannah deserved to know what little he knew. He'd see her first, then check out the crime scene and see what the forensics team had found. He might be off the case but, damn it, this was still his town. He'd do whatever he could.

He drove the three miles to Hannah's in record time. Barreling up the dirt road to the trailer, he was relieved to see only the old Dodge Dart.

He knocked on the rusted door. Hannah peered through the sheer curtain before opening the door.

"Norm, what are you doing here?"

"Just wanted to see how you're doing. Can I come in for a minute?" Norm ducked his head and stepped into the kitchen. He had forgotten how cramped the trailer was. "Did it go okay with Detective Whitcomb?"

Hannah nodded. "He took Mel's computer and some other things from her room."

Norm didn't question her further. Her eyes were glassy. She rubbed them like she'd been sleeping. It was after one in the afternoon. "Are you going back to Carrie's place?"

"No, I need to be home."

"I hate the thought of you being here by yourself."

"You don't have to worry about me, Norm."

"I have some news, Hannah. The state police questioned a suspect today and may be close to an arrest. This has to stay between us. No leaks until it's official."

Hannah sat down at the table where Norm suspected she had waited many nights for Mel. She put her head in her hands and said nothing.

"Hannah?" Norm sat down beside her. "I thought this would be good news.

She looked up. "It is. I'm sorry. I'm grateful to the police, but it won't bring Mel back." Her eyes teared up.

Norm didn't know what to say. He was suddenly aware of his big frame taking up too much space in the small confines, of using up more than his share of available air.

"Who?" Hannah's voice croaked.

Norm heard the tremor in her voice, the difficulty in saying that one word. "I really can't say. I'm sorry. As soon as I know something, you'll be the first to know."

Before she could respond, the door opened and Dr. Glenn Braddock walked in. Norm hadn't heard him drive in, or knock. Did he have a key?

"Constable Johnson, I didn't expect to see you here."

"Doctor." Norm nodded.

Hannah got up. "Norm said the police may be close to making an arrest."

Norm shook his head a fraction of an inch, signaling Hannah not to say more.

"Impressive police work," Braddock said and took Hannah's hands in his. "What happened when you came here with Detective Whitcomb this morning? Did he find anything he thought might be useful?"

Hannah shrugged. "He took her computer, a calendar on her desk, some papers and books. Things like that. I'm not sure how they will help."

"Have they located her phone?" Braddock said.

"I don't know."

Glenn Braddock looked at Norm with an edge of superiority. "Mel had a lot of friends, like any teenage girl. I expect that detective is going to be quite busy, even without the phone, going through her social media accounts and emails." Braddock picked an invisible piece of lint off his pants. "I don't suppose you can tell us who this person of interest is who may or may not be arrested."

"That's privileged information, Doctor, until the suspect is apprehended and in custody."

"Ah, the company line. Well, I imagine we'll know soon enough. Mel was a popular girl. She'll be missed by many, but by none as much as her mother and me." Braddock put his arms around Hannah. She lay her head against his chest.

Norm's neck and jaw muscles tightened. "I'll call you if I hear anything, Hannah."

The door banged shut. *Hannah and Braddock! What does she see in the guy?* To Norm he was a little too polished, a little too well dressed. He didn't like him. But it was Hannah's life.

~~

It was almost noon. While the state sat on their butts waiting for lab results, the Rourke kid could bolt. Then what? Norm drove to the crime scene.

The truck slowed as the dam came into sight. He parked next to a van marked Vermont Bureau of Criminal Investigation. He ducked under the yellow police tape and walked north along the shallow channel to where the lake opened up. In the distance a state police boat searched the area directly across from the Rourke camp. A group of people wearing navy BCI shirts and latex gloves worked the shoreline.

When he got closer to them, he hiked up his gun belt and approached the nearest forensics team member. "Constable Norm Johnson. You finding anything?"

"This is a state crime scene, Constable. You really can't be here." The young guy looked barely old enough to shave.

"Well, last I checked, this is still part of my town. I worked the initial part of this case with Trooper Clayton Storrow." Norm figured some name-dropping and truth stretching couldn't hurt. "Who's your commanding officer?"

"Sergeant Duncan, up there ahead of us." He pointed to a large redhead surrounded by several men in navy shirts.

Norm headed that way but stayed back far enough not to draw attention. Duncan was briefing his team.

"We're going to continue working the shoreline inch

by inch, photographing everything we find. The booted foot-prints are probably fishermen. The smaller full and partial ones, some superimposed on each other, are likely kids swimming. Most of them are not fresh, but we document everything."

The group dispersed. Duncan eyed him. "Can I help you, Constable?"

Glad he had worn his uniform today, Norm approached the sergeant. "The second constable and I were first on the scene Saturday morning when those fishermen found her. The victim and her family are known to me. I'm just wondering how the investigation's going."

Before he could respond, an older dark-haired man called from several yards away. "Sergeant, I think we found something. Hey, Richie, get that camera over here."

Norm followed the sergeant and the photographer but hung back, careful not to touch anything or get in the way. Fresh bare footprints were visible in the mud at the edge of the lake. They seemed small. Norm could track a deer for miles through the woods, but he didn't know much about human footprints.

Duncan crouched down. "The right print in each pair is deeper, while the left is a partial. This pattern is consistent with someone with a limp or a possible injury. The right foot appears to be stronger."

What the hell? Norm thought. A limp? An injury? What does this have to do with Mel?

Low branches were broken off a nearby bush. A deep, wide depression was visible in the mud under it. "Looks like someone went down here and grabbed onto these branches," the dark-haired man said.

The photographer snapped several pictures. He leaned

over to get a closer look at the broken branch. "Is that human hair?"

Norm could see fine thread-like strands of something hanging from a low branch but had no idea what it was.

"Sure looks like it." The baby-faced team member Norm had first spoken to retrieved it with a small stick and put it in an evidence bag. "Wait. What's that?"

Norm saw the edge of something gold and shiny sticking out from under some leaves. Maybe this kid's not such a rookie.

The forensics investigator carefully removed it and placed it in a second evidence bag.

"I think it's some kind of a hair clip," someone said.

Norm tried to remember if he'd ever seen Mel wear something like that.

"The grass in this area is all matted down." Sergeant Duncan pointed up the hill. "Look. It continues in a path up toward the road."

"See that stain in the grass?" The younger one who had spotted the hair clip was squatting down. "Could be blood. We'll need samples of that and pictures," he said as he took out another evidence bag.

Norm would have missed that too, but there it was. Brownish-red and dried.

"Let's fan out and cover the area between here and the road," Duncan said. "Finn," he called to another tech. "Walk back to the dam and drive the van to the top of the hill."

The officers began a slow, deliberate uphill climb to the road. Breathing hard, Norm followed at a distance. The smudges of blood, if that's what they were, seemed to dry up as they climbed.

The trail stopped by the time they reached the road.

Norm couldn't tell where it led next. It didn't seem like the experts did either.

"The blood appears to stop here." Two BCI officers knelt and scrutinized a small patch of grass that looked to Norm like all the rest of the grass. "If it's from our victim, how did she end up in the water south of here, wedged up against the dam?"

Sergeant Duncan held up his hand. "It does no good to speculate. First, we need to find out if this *is* blood, second if the DNA matches our victim. Let's get these samples to the lab ASAP. Good work, guys."

He turned and saw Norm. "I didn't realize you were still with us, Constable. We're going to cordon off this whole area and put a uniform here to make sure nothing is disturbed. I'm going to have to ask you to leave. Anything you saw or heard stays here. You got it?"

Norm nodded just as a dark blue two-door sports car pulled onto the shoulder behind the BCI van.

"Now, who's this?" Duncan said and walked to the vehicle.

Norm saw Officer Parelli, the Rourke daughter's fiancé, step out and remove his sunglasses. Norm couldn't hear what he said but saw him flash his badge at Duncan, who talked to him briefly and then pointed to Parelli's car.

When Duncan walked away, Parelli headed toward one of the techs collecting evidence bags, instead of going to his car. The tech talked to him for a few minutes and looked to be answering questions.

What the hell? Norm walked that way. "Officer Parelli, I'm surprised to see you here."

A state cruiser pulled up and Trooper Storrow got out. "Constable Johnson, Officer Parelli, this is a restricted area.

You're going to have to leave. My orders are to secure the area and keep traffic moving."

Parelli put his sunglasses back on and headed for his car. "Have a nice day, Constable. You too, Trooper Storrow."

Norm wondered what Parelli had learned as he walked down the hill toward the dam and his truck. Sweat soaked his shirt. He wiped the perspiration from his forehead with his sleeve. Hair, footprints, a hair clip … what did all this new evidence mean?

Looking at how far he still had to go and feeling the heat, Norm was glad he wasn't walking uphill.

22

For the rest of the ride home from the police substation, Tim leaned his head against the rear passenger window and let the sun warm his face. If they pinned this on him, he wouldn't feel the sun for a very long time.

It was after one o'clock when Grady pulled into the driveway. Tim stepped into the afternoon sunlight and turned his face toward it.

His father was on the side deck, yelling. Tim tuned him out, walked past without a word and went into the house. Everyone followed. His mom had put out sandwiches but Tim knew no one would eat.

The door crashed against the frame as his father continued his tirade. "Okay, out with it, Grady. Where the hell have you been? Kate and I got here about forty minutes ago. And what happened that had the three of you running out of the interrogation like a bunch of girls?" His face was inches from the lawyer's.

"Mr. and Mrs. Rourke, let's sit down." Grady spoke

in a calm, measured tone. "I think there's a strong possibility that Tim will be arrested for the murder of Melody Ward."

"What? NO!" His mother looked from Grady to Hutch with wide, pleading eyes.

Tim couldn't stand to see the pain on her face and looked away.

"What the hell is he talking about, Hutch?" His father turned to his best friend. "We were just *at* the police station. No one arrested him."

"They have a shirt of Tim's with Melody Ward's blood on it," Hutch said.

"What shirt? Is this true, Tim?" His mom came closer. "How did Melody Ward's blood get on you?"

His father grabbed his arm and spun him around. "You didn't think to mention this?" The waves of rage coming off him plowed into Tim like a rip tide.

His mom pushed between them. "Talk to me, Tim," she said in a gentle voice. "Make me understand."

His eyes filled when he saw the ache in hers. "It's not what you think, Mom."

She shook her head. "Just tell me."

"Mel cut her foot and I gave her my shirt to wrap around it." Tim squeezed the sides of his head. "I totally forgot about it. How could I be so stupid?"

"How did the police get it?" She looked at Hutch but Tim answered.

"I think she flung it at me during the argument and I kicked it away. The cops found it in the boat."

"Doesn't sound to me like you're thinking at all." His dad turned to Hutch. "Do the cops know for sure it's Melody Ward's blood?"

"They don't have the lab results yet, but they will."

Hutch caught Tim's eye.

This was bad. Tim remembered all the times growing up that he had counted on Hutch and trusted him. But even he couldn't make this go away. "Can you stay, Hutch, if they—?"

"I'm not going anywhere. One call to my office, that's all it takes."

"What happens when they do get the results?" His mom asked.

"They'll review them along with all the circumstantial evidence and the medical examiner's report," Grady said. "Then … I believe they'll ask for a warrant."

Tim sat, his wobbly legs ready to give out. His body dissolved into jelly.

"That's ridiculous!" His father waved his hand to dismiss Grady. "They'll get a judge to sign off on a warrant on a Sunday?" His tone was laced with the bite of sarcasm.

Tim had felt the sting of that all his life.

"If the judge thinks they have enough evidence, they will." Grady's voice was firm, matter of fact.

They heard a car. Tim's insides flipped as he imagined state troopers storming the outside steps.

The door opened and Joe came in. "Hey," he said encompassing the whole group. "How'd it go this morning?"

"Not good," Sarah said as she crossed to him.

Grady filled him in.

"I hope you have some good news for us, Joe," Sarah said. "Did you find out anything from all the police activity across the lake?"

"When I got there, I introduced myself to the sergeant in charge and showed him my badge but got nothing. A young guy, a tech I think, was loading some samples and evidence bags into the van. I couldn't see what they were. I introduced myself to him and asked what was going on. All he said was they had found fresh footprints on the muddy bank." Joe looked at Tim. "I wish I could have found out more."

"No, that's okay. Don't you get it? It proves she *did* make it to shore. I knew it!" Tim punched the air with his fist.

"Those footprints could be anyone's," Grady said. "And outside this house, Tim, you never show that kind of emotion or victory no matter what is said. Do you understand?"

Tim exhaled. "Man, do you ever lighten up? I need some good news here."

"Anything else, Joe?" Grady said.

"No, I'm sorry. I got the feeling there was more. Trooper Storrow came to secure the area. He told me I had to leave, and Constable Johnson too." Joe smiled and lifted one shoulder. "I guess they didn't care about his badge either."

"Was there any action around the old shack?" Grady looked at the sketch he'd drawn earlier.

"Not that I could see, but I was ushered out of there quickly."

"Well, if they make an arrest, we'll find out soon enough what they have or don't have," Grady said.

"Isn't it a good thing if there's evidence that Mel made it to shore?" Tim needed to hear *something* good.

Grady looked at him hard. "Thinking like a prosecutor—you could have tied up the boat somewhere and pursued her on foot. They'll comb that whole area for any shred of evidence. And remember, no one as far as we know, can verify you went directly back to the party as you claim."

"But I did! Will you listen to me?"

"*I* told you the boat left and headed north, from the same direction it had come." His mom sounded desperate.

"But then you went inside," Grady said. "How long did it take you to convince your husband to go out on the lake with you? The boat could have doubled back. You wouldn't know."

"Whose side are you on, Grady?" His dad exploded. "You just built one hell of a case to make my son look guilty of murder. We don't need this, or you." His father's face darkened.

"I'm just thinking like the DA, Jack. We need facts and evidence to repudiate any possible scenario the prosecution comes up with."

"What about your idea that someone could have picked her up on the road?" Tim said.

"It's a possible theory but like I said, we need proof. We have a lot of work to do."

They spent the next several hours until dusk spinning possible scenarios, discussing ways to prove or disprove them, making more lists of people to interview. Grady made numerous phone calls. Tim didn't know to whom but hoped it would help.

"It's getting late." Grady checked his watch. "Let's order a few pizzas, my treat. We'll go over everything we've got."

A deafening sound in the driveway silenced them. Car doors slammed in one, two, maybe three vehicles. Everyone froze, seven pairs of eyes riveted on the side door.

A knock. "Police." The door opened. Detective Chuck Cobb and someone else entered.

"Timothy Rourke, you are under arrest for the murder of Melody Ward."

"I didn't do anything, I swear!" Tim stood in the center of the room. Panic welled up inside him. He could taste it. His whole body shook. He heard his mom and dad yelling but couldn't make out the words. He thought maybe Sarah was crying. People seemed to be moving around the room. Hutch came and stood beside him.

Through the haze that engulfed him, Tim saw the detective's mouth moving. He heard bits and pieces of what was said, a word here and there. "right … remain silent … against you ... court … attorney … appointed."

Tim's arms were jerked behind him. Metal handcuffs bit into his wrists.

"What's he doing?" Tim scanned the room. "I didn't do it." His breathing was shallow and labored. The room was closing in on him. He looked onto the deck as twilight faded. A state trooper, hand on his gun, was stationed by the French doors. Another one was by the side door.

Andrew Grady stepped forward. "Detective Cobb, do you have a warrant?"

"Right here, Counselor." Cobb pulled a paper from his back pocket. "Judge Amelia Oberman just issued the warrant. The arraignment will be tomorrow in Rutland district court."

"Arraignment Monday? What does that mean?" Tim searched Hutch's face.

Hutch placed a hand on his shoulder. "It means you'll have to spend the night in jail."

"What? Where?" Tim was unable to form a complete thought.

He was aware of his mother on his other side. He saw strength in her eyes. She was tougher than she looked. He knew she meant to comfort him. But all he felt was terror.

"We have a holding cell in Castleton," Detective Cobb said. "The accommodations could be worse. Your attorney will be allowed to meet with you privately once you've been processed."

"Don't say a word, Tim. Nothing. I'll be there as soon as I can." Grady had his car keys in hand.

His mom tried to hug him, but Detective Cobb had him by the arm. "You need to come with me now."

"Right now?" The panic that was building erupted. *Jail? Now?*

Flanked by two armed detectives and uniformed troopers, Tim was taken from his parents' home. The crunch of gravel under his feet, something he'd heard a million times, was magnified and seemed important to remember.

His mother ran after them and stood by the police car. She reached out to him and gave him a reassuring look, despite the tears in her eyes. Out of the corner of his eye, he saw Sarah holding on to Joe.

Where was his dad? He looked for him and saw him standing on the deck, gripping the railing—an unreadable expression on his face.

Someone pushed his head down. He was thrust into the back seat of the marked car, behind a wire screen. In a cage.

His brain registered the frightening, metallic sound of locks clicking into place.

23

Kate stood rooted in the driveway and watched until the taillights of the police cars disappeared. Tim looked back at her, confusion and fear contorting his face, and there was nothing she could do.

Back in the house, everyone was talking at once. Their words swept around her in a violent storm. Sifting through the chaos, she focused on random comments.

Jack's voice booming. "Can they just do that? Come in here and take my son?"

Hutch's voice calm and placating. "We'll get it straightened out."

Grady's no-nonsense lawyer's tone. "They had a valid warrant. Evidently, the judge thought the evidence was sufficient to sign off on."

Sarah crying, "What happens now?"

Joe's soothing voice as he spoke to Sarah.

"Please stop!" Kate yelled.

They quieted and looked at her.

"You're all talking but no one's listening. This isn't helping Tim." She let her words sink in. "Imagine what he's going through." She looked at their lawyer with clear eyes, holding back tears. "What do we do now, Mr. Grady?" Her voice cracked.

"I know you're worried and you want to do something," Grady said. "But you need to let me take it from here. I need to call my office, explain the situation, and get to Castleton. That's what you're paying me for."

"And you've done a hell of a job so far," Jack said. "My son was taken out of here like a common criminal. How much do I owe you for that?"

Grady ignored the comment.

"Stop it, Jack," Kate said. "This isn't about you. It's about Tim." Turning back to their lawyer, she said, "When can I see my son?"

"That's one of the things I'll find out, but it's my guess it won't be until after the arraignment tomorrow. I'm sorry. I'll request a copy of the official arrest warrant and a copy of the ME's report too." Grady looked at his cell. "Damn. I have no service."

"Try the deck." Kate turned away, her eyes glistening.

Hutch and Joe took their phones and followed Grady outside.

Sarah put her arm around her mother. "You know Joe has to head back, Mom. He has to go in tonight at midnight. He's trying now to get some time off later in the week. I'm staying here with you."

"No. You go. There's nothing you can do here." Kate caressed her daughter's cheek. "I'll call you when I've seen Tim after court tomorrow. Promise." She crossed her heart with her finger and attempted a reassuring smile.

"But, Mom—"

"Sarah, there's nothing you can do for him."

"But I can be here with you."

Kate put her hands on Sarah's shoulders. "Listen to me. You start your fieldwork at Child Services tomorrow. That's important."

"Yes, but—"

"You go, honey. I'll be fine. Dad's here with me and Hutch is staying on to help Grady." She hugged her daughter. "I'm so glad you were here. I needed you to be."

Joe came in. "I'm so sorry that I have to leave."

Kate went to him. "Don't worry about that. We're glad you were here. This is pretty foreign territory to us. It helps to have a policeman in the family."

Joe hugged her. "I'll be back later in the week if I can."

She smiled and put her arms around their shoulders. "You two better get on the road. We'll be fine."

Kate and Jack walked them to the car. Jack shook Joe's hand. "Thanks."

"Bye, Dad." Sarah hugged him. "You call me, Mom. If you need me, I'll be here."

Kate nodded. "I know."

She looked at Jack when they were alone. *How are we going to get through this?*

Back inside, Jack sank onto the couch. He stared straight ahead. "Murder … arrested for murder! How the hell did this happen?" He stood up. "I need a drink."

"No. I need you sober." Kate stood in front of him. "And so does Tim. He left here without anything, no clothes, nothing. He doesn't even have a toothbrush. Maybe we can bring some things to him."

Jack glared down at her then headed for the kitchen. "He's in jail, Kate! He didn't go to Boy Scout camp. Why don't you sew labels into his underwear too?" He came back with a full bottle of Jameson and a glass.

Kate felt only disgust. "What are you doing?"

Jack poured a shot of the Irish whiskey. "What does it look like? Maybe if you hadn't babied him his whole life he'd be better off now, toughened up for his night in jail."

"Damn you, Jack. Don't you dare throw that at me, not now."

Hutch came in off the deck. Kate wasn't sure how much he had heard.

"Hey, you two," he said. "This doesn't help. You need to be together on this, for Tim."

"Yeah, for Tim." Jack put down the empty glass and picked up the open bottle. "It's always about Tim." He headed for the door.

"Where are you going?" Kate said.

"I need to clear my head, get some air."

"You can't drive, Jack. And you don't need that." Hutch nodded his head toward the bottle.

"I'm a big boy now," Jack said. "You're not my keeper anymore. In fact, you're a guest in my home. So fuck off." He left and slammed the door behind him.

"What the hell was that all about?" Hutch threw his arms up in the air. "I thought the drinking was better. He's my friend, but right now he's being an ass."

"It was. It is. He's upset. You know Jack. He can't stand not being in control. So, he lashes out. And he drinks."

"That's no excuse. You need him right now."

Andrew Grady opened the deck door. "The

arraignment's set for ten tomorrow in Rutland District Court. Meet me there at nine. You'll be able to see Tim in the courtroom, not before. I'm on my way to see him now. I'll get in touch with the prosecutor and call you later."

"Can I send some things with you like clean clothes, toiletries?" Kate asked.

"I'm afraid not. I'll see you and Jack in the morning?" He glanced at the empty couch, the abandoned glass.

Kate knew the smell of whiskey permeated the room. "Yes, we'll be there. Thank you." She shook hands with the lawyer and walked him to the door.

"Hutch," Grady said. "Will you go over everything again with Mr. and Mrs. Rourke beginning with early Saturday morning? Also anything Tim may have ever said about Melody Ward. We need everything we can get before we meet with the prosecutor. I'll call you after I've met with Tim. Thanks for staying on to help."

Kate sat on the couch. The tears she'd been holding back began to stream down her cheeks. Now that she'd started, she was afraid they'd never stop. She shuddered and rubbed her arms to warm them, despite the heat of the evening.

Hutch got the afghan from the guest room and put it around her shoulders. "Do you feel up to going over everything again? It may jog your memory. I'll talk to Jack when he gets back."

She didn't respond to the last part. Jack wouldn't be in any condition to do anything by then, and Hutch knew it. Kate wiped her eyes. She calmed herself with a couple of deep breaths. "I'm ready."

She went over every detail she could remember. Had it really only been two days?

Her eyes filled. "From the minute I heard that voice

carry across the water, I tried to ignore it, deny it, convince myself it couldn't be him. But a mother knows. Deep down in her gut, she knows." She shivered and pulled the blanket tighter around her.

"I also knew a girl was in trouble, still in the water. She could have hit her head, been in danger of drowning. What if it were Tim or Sarah, and someone heard them and did nothing? I had to do *something*."

She held her hands between her knees. "When Jack and I found nothing, I knew I had to call the constable. Even if it meant…" Hair flew in her face as she shook her head back and forth. "I didn't tell him about the male voice. I didn't even tell Jack. I couldn't!" Her tears fell.

"I don't know what to say." Hutch put the notepad down and placed his hand over hers. "This has been hell for you."

"No." She pulled her hands away and clutched at the blanket, burying her chin in the soft yarn. "It's not about me. My only concern is my son. If you want to help me, tell me exactly what will happen tomorrow."

Hutch kept his eyes on her but settled back into the cushions. "Okay. The prosecutor will state the charges and Tim will be asked how he pleads. The judge will set bail. Tim doesn't have a record, so that should work in his favor. But these are serious charges, Kate. You need to be prepared. Bail will likely be denied."

"You mean he'll have to stay in jail? For how long?" Her hands trembled as her nerves frayed.

"Until the trial, and I don't know when that will be."

"Oh, my God." She squeezed her hands together so tight her nails dug into her knuckles. "He's a good boy, Hutch. There's no way he could have done this." Kate searched his face. He had to believe her. She began to shake, to crumble, as if pieces of her were coming apart.

"I know he's a good boy, Katie." Hutch put his arm around her.

She rested her head on his shoulder and let the tears flow. Breathing in the long forgotten scents of pine and musk, she felt warm and safe. His grip tightened.

An electric shock jolted through her. She leapt to her feet, the afghan slipping to the floor. "It's late. Tomorrow's going to be a long day. I need to get to bed." She started for the stairs.

"Katie, wait."

"No. Thanks for being here. I'll see you in the morning."

"What about Jack? Do you want me to go look for him?"

Kate paused, halfway up the stairs. "No, he'll come back when he's ready. He'll probably pass out on the couch."

"He's done this to you before." His voice was husky.

"Good night, Hutch."

Upstairs, she heard the door to the guest room close and Hutch's cell ring.

Kate lay awake and alone in the king-size bed. Old and very dangerous memories spun through her mind. She hadn't thought about any of this in a long time. *What am I doing?*

Trying to dislodge the images, she kicked off the thin sheet and went to the bathroom to splash cold water on her face. She halted—her feet riveted on the cool tiles—when she heard the front door close.

Jack stumbled in and dropped his shoes. "Fuck." He must have stubbed his toe. She glanced at the bathroom clock,

midnight. Not bad, but then he'd taken only one bottle. She
half-ran on her tiptoes back to bed. Turning toward the wall,
she feigned sleep.

She waited to hear the creek on the fifth stair as he
came up. Nothing. Kate slipped out of bed again and tiptoed
down. In the glow from the nightlight in the adjoining kitchen,
she saw his form stretched out on the couch. He was already
asleep, or passed out. She bent over him to be sure he was
breathing and covered him with the blanket Hutch had put
around her. He moved slightly but didn't open his eyes.

"I'm sorry." The words were thick and distorted by
liquor and sleep.

Sorry for what? For leaving? For getting drunk? For
not getting up when she'd first asked him early Saturday
morning? Maybe then that girl would still be alive—and Tim
wouldn't be sitting in a jail cell charged with murder.

Whiskey breath overpowered her as he began to snore.
A flush of heat and anger moved through her. She straightened
and went back upstairs to bed.

Kate prayed for sleep and tried not to think about the
next day. But she tossed and turned and was plagued by
images of Tim in a prison cell, superimposed on happier times:
his five year-old whoop of victory when his three-legged frog
won the Willow Bend frog jumping contest, his joy at making
the little league team after countless games of catch in the
backyard with Jack and Hutch, his fresh scrubbed face and
trembling hands when he gave his prom date the wrist corsage,
his fourth grade tortured performance of "Twinkle, Twinkle
Little Star" on the French horn in the school concert, his
angelic face as a shepherd in the children's Christmas pageant
at church. But the tape continually looped back to a stark
prison cell, handcuffs, and the echoing clang of prison locks.

By six on Monday morning, Kate was showered and dressed. Her swollen, tear ravaged eyes required extra time and skill with makeup. A last look in the mirror didn't convince her it had been a success, but she steeled herself to face the day and whatever was downstairs.

Jack was still sprawled on the couch but he hadn't gotten sick. She couldn't have dealt with that today. The smell of fresh coffee lifted her spirits.

Hutch was pouring himself a cup. He walked over and handed one to her. "Did you get any sleep?"

"Some. Thanks."

"I see our friend made it home last night. I thought I heard him come in around twelve. You okay?"

"I'm fine. I need to get him moving if we're going to make it to Rutland on time. He's going to need lots of strong, black coffee and a long cold shower."

"I remember the drill." Hutch went to the couch.

Jack stirred. "What the hell time is it?"

"Come on, you need to get up," Hutch said. "Coffee's ready."

Jack sat up and rubbed his face with his hands. "What a mother of a headache. What time do we have to be in court?"

"We're meeting Grady at nine," Kate said from the kitchen and handed Jack's coffee to Hutch. "You need to get moving. Now."

Jack looked over at her white slacks and navy and white cotton sweater. "Jesus, you look like you're going on a yacht instead of to an arraignment."

"Just get showered, Jack. I don't want to be late." She turned her back to him. Curt responses were all she had to give, and she dug deep for those.

24

Jack nursed his third cup of black coffee as Hutch drove the white BMW to the courthouse. Hutch had suggested they all go together. He'd go back later to do what he could for Grady.

"Nice car," Jack said. "Must be nice to make the big bucks. And you don't have to share them with a wife or kids." Jack laughed.

Hutch didn't respond.

In the backseat, Kate silently applauded Hutch for not rising to Jack's bait. She fingered the silver pendant engraved with Sarah's and Tim's names. It was the only jewelry she wore in addition to small pearl studs.

She was grateful when Jack fell asleep for the last half hour of the ride. Blessed silence.

When Hutch pulled up in front of the Rutland District Court, Kate stared at the building. She took a minute to process what was happening. As she gathered her things and opened the car door, she said a silent prayer for strength.

After going through security, Kate, Jack, and Hutch

sat in the waiting area. Kate watched the court traffic: young boys and men in baggy pants and hoodies, teenage girls in short tight skirts, disheveled men, distraught mothers trying to control active toddlers, security guards, officers of the court, the occasional presumed attorney in suit and tie. She was drawn to the families, looking lost and stunned. So intent on the sights around her, Kate was startled when Andrew Grady approached at exactly nine o'clock. He shook hands with all three of them.

"How is he?" she asked.

"He's holding up."

They followed Grady into a small conference room. He didn't waste time. "There're going with second degree murder, which differs from first degree only in the sense that it is not believed to be premeditated."

"Jesus Christ," Jack said.

Kate went cold.

"They're also charging him with aggravated sexual assault of a child. DNA results on the semen are not back, but will be within days. They've put a rush on it."

Kate couldn't breathe. She was hyperventilating. Grady passed her a paper bag to breathe into. She could tell she was not the first to experience this reaction. Hutch poured her a glass of water.

"Why a child?" Jack said.

"Because Tim is over eighteen and the victim is under sixteen. It's math," Grady said.

"What does aggravated mean?" Kate sipped the water.

"That there was serious bodily injury inflicted and/or a weapon used during the commission of a sexual act, according to the statute," Grady said.

Kate shuddered. She squeezed her eyes shut and

pinched the bridge of her nose.

"I'm sorry, Mrs. Rourke," Grady said. "You're going to hear this in court."

She nodded, not opening her eyes. "Does Tim know all this?"

"Yes."

All she wanted to do was hold her son, make it right.

"What kind of penalties do these charges carry?" Jack asked.

"That's getting ahead of ourselves at this point. I really don't want to—"

"No, dammit. He's my son. Tell me." Jack stood and gripped the back of the chair.

Grady looked at Kate who nodded. "Second degree murder carries not less than twenty years to life. Aggravated sexual assault can be ten years to life with or without a fine of up to $50,000. But I don't want you to focus on the penalty phase. We're nowhere near there."

"Oh my God." Kate's entire body shook as she lay her head in her arms on the table. Her sobs were the only sound in the room. The men were silent. Jack placed his hand on her back.

Grady cleared his throat. "I believe Tim is telling the truth but we've got a fight ahead of us. He needs you all fully present and focused. And you need to be prepared. It could get ugly."

Kate raised her head. She prayed silently.

Grady scanned the room. "There's also a third charge of larceny for stealing the property owners' boat, but I'm not worried about that. I should be able to get that dismissed or reduced since he did return it."

"Well, there's a bright spot." Jack's voice was sharp.

sarcastic.

Grady went on. "I'll request bail but doubt that we'll get it due to the seriousness of the charges. We've drawn Judge Amelia Oberman. She's smart and fair, and holds to the letter of the law. She's also a woman, and a young girl's been assaulted and murdered."

"That's sexist," Jack said.

"Yes, it is. But it's what we've got. Does anyone have more questions?" He waited. "Okay then, let's go. Judge Oberman is also a stickler for punctuality. She does not like to be kept waiting."

Jack took Kate's elbow and the three of them followed Grady down the long courthouse corridor, bright with fluorescent lights. As they entered the courtroom, she thought she saw Constable Johnson in the back row.

They filed into the scarred wooden bench behind the defense table; Jack and Hutch were on either side of Kate. She sat still and concentrated on breathing—in and out, in and out. She took in none of the details of the room, her eyes focused on the side door at the front.

An audible gasp escaped when she saw him. He looked as if he hadn't slept and he had a night's growth of beard. His hair was matted. His shirttail hung outside his pants, which were stained and ripped at the knee. He made brief eye contact with her without moving his head. She nodded to him and willed him to be strong.

Handcuffed and shackled, Tim had difficulty walking to the defense table. His eyes were wide with terror.

"All rise for the honorable Amelia Oberman." The bailiff's voice filled the room.

Kate didn't think her legs would support her and leaned on Jack. She couldn't take her eyes off the back of

Tim's head and had to restrain herself from touching him.

When they were seated again, except for Tim and Grady, the state's attorney began to speak. His words faded in and out of her consciousness, her attention riveted on Tim.

"The state of Vermont Criminal Code and Statutes … Chapter 53 section 2301 second degree murder … Chapter 72 subsection 3253 aggravated sexual assault … child … Chapter 57 section 2505 unauthorized use … boat…"

Kate reached for Jack's hand and held tight.

The judge lowered her glasses and spoke to Tim. "How do you plead?"

"Not guilty, Your Honor." Kate hardly recognized his voice.

Grady was asking for bail. She heard "no previous criminal record" and held her breath.

It was the prosecutor's turn. "Due to the seriousness of the charges and possible flight risk, the state requests that bail be denied."

Kate looked at Jack whose face betrayed no emotion. He rubbed her hand, still clutched in his, with his thumb.

Judge Oberman's words hit Kate hard. "Bail is denied. Case to be continued September eighth of this year. The defendant, Timothy Rourke, will be remanded to custody at Slate Valley Correctional Facility immediately and remain there until the case is continued."

The bang of the gavel. "Next case."

Kate sat frozen and rigid as she watched her son being led away in handcuffs for the second time in two days. He looked back at her, eyes brimming with tears.

And then he was gone.

Unable to garner the will or the ability to rise, she continued to sit on the hard, unyielding bench. The next case was beginning before the men could get Kate to leave. "Where is this Slate Valley place?" she said.

"In Rutland, not far from here." Grady had gathered his papers. They were leaving the courtroom.

"I want to see him right now." She would not be placated, or concede this one demand.

"I'm on my way there now," Grady said. "You can follow me."

Kate and Jack followed their attorney down the hall, leaving Hutch to trail behind.

25

At nine a.m. Monday morning, Hannah lay awake looking at the overhead ceiling light, as she had for the last two and a half hours. Intending to make coffee, she padded toward the kitchen. As she passed Mel's room, she stood riveted in the doorway. The bedroom was just as Mel had left it on Friday night.

Hannah was embarrassed when Detective Cobb had seen it.

Discarded clothes were strewn everywhere with no indication whether they were clean or dirty. Bureau drawers gaped open, their contents jumbled and spilling over. Makeup containers littered the tops of several surfaces. Open nail polish bottles spewed alcohol fumes and competed with the smell of running shoes and dirty socks. Hannah opened the narrow window wider.

She sat on the unmade twin bed and smoothed her hand over the faded pink stuffed bunny resting on the pillow. Lying on her side, Hannah inhaled Mel's scent on the pillowcase and began to cry. She hugged the pillow to her and buried her face in the worn soft cotton.

Forty minutes later she awoke in a fetal position with the wet pillowcase stuck to her cheek. Hannah picked up the scattered clothes and clutched them to her breast. The shiny green skirt she had bought Mel with her K-Mart discount, the mid-drift top Hannah had forbidden her to wear, the strappy sandals she had begged Hannah to buy each told a story.

She was reluctant to wash them, their scent the only tangible reminder of her daughter. So she sat on the bed with an armful of clothes and waited for Norm's call. He had called last night to tell her that Timothy Rourke had been arrested and was spending the night in jail. Today was the arraignment.

The phone rang in the kitchen. She ran and was out of breath in that short distance. "Hello," she said still holding the clothes.

"Hannah, it's Norm. The arraignment is over. Timothy Rourke has been remanded to custody. No bail."

"What does that mean?" She put the pile of clothes on the counter and sat down.

"He stays locked up until trial due to the seriousness of the charges. He's also considered a flight risk since his legal residence is Connecticut."

"That's good." She rubbed the top item between her fingers absently. "He won't be able to hurt anyone else. Was his family there?"

"Yeah. They were pretty shaken up. Is anyone there with you, Hannah?"

"No, but I'm okay. Dwight is coming by. He's picking up Mel ... um, her body ... to take her to the ... to his funeral home. He said he would sign for her personal effects if I wanted. So I called the ME's office and gave my verbal permission. They wanted something official but I don't have access to a fax or anything."

"I do. I can do that for you."

"No, they finally agreed as long as I accepted responsibility. I mean, what's Dwight Atkins going to do with Mel's stuff? Keep it? Sell it? God, I've known him since first grade. The state has to make everything so difficult. Anyway, I think he may want to discuss arrangements too, but I don't know if I'm ready.

"Don't do that alone, Hannah. I can be there in less than an hour. I'm already on the road."

"It's okay, Norm, I'm fine. Mel's room is a mess, clothes everywhere. I'm keeping busy trying to clean up. But I can't bear to wash them." She dissolved into sobs.

"Hannah, I'm coming as soon as I get back to town."

"You're going to the candlelight vigil tomorrow night, right?"

"Of course. I'll pick you up."

He hung up before she could tell him that she'd be going with Glenn. *Oh, well, I can't worry about whatever's going on between those two.*

A knock at the door startled her. She had dozed off again, wrapped in Mel's comforter, despite the heat. She hadn't been able to wash those clothes after all.

"Just a minute, Dwight." She opened the door. "Norm, what are you doing here?"

"I told you I was coming. Dwight's right behind me." He gestured to the van. "I couldn't let you do this alone."

Tall and lanky, Dwight Atkins was almost a caricature of what the local undertaker should look like. How they'd teased him all through school because of his father's profession.

"Dwight, come in. Do you have…"

"Yes. We can talk about arrangements whenever you're ready. I just wanted to give you this." He held out a sealed manila envelope. "They needed to keep her clothes but I signed for her personal effects as you requested."

She hugged the envelope to her chest. "Thank you. You saved me a long drive." *And the raw pain of collecting these myself.*

"We're all set for the vigil. Everything you wanted is included."

"You've been so good to me, Dwight. You're a very kind and compassionate man."

Hannah continued to hug the envelope to her after he'd gone. "Norm, I don't know if I can do this, see and touch the last things Mel had with her when she…." Hannah wept.

He touched her shoulder. "Would it help if I stay?"

She nodded and with hands shaking, emptied the envelope onto the counter. Norm read the typed list aloud. "Two silver earrings, one silver pinkie ring, one silver toe ring, one cubic zirconium navel stud. That's it. No phone."

"Wait. Where's her bracelet?" She spread out the items. "Mel *always* wore that bracelet, every day since I gave it to her for her fourteenth birthday. It was a chain of silver hearts. Where is it?" Hannah went through the items again, picked each one up and put it back on the Formica. "Where is it, Norm?" Her eyes scanned the few pieces again. "Where!"

"Well, I'm sure Dwight didn't take it," Norm said. "Let me call the medical examiner's office." He scrolled down the numbers in his phone. "This is Constable Norm Johnson in Willow Bend. Would you check the list of personal effects from Melody Ward? Her mother is inquiring about a silver bracelet. Thank you, I'll hold."

Hannah watched until he hung up. "What did they say?"

"No bracelet of any description was found. I know the police checked the crime scene and the shoreline too. I'll call the trooper I know. He might have some information. Maybe it was overlooked somehow."

Her eyes were moist as she held the few trinkets close to her chest. "I'm glad you were here, Norm."

"Do you want me to call Carrie to come stay with you? I have to get back to the office."

"No, that's okay." She swiped at her eyes and nose with a rumpled tissue. "I have some things to do before Glenn comes over."

Norm said nothing but didn't look happy. *He'll just have to get used to me and Glenn being together.*

"What did you mean yesterday when you said Mel was spending a lot of time with him?"

"I told you she's been working for him in the stables after school three days a week. Now that it's summer, she goes every day for four hours. He's trying to get her interested in riding. He wants her to quit her job at Jenny's but she doesn't want to." Hannah paused. "Didn't want to, I mean. She liked seeing her friends at the store. Glenn thought more responsibility and a new interest would be good for her and boost her self-esteem."

"Sounds like a lot of psycho-babble to me." Norm picked up his keys from the table.

"Don't ridicule what you don't understand, Norm. Glenn is a good person. He's been very good to us."

"Did you ever go over there to watch her ride?"

"I wanted to, but Glenn thought Mel needed some space."

"Right. Did the three of you spend time together too?"

"Sure. Sometimes I thought she'd rather be with her friends but Glenn thought it was important we spend time together as a family. Why the third degree? Don't you have some police work to do?" She sighed and shook her head. "I'm sorry, Norm. I don't know why I said that."

Norm hesitated like he was going to say something but didn't. He looked back when he got to the door. "I'll call you if I find out anything about the bracelet. You sure you're all right?"

"Yes. I'm going to tear this house apart until I find it."

26

Entering the one-story brick Slate Valley Correctional Facility as visitors was intimidating. Kate tried to imagine what it had been like for Tim, as a new inmate. *Inmate*—the word didn't belong in her vocabulary, or his.

Kate, Jack, and Hutch signed in and sat in silence in the visitors' reception area. Although this was not a regular visiting day, Grady had managed to secure Kate and Jack a few minutes with Tim. Immediate family only. Kate was thankful she had reached Sarah from the car to tell her about the arraignment. This wasn't a place for conversation. She wondered about surveillance, if prison officials listened in.

Grady, as the attorney of record, met with Tim for over an hour while they waited. A metal door buzzed and their lawyer appeared. "Tim's anxious to see you," he said.

He led them to a window where Kate and Jack showed photo IDs. The guard checked their names against a list of approved visitors. A metal door clanged open. When it locked behind them, Kate felt claustrophobic. She concentrated on breathing.

Jewelry, phones, all items in their pockets and Kate's purse were removed, checked and placed in a secure lock box. Stepping through the metal detector, she prayed nothing would set off the alarm. The underwire of her bra? A belt buckle? She knew they would be searched further by hand if necessary. The entire process, done with a minimum of verbal interaction, was demeaning and demoralizing. Finally admitted to what must be the visitors' room, antiseptic in feel if not in cleanliness, they sat down without a word. She glanced at Jack whose eyes were riveted on the counter and glass partition that divided the room.

Within minutes, Tim, wearing a one-piece orange prison jumpsuit, was brought in through a side door on the other side of the partition. He looked dazed, a returning soldier or POW not quite sure how he'd gotten there. Kate sat forward and placed her hand on the glass. He did the same, his hand so much larger.

"How are you doing?" Jack spoke into the telephone receiver.

"Okay, Dad. I'm glad they let you guys in."

"We are too. Grady and Hutch are working very hard to get you out of here."

"I know, but it's going to be a long time." He blinked back tears.

"We love you, Tim," Kate said into the receiver. "We'll be here as often as they'll let us come."

"I didn't do it, Mom. I loved her." He began to sob.

"We know." Kate pulled up reserves she didn't know she had.

"You have to keep it together. For your own protection." Jack's voice cracked.

"Yeah, I can't let them see me cry." Tim wiped his eyes.

The guard stepped forward. "Time's up." He grabbed Tim's arm above the elbow.

"No! Please! It took us longer just to get into this room." It tore at Kate's heart to see him like this, to leave him like this. She wanted only to hold him, to soothe him as she had when he was a little boy.

Her hand was still against the glass as he was led away. "I love you, Tim," she said to the empty room.

Jack said nothing as he wiped his eyes, and helped her up.

Kate didn't speak of the visit, if you could call it that, or talk all the way home. She rested her head against the side window in the back. Trees and farmland blurred past. Any conversation between Jack and Hutch in the front went unheard. Grady was meeting them at home.

"Do we have anything for lunch?" Jack's voice stirred her and she sat up straight. They were home.

"Um, I don't think so. Give me the keys and I'll make a quick run to Jenny's for sandwiches. What do you want? How about Grady?"

"I can do that," Hutch said.

"Thanks, but I need some time to myself. I'll be right back."

When she got to the general store, it was unusually crowded for mid-afternoon. The lunch rush should have been over. All conversation stopped as Kate stepped up to the deli counter to place her order. Several pairs of eyes bore into her back. "Jenny," she said twice before the owner seemed to notice her, even though Kate was the only one standing there.

"One of the girls will take care of you. It will just be a

few minutes."

Kate stood there another five minutes before reciting her order to the teenage girl. No one spoke while she waited another twenty for the sandwiches.

They know who I am. They know Tim's been arrested. This is how a small town works. They close ranks, and we're the outsiders.

A multi-colored flier on the bulletin board caught her attention on the way out. "Prayer Vigil Tuesday Night for Melody Ward. 8 p.m. on the Town Green."

"What took you so long?" Jack met her at the door.

"It was pretty crowded." It had been a stressful day. She didn't need to upset them any further.

She, Jack, Hutch, and Grady gathered at the kitchen table for a strategy session amid sandwich wrappers and cans of soda. Kate had three voice mails from Ellen and two from Sarah. She would call them after this meeting.

Grady had met with the state's attorney for "discovery" Kate thought he called it. "Much of what they have is circumstantial," he said. "The last time anybody saw Melody Ward alive she was with Tim, when they left the party in the boat. Then there's the constable's report of the supposed argument and all that followed on the lake."

Slicing pain seized Kate's stomach and cut around to her lower back as Grady reiterated her unwitting role in incriminating Tim. She started to rise and excuse herself when Hutch took her hand.

"You can't blame yourself, Kate. You thought a girl was in danger."

"To tell you the truth," Grady said. "The most damning evidence they have right now is Tim's T-shirt covered in the victim's blood."

191

"He explained that," Jack said.

"No one that we know of saw her cut her foot or Tim wrap his shirt around it. Melody Ward's skull was fractured, along with other injuries. The oar is being tested for latent traces of blood and DNA. I know Tim has no memory of handling it. But if his fingerprints are on that oar, it won't matter."

"Oh, my God," Kate said. "Why didn't we just leave it in the water? It might never have been found."

"What about that Shane character?" Jack said.

"The detectives have interviewed him extensively and checked out his alibi during the estimated time of death. Rock solid," Grady said.

"Do they have evidence that Melody definitely made it to shore?" Hutch asked. "What about the footprints Joe told us about?"

"They do have photographs of footprints but that's a popular swimming area for locals," Grady said. "More important, the forensics team found hair on a low lying branch near the water, a hair clip identified as Melody Ward's by one of her friends during an interview, and a blood-spotted path through the high grass up to the road. Everything will be tested for Melody's DNA."

"How long before they get results?" Jack asked.

"They put a rush on it. We don't have the backlog like Boston or New York, so days maybe? If it's a match, we'll maintain that once on the road, she was met or picked up by someone. That's our focus right now—the hill and the road. But you have to understand. The most important evidence will come from the body." Grady looked around the table at each of them. "If there's skin or blood under her nails ... or semen."

Everyone was quiet.

"Now that Tim's in custody, there's a court order to get a sample from him. They probably already have it. We'd better pray it's not a match."

"The good news is that Tim didn't have sex with Melody that night," Hutch said.

"If he was telling the truth. Recreational sex and rape both leave semen in the vagina," Grady said.

"Ever the cynic, Mr. Grady. Glad to know you're in my son's corner. I have some phone calls to make." Jack went upstairs.

Leaving Hutch and Grady to strategize further, Kate excused herself and went onto the deck. She stared at the hill directly across. Did it hold the key to the investigation? What piece did they still not have to prove Tim's innocence?

The sun was positioned just above the hill. Soon the lake would mirror the pinks and purples, the deep magentas of the setting sun. This was her favorite time of day. Her dad used to say his favorite color was sky blue pink. After he died, Sarah and Tim thought Grandpa painted the sunsets for them. Kate smiled at the memory.

She wished her dad were here right now. He always knew how to make things right. "Where are you, Dad?" she said to the changing sky. "How are we going to get through this?"

The peace was jolted by the sounds of raised voices inside. *Now what?*

"What do you mean you're leaving?" Hutch was striding toward Jack.

Was that an overnight bag at Jack's feet? She opened the slider and walked in. "Where are you going?"

"I told you I had an important meeting tomorrow. It's our biggest client and I'm lead man. You know I've been working around the clock on this presentation."

"You're still going?" Kate stepped back as if pushed. She shook her head in disbelief.

"I've been on the phone for forty minutes trying to reschedule or have Jim take over but no luck. There's nothing I can do here. I'll be back Wednesday night."

"Wednesday? Nothing you can do? What are you talking about?" Kate stepped closer. "How about going to see our son? How about being here with me? I need you!"

"I can't do it again, Kate. He looked so ... I don't know ... so sad, so frightened. I don't know what to say to him, what to do." He paused and got his voice under control. "You'll be fine for a couple of days. Isn't Ellen up all week with the kids?

"Ellen's my *friend*, Jack. She's not you. And I'm not about to ask her to go with me to visit my son in *prison*!"

"I'm sure she'll let you borrow her car."

"You have it all figured out, don't you?" Kate moved so she was right in front of him. "Think of someone besides yourself. Do you think I enjoy seeing him like that? It's hard, but nothing could keep me away."

"Listen, Jack," Hutch cut in. "I can't tell you what to do. I couldn't do it at twenty and I sure as hell can't do it now. But your family needs you. Kate *and* Tim."

"I'll be back in two days. I think they'll survive for two days. I need to work for a living. I don't have a trust fund as back up."

If she cared enough, Kate would be embarrassed for him.

"You do what you need to do," Hutch said. "I'll get a room nearby and be here if Kate needs anything."

"Ah, the gallant Hutch steps up to the plate once again.

Always there when I fall short." Jack saluted and picked up his bag. "Why not just stay here?"

"No. That's not necessary," Kate said. "I'll be fine."

"That's not what you said a minute ago. You can't have it both ways, Kate." Jack looked from his wife to his best friend. "Which is it?"

"I don't know what's going on here," Grady said. "But our focus has to remain on Tim. I'd like to bring my fax and a few other things from my office and set up right here if that's okay." Kate nodded. "Just until I can rent a temporary office in Rutland near the courthouse. I can't keep driving back and forth to Burlington. I won't impose on you any longer than I have to. I've arranged for one of our junior associates to follow up on my other cases." He looked at Hutch. "A friend of mine has a fishing camp nearby he's letting me use. You can bunk with me if you want."

"Great. Sounds like everything's under control." Jack opened the door. "I'll call you tonight, Kate." And he was gone.

Kate stood in the middle of the room and stared at the closed door. The hurt was potent. "I need to call Sarah back," she said. "And I really need to be alone right now."

"Of course." Grady packed up his briefcase. "We'll talk in the morning."

Hutch walked to her and bent his knees to be at eye level. "Is there anything I can do?"

Hurting and stunned, she shook her head.

"You call me anytime, Katie. Whatever you need."

"Thanks." She forced a small smile and locked the door behind them.

She called Sarah and asked about her first day. Sounded like a lot of meetings. Kate filled her in on their visit with Tim, leaving out the worst of it. "He'll be all right, Sarah. You concentrate on your placement. I'll keep you up to date."

There was no need to tell her that Jack had left.

"Okay, Mom. But I'm only a car ride away if you need me."

Kate poured herself a glass of white wine. On the deck, she watched as the night sky consumed the sunset.

~~~

Sleep eluded Kate for most of the night. Tim had looked terrible when she'd seen him in the courtroom and later at the … God, they could call it a correctional facility but it was a *prison!* He was in there for a crime he didn't commit, and there was nothing she could do about it. He had evaded responsibility and made a lot of bad decisions. But rape and murder? Never. She's stake her life on it.

She finally gave up on sleep, took a hot shower and dressed in running clothes. She hadn't eaten anything since yesterday afternoon and forced down a piece of dry toast. It was early but she made the call.

Ellen answered on the first ring. "I've been trying to reach you. Are you all right?"

"Not really. Could you maybe come over?"

Five minutes later, Ellen stood in the kitchen and enveloped Kate in a big hug. "What's wrong? Is it Jack? I thought he was doing better."

Kate shrugged. "Jack's Jack. We've done this dance before." She paused. "It's Tim."

She felt physically lighter as she spilled the whole story. Her friend's silence unnerved her until Ellen squeezed her hand. "I've known Tim since he was a little boy. There is no way he could have hurt that girl."

"Thank you, Ellen. You're a good friend." Kate's eyes filled. "This has been a nightmare. I can only say this once, so please let our friends know. They're going to find out anyway. If you tell them, at least they'll hear the truth."

"I can't imagine what you're going through. Where's Jack in all this?" She glanced upstairs.

Kate pulled her hand away. "He's gone home."

"Home? What could be so important?" Ellen frowned.

"Work. Like always, it comes first." Kate couldn't look at her, didn't want to see pity in her friend's eyes. "He called late last night but I let it go to voice mail."

Ellen shook her head. "You know how I feel about Jack. I can't go there. Where are they holding Tim? He's the important one in all this."

"Outside Rutland in a correctional facility. It's a *prison*, Ellen! A terrible place. I couldn't even touch him yesterday." The tears let loose.

Ellen put an arm around Kate's shoulders. "You should not be doing this alone. Come over later and stay for dinner. Do you want me to take you to see him?"

"No, thanks. I need to do some things here. And Tim wouldn't want you to see him like that. Hutch is here. He'll take me if I'm approved for another visit. You've met him, Jack's friend and our lawyer." Kate dug in her pocket for a used tissue and wiped her nose. She could always count on Hutch.

She clutched the shredded tissue in her lap. "Ellen, there is something I'd like to ask you. There's a candlelight vigil on the green tonight at eight for Melody Ward. Will you go with me? Tim's car's been impounded. Can you drive me?"

"Of course, but do you think you should be there?"

"I'm sure Jack would say no. The lawyers would probably agree. But in my heart, it's something I need to do. I can't fathom her mother's pain. Her fifteen-year-old daughter brutally murdered." Kate shivered although there was no breeze. "We'll stay in the back and no one will even know we're there. We'll leave as soon as it's over."

"All right," Ellen said. "I'll pick you up at 7:30 but I'm not telling Gil."

Kate hugged her.

27

Early Tuesday evening, Hannah brushed her hair and pulled it back into a pearl colored hair clip she'd found under Mel's bed. She'd searched every inch of that bedroom and the rest of the trailer without finding the bracelet. Maybe Mel had lost it and didn't want to tell her.

"Are you about ready?" Glenn called from the kitchen. "We need to get going if you want to talk with Dwight before people start arriving."

"All set." Hannah checked the clasp on the hair clip. It was important to her to wear something of Mel's tonight.

"You look nice," Glenn said as she came into the kitchen.

"Thanks." Hannah's cheeks grew warm. She still wasn't used to his compliments. "I'm glad you're here. I couldn't get through this without you. And I don't just mean tonight."

Glenn patted her arm as he took it and guided her down the steps to his car. "The vigil is going to be beautiful,

Hannah." He kissed her forehead.

They parked at the edge of the town green and spotted Dwight Atkins directing members of the high school choral club to the risers set up behind the microphone. The music teacher, Mr. Crawford, was checking the sound equipment.

"Ms. Ward?" Hannah turned to see Molly Townsend. "I'm so sorry about Mel. I miss her so much."

Hannah drew the girl to her. "I know, Molly, me too." The girl sobbed as Hannah stroked her hair. "She would be happy you're here tonight."

Molly stepped back and wiped her face. "I have to pass out the candles."

Pastor John made his way toward them. "We're all praying for Mel and for you." He clasped Hannah's hand.

"Thank you, Pastor."

"We're all set." Dwight came up behind her. "How are you holding up?"

Hannah nodded, unable to respond.

"Come with me. I set up a few chairs beside the podium."

Glenn joined her and looked out over the assembling crowd. "I saw Timothy Rourke's mother at Jenny's today. Someone pointed her out to me. I can't imagine she would come."

"Please, Glenn. I can't think about any of that now. Tonight is for Mel." Hannah waited in silence, barely registering the activity all around her as friends and neighbors arrived and took their places.

28

Kate was waiting on the deck when Hutch drove in. She had her white jacket over her arm.

"Hungry? I brought pizza," he said as he got out of the car. Part way to the stairs, he stopped. "Are you going somewhere?"

She tried to sound casual. "There's a candlelight vigil in town tonight for Melody Ward. I'm going. Ellen's picking me up."

Hutch came onto the deck and put the pizza down. "I don't think that's a good idea. I'm speaking as your friend, *and* your lawyer."

"I knew you'd say that, which is why I didn't tell you. I need to do this, Hutch. My heart aches for that mother."

"Then I'm going with you, and I'll drive," he said as Ellen drove in. "By now the whole town knows about Tim. I'm afraid of repercussions against you."

"Ellen and I decided we'd stay on the sidelines, back from the crowd. No one will know we're there."

"Staying in the back is a good plan, but I'm still going. Unless I can change your mind."

Kate shook her head.

"Okay then, let's go." Hutch opened the car doors.

A large crowd, maybe a couple hundred people of all ages, had gathered on the green.

"I hope you don't mind walking," Hutch said. "There are closer spots but I want to be able to get out of here fast if we need to."

Kate, Hutch, and Ellen stood on the periphery of the crowd, not drawing attention to themselves. Kate scanned the group. She saw Constable Johnson in uniform and another man flanking a very distraught woman at the front of the crowd. The woman was sobbing; each of the men held her by an elbow. Kate knew without question this was Melody Ward's mother.

"I know that man," Ellen said, pointing to the man on the woman's right. "He's the doctor that stitched up Gil's foot last week."

One of the young girls Kate had seen at Jenny's Saturday morning was passing out thin white candles set in circles of white paper. A young man followed and lit each one. When he got to Kate, her hand shook causing the flame to flicker. Hutch entwined her other hand in his.

The crowd was quiet, reverent. Kate recognized very few of them. An older man, introduced as the pastor of the Methodist Church, came forward and stood at the podium. He led an opening prayer and read two scripture passages. Ms. Ward sat with the men's assistance. Music came over a loud speaker and a group of teenagers, a choir maybe, led the crowd in two hymns, which the majority seemed to know.

The minister then spoke of a young life tragically cut

short and acceptance of God's will. He may have thought he spoke words of comfort, but one look at the sobbing woman told Kate otherwise.

After a final hymn, the crowd began to disperse in silence, many stopping to say a few words to the woman now standing, supported by the constable and the doctor.

On impulse, Kate made her way in that direction before Hutch or Ellen could stop her. Face to face with the grieving mother, Kate extended her hand. "I'm so sorry for your loss."

Hannah frowned. "Thank you. Do I know you?"

"I don't think you should be here," the constable murmured.

"I know who you are," the doctor said. "I think you should leave."

Kate turned, head down, and walked as fast as she could toward where she'd left Hutch and Ellen.

"That's Tim Rourke's mother," someone said loud enough for bystanders to hear.

"What's she doing here?" someone else shouted.

Word of Kate's identity spread through the crowd like a spark in dry kindling. The crowd began pushing and shoving, closing in on her. She felt searing pain as the candle was knocked to the ground and singed her hand. Someone pulled at the jacket she carried. Hands landed on her. Kate was thrust one way and then the other, tripping and almost losing her balance. She lost all sense of where she was in relation to Hutch and Ellen.

Someone grabbed her hand. Hutch pulled her to the waiting car. He pushed her into the back seat and jumped in beside her. Slamming the door, he yelled, "Go!" Ellen floored the gas.

Kate covered her face with trembling hands. "How did you get to me? They were all around me. I was afraid I would fall."

"When you headed toward Ms. Ward, I tossed the keys to Ellen and ran after you." Hutch put his arm around her shoulders.

Kate stared unblinking at the road before them. She could feel the bruises forming on her arms and torso. Her hand burned from the candle's flame.

"I know some of those people. We've been in this town for eighteen years."

Hutch held her closer. "Eighteen *summers*. There's a big difference."

Once home, Ellen helped Kate change into pajamas. She was still shaking and tossed down a couple of Advil before coming back downstairs.

She sat on the couch and Ellen handed her a cup of tea. The heat from the ceramic cup warmed her hands but went no further. The rest of her body was ice. She assured Ellen she was fine and persuaded her to leave. She wondered what Gil's reaction to their escapade would be, to say nothing of Jack's.

Hutch closed the door and eased down beside Kate. He examined her face, now washed clean, and the small burn on her right hand, shiny after the application of ointment.

"I'm fine, really," Kate said. "I just can't seem to stop shaking. I thought I was going down a couple of times." Hutch covered her with a blanket and rubbed her back. She relived the chaos on the green, felt the crush of bodies closing in on her. "I didn't think I was going to get out of there."

"I never should have let you go." Hutch's eyes were intense.

"*Let* me go?" She frowned. "You do know me, right?"

He smiled. "I thought maybe that 'I'll do it my way' girl was gone for good."

"Marriage can do that sometimes," Kate said. "But deep down, I'm still me."

A distinctive ring tone intruded. "That's Jack." She angled her body away from Hutch and answered. "Hi, I tried to get you earlier. Where were you?"

She felt Hutch get up and leave the room. To give her privacy?

Loud music and people laughing drowned out whatever Jack said.

"I can't hear you. Where are you?" Kate pressed the phone closer to her ear. Were those slot machines ringing in the background? "Are you at the casino?"

"It's a work thing," he shouted. "The big clients, remember?"

"Are you kidding me? You're willing to risk losing what money we *do* have? Like this?"

"Relax, Kate. I'm feeling lucky. Do you have anything else to tell me?" He sounded distracted.

You mean like I narrowly escaped a mob tonight? He would be furious she'd gone to the vigil. "I need you here, Jack. I'm hoping we'll be allowed to see Tim again. You'll be back tomorrow, right? You said Wednesday."

"I'm not sure. Wednesday or Thursday. It depends."

"On what?" She was shouting now.

"I'll have another double," he said. Then into the phone, "Aren't you going to ask how my presentation went?"

Kate wanted to reach through the phone and shake him. Instead, she took a calming breath and drew upon years of yoga practice. "From the sound of the celebration I'd guess it went pretty well. I have to go, Jack."

She broke the connection before he could respond. She didn't care about his presentation or any deal he made. He could very well lose it all tonight at the tables.

Slamming the phone on the coffee table, she sensed Hutch's presence. He looked at her, his eyes questioning. What could she say—*my husband's an asshole*?

"Don't ask," she said and stood up carefully, feeling some stiffness and a twinge of pain.

"Are you hurting a lot? What can I do?"

She waved him off. "I'm fine. Nothing a couple of Advil can't take care of."

"I guess I should go then." Hutch hesitated and took a step closer, studying her face. "I can stay, Katie, if you don't want to be alone."

She warred with her feelings. Seconds ticked by in silence.

"I know, but I think it's best if you go. Thank you for going with me tonight." She suddenly felt shy. "You were there for me—like always."

He kissed the top of her head. "Call me if you need anything at all." His fingertips touched her cheek.

After securing the deadbolt, Kate leaned against the door. She would not let old feelings in, feelings that had been buried for decades. Why then was her heart racing?

She shut off the lights and locked the French doors to the deck. A thin sliver of the new moon shone down on the lake—so different from the total blackness of Friday night.

Her cell rang. "Sarah." She bit back the tears.

"It was great, Mom. I met some of my clients today. Is it too late?"

"Never, sweetheart. Tell me all about your day." She saw no need to tell Sarah about the vigil.

Sarah gave an excited rundown of her day. "Is Dad still awake? Can I talk to him?"

"He's not here, honey. He's gone home."

"Are you kidding me? What the hell's wrong with him?"

"He had to work, Sarah. And be respectful. He's your father." Why did she always defend him?

"Sorry, Mom. But he left you alone—now?"

"I'm fine. He'll be back tomorrow or Thursday. Ellen's here. And Hutch stayed to help Grady. He's staying nearby if I need anything."

"You knew Hutch before you met Dad, right?"

"Yes, you know that. He introduced me to Dad when he came back from his semester abroad."

"Did you ever date Hutch?"

"For a short time, but we were really just friends."

"You never loved him, Mom? I mean as more than a friend?"

"Sarah, I married your Dad. I love *him*. He swept me off my feet. And that was that."

"You knew right away?"

"Yep, and you know the rest of the story. Hutch was our best man and your godfather. He's been our best friend for years. Why all the questions, Sarah? Is it you and Joe?"

"No, Mom. We're fine. It just seems that Hutch is always there for you whenever Dad screws up."

Kate laughed. "It does seem that way. That's what friends are for, I guess." She hoped she was projecting a light-heartedness she didn't feel. "Don't worry about me, Sarah. I'll call you tomorrow."

"I can be there tonight, Mom. I'm not that far away."

Kate felt a surge of love for her first born. "I know,

Sarah, but I'm really okay."

She hung up and headed upstairs. Holding the railing and leading with her right foot on each step, Kate paced herself. The Advil was finally kicking in. Lowering herself onto the bed, she thought about all the things she *didn't* tell her daughter.

Like how love began to mingle with friendship as she and Hutch grew closer. How they were inseparable and then intimate for a short time. In the end, they chose friendship. They knew too many couples who ended up hating each other after a breakup.

But that's not to say they never second-guessed their decision.

She'd told Sarah the truth about Jack's return from abroad. Jack Rourke had blown onto campus like a gale off the west coast of Ireland. She never stood a chance. He'd won her heart right away with his charm and handsome black Irish looks. He was bigger than life, yet familiar in so many ways. He'd grown up in the Irish enclaves of Philly, not so different from her in Boston. He had an enthusiasm and a love of life that was contagious. He was smart and partied hard, as at home in the hallowed halls of academia as he was in an Irish pub.

Easing her legs up, Kate stretched out and leaned back against the pillow. She recalled Jack's ambition even then. He craved success. The son of a small-time politician with connections in the local Democratic Party, Jack coveted entry into the world of country clubs and privilege. Hutch's world. Jack became obsessed with it.

He took lessons at a public golf course and worked to enhance his game. He got a job caddying and then bartending at an elite country club to meet the right people. He made connections and worked them to his advantage. But he was never satisfied. He always wanted more, felt he deserved more.

Hutch warned her that Jack would break her heart. And he did, again and again. Hutch was always there to pick up the pieces. Many nights she and Hutch carried Jack back to his dorm room and got him into bed. Any warning bells about his drinking and being with other girls were silenced by his contrition the next day, and his smile. That smile that undid her every time.

His behavior didn't change when they married, despite repeated promises. His drive to succeed intensified and took precedence over everything, even their family. But Kate stood by him and never again confided to Hutch or turned to him.

Not until things hit bottom that summer on the Vineyard.

Kate thought now of Hutch's constancy, the love she'd once had for him. And about the truth she had never told anyone.

The truth that could blow her family apart.

29

Shaken by the turn of events at the vigil, Hannah was deposited into the front seat of Glenn Braddock's car. Carrie followed in her own car.

Hannah wrestled with the seatbelt that strained against her. "It was supposed to be a tribute to Mel, not a riot. Pastor and I planned it all with Dwight's input—the prayers, the hymns. I wanted it to be something Mel would have liked."

Wiping her eyes, Hannah wondered about Norm. The last she saw of him he was trying to control the crowd. She hoped he had called for help.

"Glenn, why did you say who that woman was? You had to know it would cause trouble."

"She never should have come. It was her own fault." They had been traveling well above the speed limit. He eased up on the gas now that they were a safe distance from town.

"You can't mean that. She could have been seriously hurt. She's a mother just like me. Her son will be locked up for a very long time. In a way, she's lost her child too."

"You can't be serious, Hannah!" He took his eyes off the road for the first time. "Her child's not dead!"

Hannah flinched and shrank back at the bold truth.

"I'm sorry. That was insensitive. I wish you would reconsider and let me take you to my place."

"We've been over this, Glenn. I need to be in my own house. I ... it's just ... I feel closer to Mel there. Do you understand?"

"Of course I do. I'm just thinking of you." He reached over and touched her knee.

At the house, Hannah convinced Glenn and Carrie that she was fine and that they should leave. Refusing Glenn's offer of another sedative, she took a hot bath and wanted only to get under the covers, although she knew sleep wouldn't come.

She had just shut off the light when she heard a knock at the door. Now what? She parted the faded curtains and saw Norm's truck, roof light bar still in place, in the driveway.

Opening the door, she was struck by how tired he looked. "Are you all right, Norm? Was anyone hurt?"

"Everybody's fine. I called Travis for back up. But once Mrs. Rourke was gone, the crowd lost its focus and broke up. What about you? Are you okay?"

He stood in the middle of her kitchen and it seemed to Hannah that his presence filled the room. "I'm fine. You don't have to worry about me. Everyone seems to think I need taking care of. Hell, I've been on my own with Mel for years, never asked anybody for anything and nobody offered. Now people are all over me. For God's sake, the same people that went after that poor woman tonight ... most of them wouldn't have given me *or* Mel the time of day a week ago. Hypocrites, all of them. I need to sleep, Norm. Good night."

As predicted, sleep eluded her. Insomnia was her new companion. She was up at one-thirty, at three, at four. Wide awake at five Wednesday morning, Hannah was drawn to Mel's room, another familiar pattern. Clothes were piled on the still unmade bed just as Hannah had left them when she'd torn everything apart yesterday looking for the bracelet. She still couldn't bring herself to wash them, but at least she could get them into the hamper.

Hannah stripped the bed and added sheets to the pile of clothes. Ready to deposit the first armful, she saw something sticking out from under a rectangular piece of cardboard at the bottom of the wicker hamper. She lifted the stiff paper and retrieved a black and white school composition book. She held it, turning it over in her hands while she debated. This was something private, hidden. Should she open it? Read it?

She flipped through a couple of pages of Mel's careful, neat script and glimpsed references to grades, to friends. She closed the book and laid it on the bed. She couldn't do it.

But what if there was something in there that could help the police? She looked at the clock. It was almost six. She'd call Norm.

30

Early Wednesday morning Norm drove to town. He parked at Jenny's and crossed to the green. The town maintenance crew had done a good job cleaning up from the melee the night before. "Nice job, guys."

"Thanks, Norm. We found this." One of the men held up a jacket, once white but now ripped and stained. "Any idea who it belongs to?"

"Nope. I'm just glad that was the only casualty. I've never seen a crowd turn like that." Norm supposed people needed to put a face on their anger and grief, but Mrs. Rourke wasn't their target. "I'll take it in case somebody's looking for it."

His cell rang. "Hannah?"

"Norm, could you come by sometime this morning? I have something I think you should see."

Norm bought two cups of coffee, one with Sweet'n Low.

Driving to Hannah's, he wondered if Glenn Braddock

would be there. He didn't like the guy. And what about last night? He'd pretty much ID'd Mrs. Rourke to the crowd and got things going.

Hannah let him in before he had a chance to knock. Deep lines of grief and fatigue cut into her face, aging it since last night. Her eyes were swollen from crying; her hair hung limp around her face. She held one of those black and white notebooks they used in school.

"What's that?" Norm followed her to the kitchen table with the coffee.

"A journal. I found it in Mel's hamper, under a false bottom. That's why Detective Cobb didn't find it. Mel's been doing her own laundry, so I don't know how long it's been there."

"Did you read it?" He sat down across from her.

"I scanned a few pages but couldn't read more. I felt like I was betraying her, invading her privacy, you know? If it was private enough to be hidden..." She placed the book on the table between them.

Norm leaned forward. "You're not your mother."

Hannah looked up, her eyes damp. "She bared my soul, Norm. Read my innermost thoughts and feelings. I never did forgive her that breach of trust.

"This is different, Hannah. There could be something in there, evidence that will help the investigation. May I?"

Norm read a couple of random pages: disappointment over a D in chemistry, anger toward the asshole teacher, excitement over last spring's school dance. "Looks like a typical teenager's diary—where she went, who she saw, how she felt."

"You think I should give it to the police." It was a statement, not a question. Hannah smoothed a strand of hair and tucked it behind her ear. "It's just that I feel like I'm exposing her."

"Hannah, if it helps convict the bastard, it's the right thing to do. If you want, I'll take it and give it to the state police."

Hannah handed him the notebook and he headed out. After he pulled into his parking spot at town hall, Norm picked up the notebook he had tossed onto the passenger seat. He sure as hell wouldn't turn it in until he'd read it himself, cover to cover.

He closed his office door to the chatter coming from the Town Clerk's office down the hall. Those busy bodies never stopped talking! He didn't think they'd seen him come in. Maybe they'd leave him alone. He poured a cup of stale coffee, pulled out his worn chair and propped his feet up on the cluttered desk. He began to read.

The initial entries continued to be what Norm thought of as normal teenage angst, if anything about teenagers was normal: concerns about grades, complaints about teachers, worries about fitting in. It seemed teenage girls went through life as a pack. It was, however, not without drama. He recognized the names of some of the girls Travis had interviewed: Becca, Courtney, Molly..

Molly is such a little bitch. She doesn't think I should be seeing Shane because he's older. Who cares? She's just jealous. Who'd even look at her? She has a chest like a ten-year-old boy! If anyone did put the moves on her, she'd run. She won't have a drink, won't smoke. Why does she even hang out with us??? We were good friends in like 3rd grade!

Norm paused. McVeigh? Becca's brother? He read the

next entry.

Went to the quarry again last night. Mom would kill
me if she knew. The guys brought a case of beer.
Mom has no idea how easy it is to get booze. Sully
brought the pot. His brother will have his ass if
he finds out Sully's into his stash. I like the way
it makes me feel. He says next time he can get
something even better. We played strip pong—like
beer pong—and dared each other to jump in the
water. It's still sooooo cold. The guys freak when
they shrivel up! I think it's funny. Shane wants me
to be just with him, but I'm having too much fun.
Deal with it!

Norm cringed as he read more references to sexual
activity, alcohol, and drugs. Mel had definitely been caught in
a downward spiral and he had done nothing to help her. He
wanted to reach into the pages now and pull her out. He had
failed Hannah, and Mel too.

He skimmed more pages and finally there it was. A
reference to TJ. Norm's feet hit the floor and he sat up straight.

Yay! It's spring! I am so done with winter and I'm
done with this town! It sucks! We hitched a ride to
EA after school today. Kind of wandered around,
acted like we belonged. We saw a group of guys
hanging out by the soccer fields. We stretched out
on the grass pretending to catch some rays and
waited for them to notice us. It didn't take too
long!

"I bet. Hitching a ride, Jesus!"

We started talking to them. They had no clue we
weren't students. We pulled it off! Molly looked
like she was gonna bolt when the red head with the

freckles started talking to her. I thought he looked harmless enough, kind of a dork like her. But TJ, wow! I thought I'd die when he sat down next to me. He is SO HOT! He invited us to a party this Saturday night. I have got to go! I'll find a way. Mom will KILL me!

Nothing much on the next few pages. Apparently, convincing the other girls to go and finding a way to get to the campus were top priority. He guessed Hannah had no idea.

I so totally blew my curfew last night but I don't care. TJ is AMAZING! And college parties—man, I have never seen so much booze and pot in one place! Everyone was doing it and nobody cared. I was with TJ the whole time. He makes the guys in town all look like losers. We were still making out when Becca and Molly came to tell me we had to get going. I didn't know where Courtney was and didn't want to leave her but Molly had found us a ride back. When we got to the car, Courtney was there, shit-faced. I thought I was bad! Mom fucking grounded me. I hate her! What's she going to do— watch me 24/7!

Norm wished there were dates on these entries. No way of knowing when this happened.

Well, Shane is pissed! He thinks he owns me. A couple of blow jobs and I'm his? No way. He's pressuring Becca to tell him who I'm seeing. Screw him. Who cares?

Norm took a break and rubbed his face. Hannah would be sick if she read this. He got his case notes. Shane McVeigh was a person of interest early on. His pickup had been spotted driving by the party last Friday night, but he'd been cleared.

He had an airtight alibi for later that night.

Norm picked up the journal again. Mel and TJ spent a lot of time together last spring into summer, much of it lately at his apartment off campus. The entries weren't graphic, nothing incriminating that could be introduced in court as far as he could tell. He'd have to turn this over to the state police anyway. They'd know better. Norm knew Mel was spending a lot of time at the college but didn't realize she was seeing one specific guy. She was also blowing off every curfew Hannah tried to set for her. What kind of nineteen-year-old guy spends all his time with a fifteen-year-old girl? Shit. Norm answered his own question.

I hardly ever see my friends anymore. Becca's the only one who will still go with me to see TJ, but even she won't go all the time. Courtney's got her own guy. Molly's being a real pain in the ass, says I'm getting in "over my head." Says she's going to tell her mother. They're all just jealous. Molly wouldn't know what to do if a guy was naked right in front of her!

Norm checked his notes again. Yeah, Molly Townsend. She was the first girl who caved and came in with her mother to talk to Travis.

He was about to put the journal down when another name jumped off the page at him. Dr. Glenn Braddock.

I hate this stupid job. All I do is shovel shit all day. The place stinks and so do the horses. This is Mom's way of punishing me, keeping me out of trouble, but it sucks. She might let me keep working at Jenny's but not if Braddock has his way. He's trying to convince her that this is better, keeps me away from the "bad influence" of my friends. He doesn't even know my friends!

More complaining about the job. Then this entry a few days later.

Today Dr. Braddock was called out on an emergency. I took a break (which I deserved) and went looking for more bottled water in the house. I was poking around his office. He'd left some samples of meds on his desk, probably from the last patient. Birth control pills! I always make the guy wear a condom but I hit pay dirt! I pocketed them and read the inserts tonight. I think I'll start taking them tomorrow. Better safe than sorry.

"Christ! This is unbelievable." Norm read on.

I've been found out. The doctor's not as stupid as he looks. He noticed the pills were missing. Says girls need to be protected and that he'd give me more samples if I wanted but I can't tell anyone. My friends would freak to say nothing of Mom! Samples are perfect. This town is too small for me to be bringing a prescription to the drugstore! It's probably not even legal anyway. Do you have to have a parent's permission to go on the pill? I don't know and I didn't ask him. He wanted to know details of my "sexual activity," said he needed to know to prescribe the right medication. I don't think that's true. He probably wanted to get off on it but I didn't care. I want the pills!

"Son of a bitch!" Norm's fist contracted and struck hard against the desk. Heavy black lines had been drawn through the words on the next pages, making them impossible to read. Other pages were ripped out, leaving jagged edges.

There was no way of knowing how much time had elapsed.

Norm read the last entry. Mel's handwriting was shaky and very small.

Braddock wants me to "work" more hours although there's nothing to do once I clean the stables and feed and water the horses. He told Mom he's teaching me to ride, that's why I'm spending more time there. Like I'd ever get on one of those mangy flea bags! Sometimes when I'm straightening out the tack room, I turn around and he's there just staring at me. Or he "helps" me and tries to "accidentally" feel me up. I quickly get out of his way and say I have to get home. He gives me the creeps. Tells me I have nice breasts all the time. The other day he came up behind me and kind of brushed against my ass. He had a hard-on! I felt it! I'm not stupid.

"Fucking bastard!" Fury coursed through Norm's body—he was on fire. His heart beat hard against his chest. He leaned forward and forced himself to keep reading.

He texts me sometimes but I never answer. I want to tell somebody. But who? I've kind of pulled away from my friends. Mom wouldn't believe me, she thinks the guy's great. I thought of TJ. We're really close now but he can get real jealous. I wish I could still talk to Norm like when I was little, but he's a cop. And anyway he doesn't bother with me anymore.

The force of the words shoved him into the back of his chair. He rubbed his face and read on.

Braddock (he wants me to call him Glenn, right!)

says as long as I keep coming and spending time with him, talking and watching movies and stuff, he won't tell Mom about the pills. The other night he gave me some beer. I didn't have that much but I felt funny. I think I fell asleep. My blouse was untucked and the top button of my jeans partly undone when I woke up. Maybe I was moving around and did it myself but I don't think so. I'm scared. I don't know what to do. I can't go there again. I'll make up some kind of excuse. I'm done. I used to think he was being nice to me just to get into Mom's pants. Now I think it's not Mom's pants!

"Jesus Christ!" The veins at Norm's temples throbbed. His hands shook. He knocked over the cup. Cold, stale coffee soaked his pants. "Shit." He jumped up and grabbed the journal.

Thick black marker covered the next dozen pages. X's were scratched into the paper with enough force to rip the pages.

It tore at his guts.

The door opened and the town clerk poked her head in. "Hey, Norm, did you hear...?" She saw his pants. "What happened to you?"

"Don't you ever knock, Priscilla?" He grabbed the cheap paper towels from the dispenser and didn't look up as he attempted to wipe his pants with trembling hands.

"Just heard that college boy's cooling his heels up at Slate Valley. Best news we've had in days."

"Yeah, well an arraignment's not a conviction. We ain't done yet."

"I can see this hasn't improved your mood any. You better change out of those wet pants. You're not looking too professional." She headed back toward her office and he heard the women laughing down the hall.

Norm grabbed the journal and left without another word. He needed to get this to Detective Whitcomb right away.

What the hell was happening to his town? Rape and murder! Now sexual assault against a minor! He'd go after Braddock himself and see him put away for the rest of his life, right along with the Rourke kid.

~~

"Where the hell's the card?" Norm dug in his front pants pocket for Detective Whitcomb's card. He punched in the number and started the truck.

"Whitcomb." The detective picked up on the first ring.

"Constable Johnson here. I have something you need to see. It's Melody Ward's journal."

"I'm on my way to Willow Bend now, be there in about ten minutes. Do you know where the abandoned shack is north of the dam?"

"Yeah. What's going on?"

"Meet me there."

"Why?"

"Just be there, Johnson, if you need to see me." The line went dead.

Norm thought of Braddock again. His hands gripped the steering wheel. "Fucking scumbag!"

The road curved and the lake came into view. As he passed the dam, Norm looked away. Would he ever be able to look at this spot again without seeing Mel's broken and violated body mired in muck? He drove up the hill where the forensics team had been investigating on Sunday and parked near the old shack, hidden from view by overgrown weeds and old oaks.

Police cars, unmarked sedans, and a crime scene van lined the gravel shoulder. Norm parked his truck and approached as troopers unrolled police tape to cordon off this new area. One of them looked like Storrow.

Norm heard a siren just before a jeep skidded to a stop, gravel flying from the rear tires. Whitcomb got out.

"Morning, Detective." Norm walked over and shook hands. He checked his watch. "Almost noon, but I guess that's still morning. What's going on?"

"A couple of twelve year olds, planning to sneak some smokes, found what they thought was blood in that shack." He nodded toward the police tape. "They high-tailed it home on their bikes. One of the Moms got suspicious about the way her son was acting. Called 911 after she got the story out of him."

"Does this have anything to do with Melody Ward?" Norm stared at the solid wall of trees concealing the old rundown structure.

"Don't know yet. The uniforms who responded reported signs of a possible struggle with the few items in there knocked over or broken. The BCI guys are in there now. I have to talk to the lead detective, Chuck Cobb. Whatever you have, Constable, is going to have to wait."

Norm followed Whitcomb past the perimeter and inched closer to what was left of the abandoned building. He peered through the broken window closest to him.

A young woman in a BCI jumpsuit approached a big guy with a shaved head. "Look at this, Detective Cobb." She led him to the open door but didn't go in. "See that spot on the floor? Looks like dried pooled blood. The lighter lines from there to the door? Could be a body's been moved. The lab will run tests first to confirm it is human blood and then to determine if it's Melody Ward's."

Norm's breath caught. He moved closer to the door of the shack to hear better.

"Prints?" Cobb asked the woman.

"Wiped clean. Either the perp wore gloves or cleaned up after himself. But see that?" She pointed to something on the floor. Norm couldn't see what.

"Is that a partial shoe print?" Cobb bent at the waist.

"Yeah. We got photos of everything."

Cobb went in and squatted down next to the dark stain. "Why leave the blood?"

"Don't know. Something scared him off? He planned to come back later?" The forensics officer shrugged. "We're still checking for anything he may have overlooked—hair, a piece of thread, a scrap of clothing, anything."

"Weapon?"

"Nothing so far."

"Constable Johnson, what are you doing here?" The voice came from behind.

Norm turned. "Hey, Storrow. Detective Whitcomb asked me to meet him here."

They both watched as an unmarked sedan pulled in and a well-dressed man stepped out.

Norm raised his chin toward the newcomer. "Who's the suit?"

"That's Pete McMahon, the state's attorney," Trooper Storrow said and stepped into the road. "I need to keep traffic moving. Too many rubberneckers."

A dark Ford Escort came from the opposite direction and parked on the shoulder. Norm recognized the two defense lawyers from the arraignment. He positioned himself off to the side where he could see and hear the exchange between the lawyers.

"What have you got for me, Pete?" the dark-haired lawyer asked. Norm thought his name was Andrew Grady.

"Let's step over here out of the way. We put a rush on the DNA samples from the semen and the skin from under Melody Ward's fingernails. I have to tell you, Counselor, it's not what we expected."

Norm moved closer.

"The DNA is not Timothy Rourke's."

What the hell? Norm leaned in and cocked his head.

"Whose is it?" It was the blond defense lawyer.

"Don't know. FBI's working on it," the prosecutor said. "Not a word about this. I want no leaks. None. And don't you and your client go celebrating yet."

"Hell, if the DNA isn't his, it isn't his. My guy's clean." Grady looked at the other defense attorney and smiled. "I don't care whose it is. That's your problem, Pete. But we won't say a word."

The state's attorney nodded but looked pissed. Norm couldn't blame him. He was still trying to digest what he'd overheard when Cobb approached the group.

"Got something you should see, Pete. One of my guys just found shoe prints around the back of the building. They're set in mud in a protected area. A few are intact. On visual inspection, they appear to match the bloody print found inside. Forensics photographed them and will make impressions. They'll compare them and determine size and possible brand."

Norm followed them behind the shack and stayed on the periphery, his view partially blocked. The detective and the lawyers squatted down to get a better look.

"Probably not a local guy," Cobb said. "Most of the guys around here wear work boots all year long, the younger kids running shoes. These are smooth, no treads."

"Around here you only see these kinds of shoes at church," McMahon said.

"I'll tell you one thing." Grady stood up. "These prints sure weren't made by the flip flops my client was wearing Friday night."

Norm pushed his way to the front and looked down at the pristine outlines of what looked like men's dress shoes. His insides turned to jelly. Bile rose up in his throat. Images flashed in his brain like a bad movie in a high speed loop: dress shoes sinking into the mud at the crime scene, those same shoes later highly polished and sticking out from under Carrie Ryan's kitchen table. Both times Norm had been struck by how out of place they were.

With surprising outward calmness, despite trembling inside, Norm approached Detective Cobb and the state's attorney. "Excuse me. I'm Constable Norm Johnson from here in Willow Bend. Is it possible these prints could have been made by a man's dress shoe?"

"We won't know that until we examine them but thanks, Constable," Cobb said.

"Before you blow me off, Detective, I have something you need to read. It's the reason I came here."

31

Kate slept in on Wednesday. She got up slowly, holding the nightstand for support. She ached all over and inched her way to the master bath. Blasting the shower as hot as it would go, she breathed in the steam. In her mind she saw Tim in that awful place, trying to be brave, his hand pressed against hers through the glass partition.

She removed her pajama top carefully. Looking down, she touched the bruises that had formed on her torso. Her body resembled a finger painting canvas, splashed with purple and yellow designs by eager preschoolers. Kate stepped into the shower and let the scalding water sluice over her, until the water ran cool.

After patting herself dry, she downed a couple more Advil. Maybe a short walk would work out some of the stiffness in her muscles. She walked along the lake. The sun glistened off the water. Kate was stretching her lower back when her cell rang. She grabbed for it. "Jack?"

"No, it's Hutch. I only have a minute. The DNA is *not*

a match."

"What? Oh my God!" A sob escaped. "Tim will be released!"

"It's not that easy, Kate. But listen, you can't tell *anyone*, not even Jack. Grady would have my head if he knew I told you. Here he comes. I have to go. I'll check in on you later."

She nodded. Her fingers touched lips wet with fresh teardrops.

"Hutch?" She sniffed. "Thank you."

The line had gone dead. Kate turned her face to the sun and let it warm her inside and out. *Can this nightmare really be over?* "Thank you, God."

32

Hannah checked the balance in her checking account late Wednesday afternoon as she finished a dry piece of toast. Nothing more stayed down.

She'd had no word from Norm since she'd given him the journal that morning. Had he already given it to the state police? She hoped she'd done the right thing.

She checked the figures again.

She and Carrie had met earlier with Dwight to plan Mel's … her mind couldn't form the word. Arrangements sounded better.

The undertaker had brought them into the room attached to the main part of the building to view and select a casket. Hannah had walked from one to the other in a daze, not really paying attention to what she was seeing or what Dwight was saying. Did he really point out which models held up better underground, even though they were all placed in concrete liners by law? A shiver went through her.

"God, how can he do that job?" she said out loud. "And

how can he live upstairs?"

She still didn't know how much it cost, the one she'd chosen with the pale pink satin lining. She just knew Mel would like it. She'd told Dwight to just put it on her bill. She never did that!

A loud noise startled her. Someone was banging on her front door hard enough to break the frame.

She moved the edge of the torn shade over the sink just enough to see a TV van from channel five out of Burlington in her driveway. As she watched, another van pulled in. She strained to read the logo, *The Rutland Herald*. The paper had run a small piece about the vigil last night and the scene afterward. More follow up?

A smart-looking blonde, microphone in hand, stepped away from the door and nodded to a cameraman hovering nearby. Hannah watched from behind the shade.

"This is Kristen Campbell coming to you live from Willow Bend. We're at the home of Hannah Ward, the mother of the girl brutally murdered in this small town last Friday night."

Hannah's breath caught and she stepped back. She was sure no one had seen her. She listened through the open window as the reporter spouted off about Mel—the rape, the murder, the condition of her body, everything. *Can they just say whatever they want? Can they get photos and plaster them all over the six o'clock news?*

Hannah had heard enough. She flung open the hollow door, probably dented by now, to tell them to leave. A microphone was shoved in her face. A second reporter she hadn't seen rushed the steps. They launched a barrage of questions at her.

"What do you think of Timothy Rourke being arrested

for the murder of your daughter?"

"Is it true she was only fifteen?"

"Did he date your daughter for long? Wasn't he a little old for her?"

"Was his mother really at the vigil?"

"How do you feel about that?"

Pulling herself up to her full five feet three inches, Hannah raised her hand, palm out, and spoke in a clear loud voice. "I have no comment. Please leave my property." She stepped inside, not turning her back to the crowd, and tried to close the door.

The reporter with *The Rutland Herald* press badge had a toehold in the door and wouldn't budge. "Give me an exclusive and I'll be sure people hear your side of the story."

Hannah put both hands on the door and pushed. "Leave now or I will call the police."

From the bottom of the steps, the woman with the microphone yelled. "What do you think about the DNA results not being Timothy Rourke's?"

Hannah swayed backward at the force of the question. She grabbed the doorjamb to keep from collapsing. *The Herald* reporter got his arm through the small opening. With her shoulder and the side of her body, Hannah pushed all her weight against the door. She pressed it shut and locked it, not caring whose foot or sleeve might be crushed.

She threw the deadbolt and closed all the shades and curtains. Her hands shaking, it took two tries to dial Norm's office phone. It was late in the day but he answered on the first ring.

"What the hell is going on? I've got reporters camped out here, banging on my door. One of them is saying the DNA taken from Mel doesn't belong to Timothy Rourke. Is that true?"

"I'll be right there, Hannah. Don't talk to anyone. That wasn't supposed to be leaked."

"What! You knew about this? And you didn't tell me?" Hysteria was overtaking her. Her voice was getting louder. "I really thought you had changed. But you're still the same old Norm."

She hung up. Her cries were magnified as they rebounded off the aluminum walls of the trailer. The thought of Mel being attacked and raped—and murdered—by some unknown pervert was too much. In her panic, another thought took shape. What if it was by more than one person, the Rourke boy and someone else? She'd heard about gang rapes on college campuses. Her entire body swayed as she grabbed the counter. It was like it was happening all over again.

The phone rang again and she answered without thinking. "Yes?" She was sobbing.

"Hannah, don't hang up!" It was Norm. "I'm on my way. Don't open your door and don't talk to *anybody*. And I mean *anybody*, not just the reporters."

"Don't tell me what to do, Norm. I'm done with that." She hung up a second time.

Her shoulders heaved. Timothy Rourke was in jail. What about this other person? Do the police know who he is? What if he's still here? Worse, what if he's miles away and they never catch him?

Hannah slid to the floor, her back resting against a cabinet. Through gathering tears she saw the truth.

She was the mother. *She* was supposed to keep Mel safe. She had failed at that, just like everything else.

Defeated, Hannah got to her knees and pulled herself up. The pervasive buzz of reporters still swarmed the house.

She had to get away and she had to do it before Norm got there.

Glenn's private line rang and rang. She twisted the phone cord around her index finger. *Pick up!* Glenn would know what to do. He always knew what to do. After all these years of taking care of herself, it was nice to lean on someone else.

"Doctor Braddock."

"Glenn, I'm sorry to call you at the office. I have to get out of here. Reporters are all over the place with cameras and microphones. They're banging on the door and won't leave!"

"It's okay, Hannah. I'll come and bring you to my place. You'll be safe here and the press won't be able to find you. Don't tell anyone where you're going just to be sure."

She agreed and pictured Norm still sputtering into the phone when she'd hung up. Why had she thought he'd changed? She left the phone off the hook.

Checking left and right out the back bedroom window, Hannah saw no reporters or photographers. Hungry for a glimpse of the bereaved mother, they were still camped out in the front yard.

Hannah silently thanked her ex for providing the means of her escape. Years ago Bobby Jenks had built a small porch off the back of the trailer to give Hannah easy access to the clothesline and Mel a sunny spot to sit in her playpen. A welder by trade, he boasted the only mobile home in the area with a rear door cut into its aluminum skin.

After waiting what seemed a reasonable amount of time, she eased the door open and stepped onto the porch, now listing to one side from rot and decay. Bobby hadn't used pressure treated wood, too expensive. Hannah scanned the yard and the edge of the woods about fifteen yards from the trailer. Had something moved? Was that the sign she was watching for?

There he was! She waved and waited for the pre-arranged signal back from Glenn. He gave the all clear and Hannah moved as fast as she could across the exposed roots and scrub grass to the trees. She fell into the doctor's arms.

"I'm so glad to see you," she said and meant it.

"Let's get you away from here. My car's on the other side of these trees. We'll be at my house before they realize you're gone."

33

The phone rang just as Norm was leaving the office. *Damn!* "Johnson." He had to get to Hannah's. He didn't have time for this.

"It's Detective Cobb. You were a big help today, Constable. We've turned the journal over to our sexual assault team. Forensics is working on identifying the shoe prints. It's likely they were made by a man's dress shoes, as you indicated."

"Yeah, and I told you whose they were. The same guy whose name is all over the damn journal!" Norm shifted his weight from one foot to the other. "When are you going after the pervert?"

"When we have all the evidence. The blood on the floor of the shack is A positive, consistent with Melody Ward's blood type. We're waiting on DNA results for further confirmation. We put a rush on it. Looks like that was the crime scene."

"So she was either dragged or transported to the

location where she was found?"

"That's what we think. My guys are searching the area around the shack now for a murder weapon but there may not be one."

"What do you mean?"

"Official cause of death is blunt force trauma to the head. Marks on the victim's neck indicate strangulation, which often indicates a personal connection between the killer and the victim. It could be that the killer choked her and slammed her head against the floor, causing the head trauma. That could also explain the pooling of dried blood."

Norm was quiet and rubbed a hand across his face.

"Are you still there, Constable?"

"Yes."

"I know you're a friend of Melody Ward's family. This is hard to hear. All these details are also confidential."

"I know that. I'm not going to do anything to tip that bastard off. But *you* need to know there's been a leak about the DNA match. Some bozo reporter confronted the victim's mother about it. As you can imagine, she freaked!"

"That information was not to be made public."

"No shit. I need to get over there right away. Can we continue this on my cell?"

"I need for you to stay put at your office for a few minutes, Constable. The FBI ran the semen and the skin samples through CODIS. They got a hit. A known sex offender, Clive Wheeler. He has several aliases. Last known location is Jacksonville, Florida, three years ago. Nothing after that."

Norm sat. "Holy Shit."

"The Albany FBI office just faxed us a picture of him.

We need to know if he's the guy Melody Ward refers to in her journal. You know what Glenn Braddock looks like. If it's him, we'll nail him. Do you have a secure fax line there?"

"We're pretty small time here, Detective Cobb. The only fax machine is in the town clerk's office and that's like Grand Central Station most of the time. People coming and going, hanging out."

"You'll need to secure the area and get everyone out of there. Call me as soon as you're ready."

This is not gonna go over well. Norm walked into the clerk's office. "Priscilla, there's a confidential fax coming in a few minutes. I need for you ladies to vacate the area."

"Vacate the area? You on one of those cop shows now, Norm?" The women laughed.

"I'm serious. It will only take a few minutes then you can get back to doing whatever it is you do in here all day."

"Nice, Norm." They grumbled but went out into the hall.

"And don't let any of the public in here either," he called after them.

Norm called the detective and listened for the beeping sounds that indicated a successful fax transmission. Seconds stretched into minutes. Norm was aware that he was holding his breath.

As soon as it came through, Norm shoved the picture into an empty manila file. He opened the door. "Okay, ladies. Thank you very much."

After locking his office door, Norm opened the folder. Certainty rammed into him like a runaway logging truck. The fax fell to the desk. Rage rocketed through him, taking his blood pressure to new heights. His fist came down hard on the desk, splintering the wood. His hand ached as he dialed Cobb's direct line.

"The prick is so arrogant he didn't even try to conceal his identity!" Norm's fury burned through the phone line. "The hair's a little longer and lighter, and he looks younger without the glasses. But it's him, goddamn it! Glenn Braddock. I'm sure of it."

"Okay, Constable. That's what we needed to know. I'll notify the FBI field office in Albany of your positive ID. And we'll go get him. We'll also get a search warrant for his house, his office, and his car. If he transported the body, there will be blood." He paused. "Johnson, you said the victim's mother is acquainted with Braddock?"

"Yeah." His insides sank. Where was Braddock right now?

"If this guy suspects we're on to him, there's no telling what he'll do. He's done time in Georgia and is wanted for sexual assault in Tennessee and Florida. I think it's a good idea if you get over there and stay with her."

"I'm leaving now. You have my cell number. Call me if there's anything I need to know."

After cranking up the siren and turning on the lights, Norm sped toward Hannah's taking the curves on two wheels. It had been close to a half hour since he'd talked to her. He got a busy signal every time he called the house. She was so pissed at him, she probably took the phone off the hook. Her cell went right to voicemail.

He parked in front of the trailer. The news vans were still there. Getting out, he got himself under control.

"All right, folks, show's over," he said in a calm, authoritative tone. "I need for you to clear out of here. Ms. Ward's not making a statement today."

Despite objections and protestations of First

Amendment rights from the reporters, Norm stood firm with arms crossed over his chest in front of Hannah's trailer. *First Amendment be damned!*

As the journalists packed up, Norm pounded on Hannah's door.

"It's me. Open up."

There was no response, no furtive glances from behind drawn curtains. The old Dodge Dart was parked in its usual spot.

"Come on, Hannah. Let me in." He banged again.

Norm walked to the back by the porch. There was no sign of her anywhere.

Panic kicked in and Norm busted down the door. "Hannah," he called as he went from room to room. The kitchen phone was off the hook.

He called Carrie on his cell. "It's Norm. Is Hannah there?"

"No. Why? What's the matter?"

"I just need to find her. She was upset earlier. Reporters were hounding her."

"Well, she's not here. My guess is she's at Glenn's." *Damn!* "Thanks."

Fingers fumbling, he punched in Detective Cobb's direct line as he ran back to the truck and turned on the ignition. "She's at Braddock's. I'm on my way."

"Don't do anything stupid, Constable. Wait for back-up."

Norm hung up. Throwing the truck into reverse, he jammed his foot on the gas and backed out of Hannah's driveway.

He hadn't prayed in a long time. He prayed now to whomever might be listening.

34

"Did you tell anyone where you were going, or that you called me?" Glenn asked as soon as they were buckled in and on the road.

"No." She shook her head. "Norm told me to stay put, not to talk to anyone, that he'd be right over. But I couldn't wait. I was afraid they'd break the door down.

"You did the right thing, Hannah. I'm glad you called me." Glenn smiled and patted her knee. It felt good when he kept it there.

They drove to his farm on the outskirts of town. When he turned into the long drive, she saw stables and horses grazing in fenced in pastures. She wondered which of those beautiful animals Mel was learning to ride.

Glenn pulled the car into the garage and closed the automatic door. To a passerby, it would look as if no one were home. She was safe.

Entering the kitchen through the connecting side door from the garage, Hannah trailed her hand along the spotless granite counter and sank into a comfortable cushioned chair in the breakfast nook. She put her head into her hands. "What am I going to do?"

"You're going to stay here for now and not worry about anything beyond that. No one knows you're here. You won't be disturbed. I'll shut your phone off too."

She felt the pocket of her dress. "I must have left it home. I just wanted out of there."

"It doesn't matter," Glenn said as he massaged her shoulders. "You won't need it. I'll bet you didn't sleep last night, did you?"

She rubbed her face. "I *am* tired."

"I can give you a sedative, something light."

"No, I don't want anything. But I may just close my eyes for a bit."

He led her to his bedroom. "I have to go back to the office to finish up a few things. I had my nurse clear all my appointments for the rest of the day. I'll be back as soon as I can."

Hannah lay down on the king-size bed and Glenn covered her with a quilt. She'd never been in his room. It was spacious and bright.

"Do you want me to draw the drapes?"

"No, I'm fine." She was already drifting off.

"I'll lock the kitchen door on the way out. No one will disturb you."

Hannah nodded into the pillow. She took comfort in knowing Glenn was just through the garage in his adjourning office-clinic. It was so quiet; she heard the lock fall into place.

Her sleep was restless, plagued by scenes of death and violence. Mel was calling to her for help. Hannah startled awake and looked around, not knowing where she was at first.

Pushing her sleep-tousled hair out of her eyes, she glanced at the bedside clock. Only twenty minutes had passed.

Awake now, her mind ran rampant—thoughts of the upcoming funeral, the reporters, and Norm jumbled together. Norm. Had he come to her house? Would he guess where she'd gone? Why was she thinking about him? She had loved him once and he'd let her down, broke her heart. Glenn was a good man. He really liked her. He had been good to Mel, had wanted to take care of them both.

Rolling onto her side, Hannah sobbed until she had nothing left. Her head throbbed as if it had been bludgeoned. She needed aspirin.

She padded into the adjoining bathroom and riffled through the medicine cabinet. Knocking over several prescription bottles in the process, she searched every shelf. No aspirin. No Tylenol. No Advil. *There has to be an aspirin in this house!*

After checking the guest bathroom, she went through the kitchen cabinets. Nothing. Glenn would have something in his office but she didn't want to bother him. Back in the bedroom she sat on the side of the bed and pressed her temples. Her head was ready to explode. She looked around and noticed a drawer in the nightstand. It blended with the wood grain and had no handle or knob. Placing her hand under the edge, she pulled.

The drawer and all its contents spilled onto the floor: a paperback novel, reading glasses, a magazine, packages of condoms. Condoms? Was he seeing someone else? Hannah knelt on the floor and quickly retrieved the items, putting them back where she thought they had been. How could she have invaded his privacy like this? He could be back at any moment.

As she replaced the drawer, something at the back caught. She eased the drawer out a little and noticed the back was uneven. The left side was higher than the right and was pulled out a fraction of an inch. In her haste to straighten it out, she pushed too hard and the piece of wood splintered and fell off.

She shoved at the drawer with clumsy and sweaty hands but it wouldn't close. *Damn!* She had to get it back in place before Glenn returned!

Hannah removed the drawer again and bent down to see the broken piece of wood wedged up against the back of the small table. She reached in up to her elbow to remove the jagged piece of wood and felt something cool and metallic behind it. Her fingers traced a delicate pattern of intertwined hearts. Her hand recoiled as if it had been scorched.

She rubbed her hand and reached in again. Hannah closed her eyes while her hand, as if operating on its own, retrieved the secret cache. She went cold, ice settling in her belly. She opened her eyes, blinded by tears, to see the chain of silver hearts reflecting the late afternoon sun coming through the window.

As she clutched Mel's missing bracelet to her heart, Hannah let out a deep, pain-filled moan. She doubled over in agony as her insides ripped apart. Her body convulsed. She struggled to breathe.

With her forehead on the carpet and her legs folded beneath her, Hannah heard the tumblers release in the lock.

Lifting her head off the carpet but remaining on her knees, Hannah looked up at Glenn. Her hair in wild disarray, tears streamed down her face.

"Hannah, what's wrong? What's happened?" He ran to her.

She shook her head, unable to speak.

"Talk to me." He reached for her upper arms but she pulled away.

"Don't touch me." She got up, leaning her elbow heavily on one knee.

"I don't understand." His eyes scanned her as if to identify the source of the problem.

Hannah opened her fist; the silver bracelet glittered in her palm. "Why do you have this?" She sobbed and tried to hold her hand steady.

"It broke one day when she was grooming the horses. I told her I would have it repaired. I hadn't had a chance to get it back to her." His eyes never left Hannah's.

"You're lying. Why was it hidden in a compartment at the back of your drawer?"

The earlier concern in his eyes was replaced with anger and coldness. Hannah shuddered.

"What were you doing in my nightstand?" He turned to inspect the opening where the drawer should have been.

"Don't turn your back on me, you bastard! This is my daughter's bracelet! What are you doing with it?" Her face and neck flushed with heat that emanated from the inside out.

He took two steps toward her. "Hannah, Hannah. I really wish you hadn't found that. It really isn't smart to go snooping around where you shouldn't. I've worked hard to establish myself in this town and I can't let you ruin it."

"What are you talking about? Just answer my question." Hannah fought to calm her voice. "Why do you have Mel's bracelet?"

Glenn smirked. His eyes narrowed and his body straightened to tower over her. His eyes squinted as they bore into her, and Hannah realized she was staring into the face of evil. "Can't you figure it out, Hannah? Come on, you can do it." His voice taunted her. "Mel was a pretty girl—that corn silk hair, those long lithe limbs. And she wasn't afraid to try anything. Had some pretty good ideas of her own too." He licked his upper lip with his tongue. "I bet she taught those college boys a thing or two."

Hannah grabbed the front of his shirt with both fists and shook him. "What are you saying?" She heard the screech in her voice.

"Wake up, Hannah." He removed her hands with a jerk. His tone was harsh and dismissive. "Did you really think I was hanging around all this time for *you*? That I was interested in *you*? A poor fat slob."

His deep laugh cut into her and laid bare her vulnerability and foolish hopes.

Her fingernails dug into the fleshy part of her palms as her fists bunched at her sides. Glenn's face morphed into someone she didn't recognize—his smile a sneer.

"Mel was much more my type, young and willing. Too much for that dumbass college boy who didn't have a clue how to really satisfy her. The cops are so stupid. He'll rot in jail the rest of his life." Another deep throaty laugh vibrated the air in the bedroom. "But Mel … oh, she was good. She was *very* good. She really knew how to—"

Hannah hurled herself at him and pummeled his chest with both fists. "Stop, goddamn you. Stop it!" Salty tears mingled with rage. "She trusted you and so did I."

"Now see, that was your mistake." Showing no effects from the blows she'd leveled, he grabbed her left arm and pulled it behind her, spinning her around. He twisted it until she cried out. She felt his hot breath as he pushed his lips against her ear. "Mothers are supposed to protect their daughters. You couldn't even do that. You're nothing."

With his free hand, he pried open her right fist. "I'll take that now." He pocketed the bracelet.

Checking her empty pocket, she cursed herself for forgetting her phone.

She kicked at him but lost her balance as he shoved her toward the living room. Landing hard on her knees, she slid across the hardwood floor toward the front door. Blood from the fresh abrasions soaked into her light cotton dress. Glenn yanked her head back by the hair. She scratched at his hands.

"Don't even think about it, Hannah. You're mine now. Just like Mel was in that old shack. She fought me too but that just made it better." He chuckled. "Like mother, like daughter they say. Let's see if it's true."

He threw her onto her back. Straddling her, he held both her wrists above her head with one hand. The coldness in his eyes changed to white-hot fury. With his free hand he pulled his belt off and tied it around her wrists. He wrapped the ends around the leg of a heavy oak table nearby and secured them.

Feeling Mel's terror, Hannah kicked and bucked. "Let me go!" She pulled her arms but couldn't budge the table. She let out a deafening scream.

"No one can hear you. I let the office staff go. And no one knows you're here."

She bucked again and tried to knee him.

"So, you want to play rough." His sneer was evil. "And here I thought you'd be the sweet passive type. Maybe you're more like your daughter than I thought."

He held her right leg down as Hannah fought him. With his other hand, he reached under her dress. In one swift violent movement, he ripped off her underwear. The sound of tearing fabric mingled with sadistic laughter. And Hannah's screams.

"Get off me! Get off!" Hannah brought her free leg up and rammed it into his groin. He let go of her and, grabbing his crotch, doubled over in pain.

"You'll pay for this, bitch."

Hannah heard him struggle to catch his breath. This was her only chance. Gathering what strength she had left, she jerked on the table leg with both arms. The antique brass lamp toppled over. Twisting and getting up onto her bruised knees, Hannah wedged her shoulder under the edge of the table. With adrenaline pumping through her, she lifted the table just enough to pull the belt free.

Untying her hands, she heaved the lamp at Glenn's head. He flung an arm up in time to deflect it. The lamp crashed to the floor.

Hannah got up and ran for the front door. He grabbed her from behind and shoved her against it, pinning her with his full weight. She elbowed him right before her cheek smashed against the dead bolt. Blood mixed with sweat poured down her face. He twisted her right arm behind her and leaving a trail of blood on the burnished oak door, wrestled her to the floor. He kicked at her side. She struggled to crawl away a few feet before she felt his knee in the small of her back, his fetid breath against her ear.

"I've got you now," he whispered. Her left arm was wedged under her body.

Grabbing her chin, he forced her head around. "I want you to see me, bitch, when I fuck you like a dog." His face contorted with rage.

Hannah let out a raging scream, torn from every cell in

her body. It was enough to make him loosen his grip on her for just a second. She sank her teeth hard into the fleshy part of his hand between the thumb and index finger. She had the strength of a rabid dog. Teeth clamped like a vise, she drew blood and tossed her head from side to side, oblivious to her victim's cries of pain.

"You fucking bitch!" He tried to pull his hand free.

Hannah shifted and lifted herself just enough to get her left arm free. She struck out behind her blindly, hitting wherever she could.

She'd lost all sensation in her jaw but willed herself to bear down harder and felt the warm stickiness of blood. Hers? His? There was a lot of it. She fought the blackness forming at the edge of her vision.

His body slumped against hers. His grip lessened. She lay perfectly still, afraid that her slightest movement would stir him.

35

Approaching Braddock's house from the south with no siren, Norm was the first to arrive. It looked deserted. Cobb's warning to wait was clear. Norm fingered his firearm—the one he had never fired, except at the state police range.

A piercing scream erupted from inside. *Wait be damned!* Norm jumped out and ran to the front door. A violation of police protocol. But this was Hannah!

Busting the lock, he burst through the door, gun drawn. Hannah was prone on the floor with Braddock slumped on top of her. Her head was twisted. Blood covered her face and smeared the floor. Hannah was pale and lay very still.

She looked up at Norm just as Braddock came to. Braddock reached into his pocket. Norm caught a glint of steel. A knife.

"Police. Drop it." Norm spoke with authority despite his racing heart.

Keeping the gun trained on Braddock, Norm approached and attempted to kick the knife out of the doctor's hand. Braddock, however, was quicker. In one swift movement he pulled his hand free of Hannah's slack jaw and yanked her head back by her hair. Straddling her body, he held the knife to Hannah's throat.

"You try that again and I'll slit her throat right now." He pressed the point until he drew blood.

Without stopping to think, Norm pointed the gun at Braddock's knee and fired. The sound reverberated and the force rocked Braddock off Hannah. He landed on his back and dropped the knife. Norm kicked it out of reach.

Hannah yelled as fresh blood sprayed her.

Crying out, Braddock grabbed his knee. "You son of a bitch, you fucking shot me." Blood dripped down Braddock's arm and pooled under his bent leg.

"Damn right, you bastard. You're lucky it was your knee. I should have blown your dick off." Norm grabbed Braddock and sat him up. Pulling his arms behind him, Norm handcuffed him. "You'll live, you son of a bitch."

Car doors slammed. Cobb and his team entered the house with guns raised. "What happened here?"

"Here's your man, Detective." Norm stood behind Braddock, his kneecap blown and blood soaking through his pants. "He needs an ambulance. And what happened is I don't follow orders well."

Cobb didn't respond. He called for an ambulance. "Someone grab the first aid kit and bandage this knee while we wait for the EMTs."

A sobbing Hannah struggled to a sitting position. "He did it. He killed my Mel."

Norm knelt and took her into his arms. He tried to wipe the dried blood from her lacerated cheek. Fresh blood trickled from the shallow puncture wound on her neck. "You're all right, Hannah." He stroked her sweat-matted hair as he rocked her.

"I'll need a statement, Ms. Ward," Detective Cobb said.

"And you'll get it," Norm said. "But right now, I'm getting her out of here. She's been through enough."

"She needs to go to the hospital, Constable."

"And *I'm* going to take her. I'm not waiting for the ambulance."

Cobb nodded. "I'm going to need a full report from you too. You discharged your weapon."

"Yeah, and it's a damn good thing I was here to discharge it." He looked the state police detective in the eye. "You'll get your report once you've locked up this scumbag."

Cobb looked down at Braddock, lying on his side now, still writhing in pain. "Clive Wheeler, aka Glenn Braddock, you are under arrest for the rape and murder of Melody Ward. You have the right to remain silent."

As the remaining words of the Miranda warning faded, Norm all but carried Hannah down the steps and into his truck. He poured bottled water onto a towel he had on the front seat. "Hold this against your cheek."

"Clive Wheeler?" Hannah asked as Norm started the truck.

"I'll tell you the whole story, at least as much as I know, once we get you fixed up."

"He was going to kill me. Just like he did Mel." She sobbed.

Norm held her hand. He hit the lights and siren and turned out of Braddock's driveway as the ambulance pulled in.

Norm willed the miles between them and Rutland Hospital to shrink.

The small knife wound on Hannah's neck had clotted by the time they reached the ER. The cheek laceration required three stitches. X-rays indicated two fractured ribs.

"Is there someone I can call for you, Hannah? Carrie?"

She shook her head.

The ER doctor approached her. "You've experienced a significant trauma, Ms. Ward. We'd like to admit you overnight for observation."

Hannah nodded. She had not spoken since they'd left Braddock's house.

Settled in a room, Hannah stared out the window.

Norm sat beside the bed. "Can I get you anything? A cold drink? Tea?"

She turned her head in response and lay very still.

"Norm." She turned to face him.

He leaned forward. "Do you want something?"

"No. I'm just glad you didn't follow orders today when it counted." She gave him a tiny smile. "Will you stay with me?"

Norm squeezed her hand. "For as long as you want me to."

36

Thursday at noon Kate parked Ellen's car in front of Andrew Grady's temporary office in downtown Rutland. He was renting space on the first floor of an old Victorian, a short drive from the correctional facility. The name on the door read *Horton and Manciewicz, Attorneys at Law*. Bernie Manciewicz was a friend of Grady's from his UVM undergrad days.

Large casement windows bathed the entrance foyer in sunlight. Kate approached the receptionist, who ushered her through a set of double oak doors. Hutch met her and led her to a dark paneled room dominated by a mahogany desk.

Grady came out from behind the desk and shook her hand. Reading glasses perched on the bridge of his nose, he looked tired and disheveled, shirtsleeves rolled up to his elbows.

"Sit down." Hutch pulled out a chair for her.

"First of all, Mrs. Rourke, I got you approved for a visit tomorrow at eleven. I wish it were today, but that was the best I could do," Grady said.

"Thank you." She fingered the clasp on the purse in her lap.

Andrew Grady placed a manila file on his desk. "Late yesterday, members of the State Police Bureau of Criminal Investigation, BCI, arrested a convicted sex offender for the rape and murder of Melody Ward. He's in FBI custody right now."

"They have him? How?" Kate looked from Grady to Hutch. "Have you told Tim?"

"I will, as soon as this meeting is over. Let me back up." Grady sat on the edge of the desk and leaned toward Kate. "As you know, Tim was arrested largely on circumstantial evidence. What sealed the deal was Melody Ward's blood on his shirt. Once forensics confirmed that, it was enough to get a warrant. Violent crime, especially murder, doesn't happen in Willow Bend. The state police wanted this case solved pronto.

"I've lived in Vermont all my life, except for three years of law school. Town folks here seem to think bad things don't happen in their towns. When they do, they can come unhinged. If those bad things can be attributed to outsiders, everyone feels better. Kind of an us versus them mentality." He looked at Kate. "Hutch told me you experienced that for yourself the other night."

Kate nodded. Flashes of the angry scene at the candlelight vigil and the coldness she had experienced earlier at Jenny's re-played in Kate's mind. "I think the good folks of Willow Bend had already tried and convicted Tim."

"The funny thing about a criminal case—it ain't over 'til it's over." Hutch smiled. "Forensics continues to do its job."

"Mrs. Rourke, I know Hutch told you the DNA in the semen and under the victim's nails was *not* Tim's. That was the turning point," Grady said.

Kate wiped a single tear. "I knew it couldn't be. Did the DNA lead you to this other person?"

"Yes. When the FBI ran the samples through the national database, they got a hit. It was a match to our boy here." Grady took a sheet of paper out of the folder. "Clive Wheeler, who goes by several aliases, served time and then skipped out on his probation. He's been off the radar for a few years. Until now."

Grady showed her the image.

"Oh my God. That's the man who was with Melody's mom at the vigil. He's a doctor."

Hutch nodded. "He's also the one who identified you to the crowd. Makes sense. Make you the target of their frustration, deflecting attention away from him."

"How'd they make the connection between this guy Wheeler and the doctor? I think my friend said his name is Braddock."

"There's a lot of evidence I can't share with you, but Constable Johnson was instrumental in putting many of the pieces together."

"Unbelievable." Remembering her first impression of the constable, Kate shook her head. "Do you know what happened to Melody after she left the boat?"

"It seems she did swim to shore as Tim hoped and made her way up the hill to the road," Hutch said. "The state's theory is that Wheeler aka Braddock picked her up there."

"Evidence suggests the old abandoned shack across the lake from your house is the actual crime scene." Grady placed his glasses on the desk.

"And they have Wheeler in custody now." Kate wanted to assure herself that the nightmare was over.

"Yes, they do." Grady gave her a full smile.

"How did they get him?" She needed details.

"With a lot of good police work," Grady said. "And some fast thinking by Constable Johnson. Again, I can't tell you everything, but by the time the state police arrived at Wheeler's home, the constable had apprehended him and rescued Ms. Ward, whom Wheeler had attacked."

"Is she all right? That woman has been through so much."

"As far as we know," Hutch said.

Kate let out a deep breath. "Constable Johnson is to be commended. Sometimes we underestimate a person."

"Constable Johnson will have his due when tomorrow's issue of *The Rutland Herald* comes out. He'll be the hometown hero then. It will be on TV too." Hutch smiled.

Kate tightened the grip on her purse. "How soon can Tim be released?"

"We have to go back to court and get the charges against Tim dropped." Hutch touched her arm.

"All of them? How soon?"

"The rape and murder charges obviously," Grady said. "And hopefully the boat theft too. The state's attorney's office has been in touch with the homeowners who may be willing to withdraw the boat theft complaint. As far as the underage drinking, Judge Oberman can be a hard ass. But considering the fact that Tim was arrested and actually *imprisoned* for something he didn't do, we may get lucky there too."

"How soon can we do this?" She stood.

"As soon as we can get it on the judge's calendar. I'm going to the courthouse right now to take care of that." Grady put the papers back in the file folder. "Then I'm going to see Tim and tell him the good news."

"Thank you. Thank you." It was finally over.

"You can use my office to call your husband. Stay here as long as you need. I'll call you as soon as we have the court date. Hutch, if you can get started on that brief for Judge Oberman, I'll be back as soon as I can." Grady closed the door behind him.

Hutch's arms came around her. After a couple of seconds, she stepped back and smiled up at him. "Thank you for everything, Hutch. I need to call Jack."

~~

It was late afternoon and Jack still hadn't returned her calls or texts, or answered his direct line at work.

At five o'clock, he finally called back.

"Tim's in the clear! They've arrested a known sex offender. I wanted you to hear it from me. Has it been on the news there yet?" Kate hadn't waited for him to say hello.

"Don't know. I was at the game with clients. That's great!" He slurred the last few words.

"You were at a game and couldn't answer your phone or return my texts?"

"I'm calling now."

"Don't you want to know how it happened or what that means for our son?" He'd been drinking. She breathed deeply and tried to stay calm.

"I'm guessing it means he'll be getting out. Who is this guy?"

"Someone the FBI has been after for quite awhile. He's in custody. Tim has to go back to court for the charges to be dropped. I don't know when that will be, but you and I have been approved for a visit tomorrow morning. Can you be here tonight?" Silence. "Jack, are you there?"

"I don't think that's going to work, Kate. I'm in over my head here. Jim quit today. I'll come for the court date. Let me know when it is. That's great news. Tell Tim I'm really happy." The line went dead.

37

A spike in blood pressure kept Hannah in the hospital a second night. With proper meds, she was discharged on Friday morning and insisted on coming home to her own house. Norm had her cocooned on the couch, propped up with more pillows and quilts than she knew she owned. This was the only way she could hope to sleep with two broken ribs.

Norm gave her the prescribed pain medication and settled himself into a chair next to her. She smiled as she remembered him sitting next to her throughout the long nights in the hospital.

"You're going to spoil me, Norm."

"It's about time somebody did." He pulled his chair closer. "Do you want to talk about it? About Braddock, I mean."

She wasn't sure. "I was such a fool. He turned my head with all the attention. I kept thinking this guy is interested in *me*? *Me.* It had been a long time." She turned away, ashamed. "I would have done anything, put myself in danger, to keep her safe. She was my whole life. Now I keep thinking my stupidity, my infatuation or whatever it was, put *her* in danger—that I caused her death."

Norm knelt beside the couch and put his arms around her. "No, Hannah. You are not to blame. The guy's a pervert and he fooled everybody. There's no way you could have known."

"I'm her mother! I should have known." Anger mixed with tears. Guilt gnawed at her.

Norm eased her back against the pillows and sat again. He cleared his throat. "I got more information late yesterday while you were sleeping. Are you up to hearing it?"

Hannah nodded. She had to face it sometime.

"When Braddock, or Wheeler, was arrested in Georgia, he was working as a coach for a girls' volleyball team. He did the minimum time for sexual assault and was supposed to register as a sex offender from then on, but didn't.

"He moved around a lot. With budget cuts, poor communication and incompetent personnel, he managed to slip off the radar. The guy's smart. He used aliases and always managed to land a job that put him in contact with teenage girls—a teacher in a private girls' school, a teenage drug and alcohol counselor." He eventually came to the attention of the FBI as a suspect in two sexual assaults in Tennessee and Florida."

Norm moved his face closer to hers. "He preyed on young, vulnerable girls, Hannah. He was a pro, a predator. They found a lot of child porn on his home and his office computer. He was also active on numerous child porn sites."

She fought the nausea. "How did he end up in Vermont?"

Norm shrugged. "Probably thought no one would find

him up here. The state police found a copy of an obituary for a Doctor Glenn Braddock on his home computer. The doctor worked in Montpelier and died eighteen months ago, leaving no family. He was sixty-three. Wheeler must have gotten copies of the doctor's diploma and medical license or just forged them."

"It's that easy?" She couldn't believe it.

"It's the age of technology. They're still investigating all that."

"But why here?"

"They're not sure. There was another article on the computer about the comeback of country doctors in rural Vermont. Willow Bend was one of the towns featured in the article as a desirable site."

Hannah mulled it over in her mind. It didn't make sense. "I just don't get how he could pass himself off as a doctor. How'd he know all the medical stuff?"

"Beats me. Like I said, he was smart and he fooled a lot of people. They found medical textbooks and drug reference books in his office. He has a military background. The FBI is checking to see if he was ever a medic. They won't stop until they know everything about him."

Norm took her hand. "I'm telling you all this so you won't think you were the only one taken in by this prick. I can't imagine a harder job than being a single parent." He swallowed. "You thought this man was helping you, showing a genuine interest in Mel."

Still tormented by self-recrimination, she didn't respond.

"You've met with Dwight about arrangements?"

"Yes." She was quiet for a few seconds. "It will be on Monday at eleven. I know it's stupid but I wanted to give

Bobby a chance to come. I got a text from his sister right before I left the hospital while you were handling the paperwork. He's in jail in New Hampshire for armed robbery. Guess he never did get his act together." She tried to smile.

"I'll be there beside you, Hannah, if that's okay. You won't be alone."

She nodded.

When Norm spoke again, his voice was low. "You've been through so much. God knows I did nothing to help you."

She took his hand. "You think I didn't know about the times you went after Bobby yourself—after you'd seen my injuries from a series of supposed accidents? And the times you brought Mel home and didn't drive off until she was safely inside?

"We both let pride get in the way, Norm. And it only got worse the more time we let go by. I was so hurt and angry when you left. I couldn't find my way back from that."

"Your parents were right not to let you come with me back then. We were too young and I was going nowhere. The Marines gave me a direction and a purpose when I had neither. But, Hannah, I tried—"

She put up a hand to stop him. "When I cleaned out Mom's house last year after she died, I found a box of your letters in the attic under a pile of junk. I don't know why she never gave them to me, or maybe I do. But I can't for the life of me figure out why she kept them."

"But you never—"

"What? Said, 'Hey, Norm, I guess I've been wrong for the past twenty years?' It was too late." She rubbed the top of his hand. "But sometimes you get a second chance. If it wasn't for you, I wouldn't be here today. You saved my life."

She didn't think she'd ever seen Norm cry.

He shook his head. "I screwed up big time on this case, Hannah. I was so sure it was Timothy Rourke. All I wanted was to get the SOB. I couldn't stay objective, didn't follow protocol, didn't follow the evidence, as they say."

"You followed me, even when I told you not too." She squeezed his hand.

"I don't think I'm cut out for this. Stopping speeders, breaking up a fight—that I can do. The new regs require constables to have extensive law enforcement training." He rubbed his face. "I don't think I want that.

"In my heart I'm a woodworker. I love the feel of wood in my hands, love using my own designs to make things I can be proud of. And if something isn't square or plumb, I can fix that. It doesn't put anyone's life in danger if I mess up."

"We've all been through a lot. Just be sure before you make any big decisions."

Norm put his other hand on top of hers. "I've been a real jerk, Hannah. And I'm not just talking about this week. You have every right to tell me to hit the road. But I'd like to make it up to you, if you'll let me. Make up for all the time we've lost."

"I think I'd like that." Hannah removed her hand and pointed to the TV stand. "There's a small box in that drawer. Would you get it for me, please?"

She opened the box and placed a piece of white marble in his hand.

"You still have it?" His eyes searched hers.

She closed her hand around his. "Always."

38

Nine o'clock Friday morning. She was an hour early. Seeing the sign for Slate Valley Correctional Facility made Kate's hands shake. Gripping the steering wheel tighter, she pulled Ellen's car into the first available parking spot. She turned off the ignition and sat in quiet until the sun beating through the windshield became oppressive.

She opened the door and stepped onto the burning asphalt. Kate walked to the main entrance, her need to see Tim dwarfing any trepidation she felt at entering that building again.

A waft of minimal air conditioning skimmed over her as she approached the visitors' desk. She turned when she heard her name.

"Hutch, what are you doing here? I told you I was fine."

He was beside her. "No, you said *we'll* be fine. I called Jack's office this morning and found out he was in a meeting."

Kate busied herself getting out her photo ID. She'd

been too embarrassed last night on the phone to admit she'd be coming alone.

"Isn't it still immediate family only?" She held her Connecticut driver's license in her hand as she zipped her purse.

"As co-counsel of record, I'm now on the approved visitors list." He smiled. "Let's see if they'll let us in early."

He was back in minutes and they proceeded through the first of a series of locked doors.

She said nothing as she surrendered her purse and cell phone.

The female guard checked the names on their IDs against her list. "Will Mr. Rourke be joining you today? Only two visitors are allowed at a time."

"No," Kate said, her tone clipped.

The woman handed each of them a copy of the Visitors Rules and Regulations and motioned them toward the metal detectors. "Please remove jackets, belts, and pocket contents."

Everything this woman said was by rote. Kate wiped the perspiration from her forehead. No one would be wearing a jacket today. It was 92 degrees!

Kate's shoulders relaxed as they passed through the metal detector without incident. She did not want to be subjected to a hand scanner or a pat search.

The guard directed them to another large metal door. "I'll call for the inmate to be brought down."

"I know I'm not Jack and I'm not trying to take his place. Tim deserves to have his dad here," Hutch said. "I just didn't want you to have to do this alone."

"Thanks." Kate nodded and tried to breathe around the lump that had formed in her throat.

Kate and Hutch were brought to a large room with several tables. No glass partitions. They were instructed to sit together on one side of the table, to keep their hands visible on the table at all times, and to have no physical contact with the prisoner.

When Tim was led in, all the air in Kate's lungs rushed out in one loud cry at the sight of her son. His right eye was swollen shut and he had a fresh raw slice on his right cheek, bruised purple and black.

"Tim, what happened to you?" Kate jumped up. Leaning across the table, she reached for him and had two guards beside her immediately.

"Please sit down, ma'am."

They didn't touch her but power and strength radiated off their persons. Hutch eased her back into her chair.

"I'm fine, Mom. It's nothing." Trembling hands contradicted his words. He looked at Hutch and then around the room. "Dad's not here?"

"He had to go home to take care of a few things. He'll be back as soon as he can. What happened?" She lowered her voice and leaned toward him. She wanted to touch him, soothe him.

Tim seemed to shrink into himself. "I don't want to talk about it." He lifted his head. "I really thought Dad would be here." His voice faltered.

Kate's heart ached. She saw in his face the disappointment he showed every time he felt he'd fallen short of Jack's expectations. "He really did want to be here, honey."

A surge of anger toward Jack rocketed through her. Jack *should* be here, damn it.

"I hope you don't mind that I came with your mom."

In some distant corner of her mind, she heard Hutch

but couldn't say anything.

When Tim didn't answer, Hutch said, "Have you talked to Grady?"

"Yeah, he said they arrested someone else?"

It was the closest to a smile Kate had seen on her son's face since this whole ordeal began.

"He said I can't get out of here right away. Is that true?" Tim looked at Hutch with such hope and trust, Kate had to look away.

"We're working on getting that done as soon as possible."

Tim looked around and lowered his voice. "It's bad in here. I try to keep to myself and not attract attention. There are some pretty scary guys in here." He looked at Kate. "But I'm okay, Mom. You don't need to worry."

Kate's eyes twinkled. "You're telling *me* not worry? How long have you known me?"

That got a small chuckle out of him, just what she was trying to do. She would not break down in front of him.

Without warning, a burly guard approached Tim from behind. "Time's up. Let's go."

"I thought we had an hour." She broke out in a cold sweat. She couldn't leave him again right now, not like this.

"It's one hour max, Mom. It's up to the guard." Tim's voice broke and his composure crumbled. "Mom."

That one word cut through her. It was the same voice he'd used as a child whenever he was afraid. She reached out to touch his hand before he was gone.

The guard grabbed Tim's upper arm and jerked him out of the chair. "Can't do that, ma'am." He pulled Tim from the room.

Keeping her eyes on Tim, she watched until the heavy

metal door clanged shut. Unable to move, she began to sob and felt Hutch's hands on her shoulders. "I just want him out of here."

Bending down he said, "Of course you do. You're his mom. Come on, let's get out of here. We'll stop at Grady's office. Judge Oberman's docket is tight but Grady will secure the first possible opening. I promise."

~~

"Three days? I can't believe he has to stay in that place for three more days! They'll kill him in there. He won't make it!" Kate screamed at Grady.

"I'm really sorry. Monday at ten was Judge Oberman's first available opening. I did my best. I've filed the necessary paperwork to have all charges dropped," Grady answered.

"Nobody seemed to have trouble finding an available spot when Tim was arrested and they wanted him arraigned."

"Point taken, Kate," Grady said and then was silent.

"I'm sorry. It's not your fault. I'm just so worried about him. He looks awful. Someone beat him up!" *Didn't anyone understand?*

"I know. I talked to him, brought him up to speed on the court date. He's trying to keep a low profile but it's tough in there. I won't kid you. I'm trying to get him moved out of the general population for the remaining time. I can't make any promises."

"Will I be able to see him again before Monday?" She pleaded with her eyes.

"I've made the request. I don't know. If not, I'll ask for permission for him to call you. I'll contact you as soon as I know something."

"Thank you." In her mind, she saw Tim's battered face. Her pulse accelerated in anger and frustration. She had to get out of there.

Hutch touched her hand. "He'll be all right."

"You don't know that!" She pulled her hand away.

"You're right. I just think knowing there's an end in sight will make him stronger." He paused. "Are you okay to drive, Kate?"

"I'm fine. I'm sorry I snapped at you. Thank you both for everything."

But she wasn't okay. Her hands trembled as she unlocked the car and left several messages for Jack—on his cell, at work, and at home. Her whole body shook, despite the intense heat of the parking lot.

In the car Kate lay back against the headrest and counted through the inhalations and exhalations of several cleansing breaths. She felt her body begin to relax as the sun on her face warmed and soothed her.

She began the drive back to the lake. With each mile, and no call or text from Jack, the slow simmer of anger returned and intensified.

How can he not return my calls? What if this were an emergency?

As the lake came in to view, Kate couldn't remember taking the last exit off the highway. Functioning on automatic, she was aware only of the steady hum of the car's air conditioning the rest of the way home.

She kicked her shoes off as soon as she unlocked the house and dialed Jack's office.

"Rourke and Associates." They had hired a new receptionist. *Was it Tracy?*

Kate spoke with confidence. "Tracy, this is Mrs. Rourke. I need to speak to my husband."

"I'm sorry, Mrs. Rourke. He's left for the day. Would you like to leave a message?"

Kate glanced at the clock. One-thirty and he was gone? "No, I don't want to leave a message. I need to talk to my husband now. I don't care if he's in a meeting or where he is. I'm sure you have a way to reach him."

"I really don't. He didn't say where he was going. I don't expect him back today. You could try his cell."

"I *know* I can try his cell." Kate took a breath and composed herself. It was none of this girl's business. "If he calls in, please tell him I'm trying to reach him and it's important."

She dialed Jack's cell. It went directly to voice mail. *Where the hell is he?* Kate hated talking to a machine. "Jack, it's me. Call me as soon as you get this. It's important." She left the same message at the house.

She called Ellen. "I'm home. I'll get the car back to you as soon as I talk to Sarah."

"I don't need it," Ellen said. "Gil's coming back this afternoon. Keep it for as long as you need it. How's Tim?"

"He's a mess. I can't ... Ellen, thank you. I'll call you later."

Sarah answered on the first ring and Kate filled her in.

"It's not right that he has to stay in that place until Monday when they know he's innocent. We'll be there Monday, Mom. Do you want me to come up with you for the weekend?"

Kate heard her daughter's unspoken question. *Is Dad back yet?*

"You know you can come anytime, honey. But if

you're worried about me, don't be. I'm fine. I'm grateful you can come Monday. I know it's a hike for you but Tim will appreciate the support."

"Is Dad with you?"

"No, but I expect him soon. I love you."

Kate hung up. How could she admit to her daughter that not only wasn't Jack there, she had no idea where he was?

Her cell rang. "Jack. Where have you been? I've left you messages *everywhere*."

"Yeah, sorry. What's up?" His voice was easy, casual.

"What's up? Are you kidding me? First of all, I saw Tim today in that horrible place. He asked why you weren't there."

"How's he doing?"

"How the hell do you think he's doing? It's prison, Jack. Prison. He has a black eye that's just about swollen shut and an angry red gash on his cheek. Somebody used him for a punching bag. He wouldn't tell me what happened."

"Did you really think he'd tell his Mommy?" She heard the familiar sarcasm in his tone.

"Damn you. I was the only one there, so yeah, I thought maybe. He has to stay in there three more days. Three more days, even though they know he didn't do it! Grady filed paperwork to have the charges dropped and the prosecutor's signed off on it. But he couldn't get it on the judge's docket until Monday at ten." She waited for him to say something. "I could use you here, Jack, and so could Tim."

"I know I've been a shit, Kate. But I can't be two places at once. I'll make it up to you. I promise." How many times had she heard that?

Kate started to hang up. She couldn't bring herself to tell him it was okay—like she always did—when she heard a woman's voice in the background.

"Come on, Jack. I'm waiting." It was more a whine than a statement.

"Who is that? Where are you?" Kate's whole body tightened with rage.

"Kate, I have to go." His words were clipped, hurried. "I'll call you tomorrow. I have to work all weekend but will try to get up there Monday."

"You have to *go*? You'll *try* to come Monday? What the hell's going on, Jack?" Her free hand was fisted on the counter, her knuckles bloodless white.

"I'm on my way into a meeting. Can't talk."

"Don't lie to me, Jack. I know you're not at your office. Who is she this time?"

Kate's volume increased with each syllable. Blood thundered through her veins; her head throbbed. She imagined her systolic and diastolic numbers rocketing out of control.

How long had she ignored the signs this time? They were all there: extra hours at work, unexplained absences from the office, secret financial transactions, withdrawal, decreased interest in sex. She had vowed the last time she wouldn't put up with it again.

So, this was how she would find out—on the phone, alone, her son in prison for rape and murder.

Phone in hand, Kate slid to the floor. The silence on the other end of the line filled the room. She touched her lips to the phone and spoke in a cool monotone. "You know what, I don't care. I'm done, Jack. I'm done."

After breaking the connection, she buried her face in her hands and cried. Twenty-six years gone— just like that.

~~

Kate didn't know how long she'd been sitting there when her cell phone jarred her. She rubbed her face and checked caller ID. "Ellen, hi."

"Are you all right? I walked by your place earlier. The car was there but no one answered the door. Jack's not back?"

Kate ignored the question and lied to her friend for the first time. "I took a long walk and then fell asleep."

"How was Tim?"

She told her friend about the beating and the court date on Monday.

"He has to stay in there all weekend? They know he's innocent. The whole town knows he's innocent," Ellen said. "There was a big article in the paper this morning with a picture of Doctor Braddock, or whatever his real name is. He's the main topic of conversation now at Jenny's. And Constable Johnson too. He's the hometown hero. I heard one old-timer say 'Norm's some kind of Wyatt Earp.'"

"It's nice to know the gossip's moved on to someone else." Kate could taste the pungent bitterness in her mouth.

"These people in town don't like to be wrong, Kate, and they don't like to be fooled. Do you want some company?"

"Thanks, Ellen, but I'm pretty tapped out. I'm going to take a long hot shower. You're a good friend. Thanks."

Twenty minutes later, finger combing her damp curls, Kate sat on the deck in bare feet, white shorts, and a tank top. She sipped a glass of Chardonnay. She had no plans other than to try to relax, soak in the last rays of sun, and wait for the sunset. There was nothing she could do right now for Tim.

Hearing a car door shut and thinking it was Ellen, she walked to the side deck.

Hutch stood holding Chinese take-out and a bottle of

wine.

"What are you doing here?"

"You have to eat, so here I am. Grady talked to the state's attorney again and everything's all set for Monday. It looks good." He looked around. "Jack's not here? I hoped he had come to his senses."

Kate shrugged. "Come on in." She led him into the kitchen and got plates out and another wine glass. "Was Grady able to get him moved?"

"Not yet, but he doesn't give up, Kate. He's a good guy." He put the cartons down and opened the wine. "Did you reach Jack?"

"Oh, yeah, I reached him." Kate set out napkins.

"What?" Hutch was right behind her.

"I can't talk about it." She moved away.

"All right. You don't have to." Smiling, he raised his hands, palms up. "I come bearing food and wine, no questions."

She laughed and relaxed. They ate in silence. "I guess I'm not much company tonight," Kate said when they had finished. "This was really good. I was hungrier than I thought."

Hutch picked up the dishes and studied her. "Whatever's wrong, I'm not leaving you alone like this. Not after seeing Tim today. I can't imagine how it was for you to see him like that. We'll just sit. If you want to talk, I'll listen. If not, that's okay too."

Bringing the rest of the wine, he led her to the couch where a quilt was bunched into a corner. Kate wanted to confide in him about Jack, but she couldn't. It seemed a betrayal, so she kept quiet. Through the wall of windows facing the lake, they watched the sun go down and the sky fade from rose to purple to darkness. He placed his arm along the back of the couch and Kate relaxed into him.

She stirred. She must have nodded off. The first stars were peeking out. Hovering between sleep and wakefulness, her body remembered. Remembered his kisses, his hands, his gentle caresses. He had always touched her as if she were made of priceless porcelain. She gave herself up to memories she'd thought long buried, to desires she'd thought dormant.

It had been so long since she'd been in Hutch's arms. Close to twenty years. And, God, it felt good—like coming home.

She felt his breath on her hair. It would be so easy to turn her face up to his.

"I know I shouldn't say this. You're vulnerable right now." His voice was husky. "But I never stopped—"

"No, don't say it." She bolted upright, pulling herself from his warmth. "I can't. I'm sorry."

"I know." He smiled and pulled the blanket over them. "Shhh … It's okay. Just sleep, Katie. That's all. I'm not going anywhere."

39

The first hints of dawn illumined the sky over the lake. Kate's back ached. She tried to shift position on the couch. The weight of Hutch's arm across her made her smile. She tried to remember the last time she'd slept the whole night through.

Hutch stirred. His eyes brightened when they met hers. "Good morning."

Kate fought the impulse to brush back the sandy hair that had fallen across his brow.

A loud noise broke the early morning silence. "What was that?" She sat up. "Was that a car?"

The next sound she heard was a key in the lock. "What the fuck?" Jack's voice filled the room. "I drive half the night to get here and this is what I find?" His gesture encompassed the room while his steely eyes focused on the bodies on the couch, the discarded quilt and the empty wine bottle.

"You're back! What time is it?" Kate jumped up and straightened her tank top.

His focus moved to her. "Not soon enough by the

looks of things."

"No, no." Kate shook her head. "We fell asleep. Nothing happened."

Hutch stood and got between Kate and Jack. "She's right, Jack. Take it easy."

"Get out of my way, you prick. This is my wife you're screwing. *My* wife." Jack's face was crimson, his eyes bloodshot. The pulse at his temple throbbed.

"Hutch and I were talking last night and fell asleep. That's all," Kate said.

She was stunned when Jack took a swing at Hutch, who ducked. "What are you doing?" she cried. "Have you lost your senses?"

Jack came closer to Hutch. "Fight like a man, goddamn it!"

"I'm not going to fight you, Jack. Nothing happened." Hutch's voice was calm.

"Jack, please." Kate laid a hand on his forearm.

"Is that all you can say?" He spit the words at her. "You're fucking my best friend for Christ's sake!" He grabbed her arm and shook her.

"Stop. You're hurting me."

"Good." He tightened his grip.

Hutch tackled Jack from behind and knocked over a reading lamp. "That's enough. Let her go."

Jack released Kate with a shove and wheeled around to face Hutch. "Don't you ever tell me what to do with my own wife."

Kate watched in disbelief as Jack's fist connected with Hutch's jaw in a bone-crunching blow. Hutch lost his balance and staggered backward over the coffee table. The wine bottle hit the floor and shattered. Holding his jaw, he looked up at

Jack and then at the blood running through his fingers and down his arm. Jack was on him again, pummeling his face, his shoulders, anywhere he could make contact.

"Stop!" Kate screamed and clutched at Jack's arm. He shook her off like a piece of lint. She lost her balance and landed in a heap on the floor.

Hutch regained his footing. He elbowed Jack in the ribs and kneed him in the groin. Jack doubled over in pain, gasping. "You son of a bitch."

Kate got up, ignoring the pain in her right hip, and brought wet towels from the kitchen. Hutch held one to his face. Jack slid to the floor and placed his head on his knees, the towel in a wet clump beside him.

"I can't believe this. Are you two through or are you going to finish it off and kill each other?" She looked at her husband. "*Nothing* happened. Why won't you believe me?"

After wiping his face with the towel, Jack leaned his head against the wall. "You've played me for a fool for the last time." Kate didn't know if he was talking to her or to Hutch.

Jack groaned as he got to his feet. Clutching his ribs, he stood as straight as he could. "I want to kill you both right now, I swear to God."

"We fell asleep. That's all," Hutch said. "But you've been a dick, Jack, and you know it."

"*I've* been a dick? Am I the one fucking *your* wife?" Jack laughed. "Oh, yeah, that's right. You couldn't hold on to your wife. Couldn't satisfy the little whore."

Hutch moved toward Jack but Kate stepped between them. "Believe what you want, Jack. But don't play the righteous husband." She was close enough to smell the stale booze on his breath. "Do you think I'm stupid? I heard her. What's her name this time? Brittany? Another Monique?" Her voice was even, resigned. "Where'd you meet this one? Work? An out-of-town conference? A strip joint? I've been here before, remember? I'm done caring."

"Don't turn this back on me, Kate." He took a step closer.

The heat of Jack's fury scorched her skin. She thought he might strike her but she was done being quiet.

"You're supposed to be so distraught over Tim." He looked at Kate and then Hutch. "It didn't take you long to find comfort."

Jack's last words were meant to hurt her and they did. "Don't you *ever* question my love for Tim," she said. "I'm the one who visited him, listened to him, supported him while you were off doing God knows what. True to form, when I need you most, you take off."

"Believe me, Kate." Jack's laugh was mirthless. "I would never question your love for Tim. He's all you care about, all you've ever cared about. I'm not stupid either."

Kate was stunned into silence. What did that mean?

"And you…" Jack pointed at Hutch. "You just stepped right in like always. But guess what, you don't get to pick up the pieces and console her anymore." He got right in Hutch's face. "Because she's my wife!"

"So act like it, damn it! Be there for her." Hutch looked his friend in the eye. "Grow up, Jack. It's not all about you."

Jack snorted. "You got it all wrong, buddy. It's never been about me, at least not for the last nineteen years."

"What are you talking about?" Kate's heart constricted.

"Are you seriously threatened by your own son, man?" Hutch shook his head. "You're a bigger dick than I thought

279

you were. I'd give anything to have a kid like Tim. You don't know what you've got here. Or how close you are to losing it all."

Jack turned on him like an animal staking his territory. "Who are you to tell me what I have and what I could lose? This is *my* family." He stopped. Eyes shining with sudden clarity, he stared at one and then the other. "How long has this been going on behind my back?"

"I told you. I've never…" Kate searched her brain for the right words.

He grabbed her shoulders. "Never what? Never screwed him? I know that's a lie."

"Jack, it was college. You and I hadn't even met yet." Kate's heart was pounding. Sweat pooled between her breasts.

"No. Not college." Jack released her. His voice was unnaturally quiet. "When we all went to the Vineyard right after Constance left Hutch. Sarah was a baby. No, not a baby. But she was little." He looked at Kate with a keener aware-ness. "We had that big fight. I got drunk and took off for two days. I left you with Hutch. I've always wondered. But I never really thought it was possible. Until now."

The room closed in around her. She couldn't breathe. She reached for something to hold onto. Her vision blurred. *NO!* She screamed in her head.

No one knew. No one could *ever* know.

She made the mistake of glancing at Hutch. She imagined him doing the math. He looked stricken, unsteady, drained of color.

"That was almost twenty years ago," Hutch's voice was hollow. It sounded far away.

Kate watched helplessly as a flood of emotions washed over his face: remembrance, confusion, understanding, and finally betrayal.

Jack watched what he had set in motion. He seized Kate's arms and shook her. "Look at me!" He bellowed, his voice bouncing off the rafters of the cathedral ceiling.

She looked away. Tears streaked her face. Her silence was all the answer he needed.

Breaking all contact, Jack pushed her away. He turned his back and walked to the door without a word. She heard the door slam and the roar of the motor as he left.

She couldn't look at Hutch, afraid of what she'd see.

"Is he right? Tim?" His voice was distant, cold. "Is he my son?"

"Hutch, please." She reached for him.

"No. Don't touch me. For more than nineteen years you kept this from me? Lied to me."

"Let me explain…" But her voice trailed off. What could she possibly say? For twenty years she'd protected this secret, locked it deep in her heart.

"You must have thought me the fool." Hutch's voice was raw. "All the time I spent with him—the games of catch, soccer tournaments, birthdays, ski trips, the Boy Scout campouts I chaperoned when Jack was too busy, his high school graduation, acceptance to college. I loved him, and you played me." He shook his head. "I don't even know you."

She raised her eyes to his, glistening now with tears. Hutch looked shattered beyond repair. He turned to leave. He never looked back.

Kate stood alone as the last thread holding her life together snapped.

~~

The sun had shifted much higher in the sky when Kate finally released her sodden pillow and stumbled from the bed to the bathroom. Splashing cold water on her face, she studied her drawn, haggard reflection in the mirror. Twenty years she'd kept this secret, held it close. Now it had all come out. Her children ... oh God. They would have to be told.

She went downstairs. The room was in shambles—bloody towels on the floor, a broken wine bottle, the dented overturned lamp. Numb, Kate sat on the couch, her hands on her knees. She relived the rage, the violence, the words spewed out in anger that couldn't be taken back. She saw again the hatred and betrayal in Jack's face, the devastated unforgiving look on Hutch's when he'd walked away. Calls to Jack's and Hutch's cells went unanswered.

How many lives had she ruined?

Kate spent the rest of the weekend alone. She called Sarah to say she was fine, and begged off invitations from Ellen and Gil. In her solitude, Kate was consumed with thoughts of how to protect her children from the coming fallout.

40

Come Monday, Kate found herself in the courthouse, which buzzed with activity. She had anticipated heavy traffic and misjudged the driving time to Rutland. The hearing wouldn't begin for another thirty-five minutes.

Kate crossed her legs and shifted her weight. The wooden bench was hard and uncomfortable. She clasped her knee with both hands to stop her leg from shaking. The hands on the large wall clock continued their tortoise-like pace.

Melody Ward's funeral was scheduled to begin in half an hour at the Willow Bend Methodist Church. A picture of her broken and distraught mother the night of the vigil flashed behind Kate's eyelids. She squeezed her eyes tight to obliterate the image as tears leaked from beneath her lashes.

So, Kate sat alone—waiting to learn her son's fate, while Hannah Ward, also alone, prepared to lay her child to rest.

Approaching footsteps intruded. "Mom." Sarah hugged her. "Where's Dad?"

"Oh, Sarah, you're here." Kate quickly wiped her cheeks. "He's meeting us here. He had some things to take care of."

Sarah frowned. "How did you get here? I could have picked you up."

"I have Ellen's car. I'm fine."

"What does Dad have to do that's so important?" Sarah shook her head. "Never mind, I don't want to know." Sarah sat next to her mother. "Look, here comes Hutch. I knew he'd be here." She stood and walked toward him.

Kate's body was fused to the bench, her eyes fixed on the grimy institutional beige wall in front of her.

Hutch kissed Sarah's cheek and gave her his full attention. "Where's Joe?"

"He's working, couldn't get the day off."

The bailiff approached. "Come on." Hutch placed his hand on Sarah's back. "They're ready to open the courtroom. Is your Dad here?" He looked up and down the hall.

"He's supposedly taking care of something," Sarah said and glanced at Kate. "He'd better get here."

"Do you want to go in or wait for Jack?" Hutch addressed Kate but his eyes remained on Sarah.

He can't even look at me! Kate said nothing. His face showed little evidence of the fight.

Sarah answered for them both. "Let's just go in, Mom. We can't be late."

They sat in the bench right behind the defense attorney's table. Sarah made room for Hutch but he shook his head. She frowned. "Are you sitting with Tim?".

He hesitated. "No. Grady's handling it this morning. You two sit here. Leave room for your Dad. I'll sit in back."

He sat three rows behind them. Kate felt his eyes burn

into her back. Or maybe she only thought they did. *Where the hell was Jack?* Didn't he remember Judge Oberman's insistence on punctuality?

She felt a hand on her shoulder. Startled, she looked up into Andrew Grady's smiling face. That had to be a good sign.

"I think this is going to go well, Kate." He looked at the empty seat in the row and his brow furrowed. "Where's Jack?"

"He'll be here." What else could she say?

The side door opened and a guard led Tim in. He looked pale and was dressed in prison garb. His cheek and eye were healing but still swollen. Her breath caught when she saw he was handcuffed. Why? Weren't they going to let him go?

The bailiff's voice boomed. "All rise. The honorable Amelia Oberman presiding."

Kate heard the back door to the courtroom open and close quietly. It sounded like someone tripped and then stumbled into one of the back rows. She didn't turn around but she knew.

Sarah whispered. "Dad's here." Kate continued to stare ahead.

Grady, the state's attorney, and the judge took turns speaking. It sounded as if the words were being filtered through a long hollow tube. Kate's eyes and all her attention were focused on Tim. In her peripheral vision, she was aware of the two attorneys standing and sitting and approaching the judge's bench. This was taking so long. Why didn't they just let him go? Sarah grabbed Kate's hand and brought her awareness to what the prosecutor was saying.

"Therefore, the State of Vermont requests that the charges of second degree murder and aggravated sexual assault of a child against Timothy Rourke be dismissed. In addition, since the owners of the boat have withdrawn their complaint, we request that the charge of boat theft also be dismissed. Pursuant to the charge of underage drinking, the State recommends accelerated rehabilitation since Mr. Rourke has no priors."

All the charges! Kate squeezed Sarah's hand.

Both attorneys sat. The room quieted as the judge read the file. It seemed to Kate that this went on endlessly. Was she reading every page? Didn't the lawyers just explain the whole thing? Weren't the DNA test results in the file? Couldn't the lawyers just tell her that the *real* killer was arrested and awaiting arraignment and trial? She looked at Tim who seemed to be trying very hard to remain calm and not fidget, despite the jerking rhythmic movements of his legs.

Judge Oberman laid her glasses on top of the file and nodded to the bailiff, who announced, "Will the defendant please rise."

Tim and Andrew Grady stood. The rush of blood throbbing in Kate's ears threatened to drown out everything. She held Sarah's hand as if it were all that tethered her to her seat.

The judge looked out on the courtroom. "Thank you all for your attention and your patience. I believe strongly in our justice system. It works. However, it is not infallible. When a mistake is made, it is our responsibility to set things right." She turned toward Tim. "Timothy Rourke, I have reviewed the new evidence submitted by the state. It appears that you have been unjustly accused of a heinous crime. In addition, you have been held without bail in a state correctional facility for the past week. It is the opinion of this court that the charges of second degree murder and aggravated sexual assault of a child be dismissed without prejudice as well as the charge of boat theft."

Kate exhaled and let her shoulders relax. Grady and Tim did not move but the crowd reacted, murmuring in agreement or displeasure. Judge Oberman banged the gavel. "Quiet. If necessary, I will instruct the bailiff to remove all spectators."

When it was silent, she continued. "As for the charge of underage drinking, the defense would like to see those charges dismissed as well and expunged from the defendant's record. However, underage drinking is of serious concern to this court and should be to society at large. It is illegal and not something to be taken lightly."

The judge looked at Tim. "Mr. Rourke, by your own admission, you were drinking the night of Melody Ward's death. While the court recognizes that you are not directly responsible for Miss Ward's death, your irresponsible behavior contributed to the circumstances in which Miss Ward found herself later that evening."

Kate couldn't believe what she was hearing. What was happening?

"It is the ruling of this court that you complete a six-hour alcohol education program prescribed by the court. In addition, you will be required to complete fifty hours of community service, the entirety of which are to be fulfilled talking to high school and college students about this experience. You will be assigned a probation officer who will certify completion of the education program and verify the community service hours, at which time your record will be expunged.

"I have seen the horrific results of excessive drinking too many times. It is my hope, Mr. Rourke, that you will learn from this experience and take responsibility for your actions in the future. Mr. Grady, your client is free to go once he meets with his appointed probation officer."

Kate registered the bang of the gavel and then heard the bailiff say, "All rise." She got to her feet and grabbed her son. It felt so good to hold him.

"Kate," Grady said. "As soon as we meet with the probation officer and Tim signs for his personal items, we'll be out. Wait for us in the corridor. It shouldn't take long."

"Thank you," Kate said and hugged Sarah as they watched Tim and Grady leave. She turned and saw Jack and Hutch leave through opposite doors.

"What's going on, Mom?" Sarah had a puzzled look on her face.

Kate shook her head. How could she even begin to answer?

They walked together into the corridor. For Kate, every minute ticked away like an hour. "Where is he?" She checked her watch again.

"It really hasn't been that long," Sarah said. "And what's with Dad and Hutch? They're standing at opposite ends of the hallway and nobody's here with us."

"Mom!" It was Tim!

Kate put her arms around her son. She didn't want to let him go and reached up on tiptoes to kiss his cheek.

Jack and Hutch came at the same time. They hugged him and slapped him on the back.

"Way to go!" Jack said.

"I knew the truth would come out." Hutch smiled at Tim.

Kate saw the wet sheen in Hutch's eyes before he turned away.

Grady was right behind Tim. "There he is, the man of the hour." Jack clasped Grady's hand in both of his. "Nice work, Counselor."

"Is everyone coming back to the house?" Sarah asked. "We need to celebrate." She held her brother around his waist.

Grady looked at Kate. "Thanks, but I have some things to take care of. I have a client coming in right after lunch."

"Thank you so much." She shook his hand. "We are so grateful for all you've done."

"I'll be in touch regarding the probation process. Tim, I'll call you tomorrow." Grady left.

Sarah turned to Hutch. "Let's go."

"Sorry, pumpkin. Another time. This is a time for family. I'll see you real soon."

"But you *are* family," Tim added.

Hutch hugged Sarah and Tim and left without acknowledging Kate or Jack.

Kate saw the confusion on her children's faces, felt the emptiness inside her. She pushed her feelings down and smiled. "Let's go home, guys."

41

They arrived at the lake in a caravan: Kate and Tim, Sarah, and Jack bringing up the rear.

"I gotta get out of these clothes and take a shower." Tim took off his shoes and disappeared into his room.

"Sarah, can you help me get the salads on the table?" Kate was already at the refrigerator.

"What a surprise! Mom made food, her solution to every problem." Jack popped the top of a Heineken.

Kate ignored him. She saw Sarah shoot him a cold look.

"Give her a break, Dad," Sarah said. "I don't know what's up with you two, but do you really have to start on the beer already? Didn't you hear anything the judge said?"

"I'm not underage." Jack shrugged and went onto the deck.

Sarah turned to Kate. "What's going on, Mom?"

Kate shook her head as they continued to get lunch

ready. She was barely keeping it together. "I can't. Not now."

Barefoot and smelling of soap, Tim came back into the kitchen. Scowling, he looked from one to the other. "What?"

"Nothing." Kate forced a smile. "Let's eat."

The four of them sat at the table, the tension palpable on what should have been a happy day. Attempts at conversation were stilted and went nowhere.

Tim set his fork down. "Will somebody please tell me what the hell is going on? I just got released from prison, cleared of a murder charge. Murder! We're supposed to be celebrating. Mom and Dad won't even look at each other. I know I screwed up big time. But now everyone knows *I ... didn't ... do ... it!*" He looked at his parents. "Can't you let it go?"

Kate placed her hand on top of his and squeezed. "Tim, it's not that. You're right. This *is* a day for celebration. The day we've all been waiting for."

"I don't think this is about you, Tim," Sarah said. "Am I right, Mom?"

Jack was at the fridge getting another beer. "Oh, it's about you all right, Tim. But not the way you think."

"Jack, shut up!" Kate was on her feet. "Just shut up. Don't do this. Please." She had never yelled at Jack, certainly had never told him to shut up. Sarah and Tim looked stunned.

"What's happening? Mom? Dad?" Sarah's voice was that of a little girl.

Jack came back to the table. "Your Mom and I are having some problems. I'm going to be moving out for awhile."

"No." "Why?" Both kids spoke at once.

Jack looked at them, turning his face away from Kate. "I'm in some financial difficulty. My business isn't doing well.

But that's nothing for the two of you to worry about. We'll figure it out, your Mom and me. But right now we need some time apart."

"That's crap," Tim said. "How's that going to fix anything?"

"How bad is it, Dad? Be straight with us." Sarah pushed her plate away.

Kate waited. He seemed to be weighing how truthful to be. "Tell them," she said.

"I'm probably going to lose the business." His voice was calm. "I've looked at the numbers over and over. Adding legal fees, filing for bankruptcy is probably the only option."

"So, it's my fault?" Tim laid both hands on the table.

"No, no. I didn't mean that," Jack said. "I've re-mortgaged the house in Connecticut already. If we sell this house, we can make it work. I've spoken to a couple of realtors—"

"You what?" Kate slapped her hand on the table and rattled the dishes. "Look at me!" She stood in front of Jack. "This is too much. Even for you."

"Sell the lake house? NO," Sarah pleaded. "There has to be another way."

"You can't!" Tim jumped up from the table and knocked over two glasses. Water ran onto the floor but nobody seemed to notice. "This sucks. Great welcome home, Dad. Thanks a lot." He left the room and banged his bedroom door.

"Nice, Dad. You know what he's been through. What we've all been through. This couldn't have waited?" Sarah walked toward her own room. She stopped and looked over her shoulder. "I have to agree with Tim on this one. It does suck!"

Jack said nothing and pounded up the stairs to their

bedroom.

Kate took a minute to settle down, then followed him up. "What are you doing?" She stood at the foot of their bed.

"Isn't it obvious? I'm packing."

"You're going to leave them like this?" She pulled a folded shirt out of his hand.

"What more is there to say? You can blame yourself for this." He grabbed the shirt and jammed it into his overnight bag.

"Oh no, you're not putting this on me. *I* didn't re-mortgage the house. *I* didn't run the business into the ground. *I* didn't borrow money to pay off casino debts."

That made him stop. She enjoyed the look of surprise on his face.

"That's right, Jack. Do you think I'm stupid?" She paused.

He took a step toward her. In a measured tone, seething with white-hot anger, he leaned into her. "*I'm* not the one who fucked around. I'm not the one who's been living a lie for nineteen years." He grabbed her chin tight enough to leave marks. "I'm not the one with a bastard child."

His words sliced into her. Venom seeped into the wound.

"I can't forgive you and neither will he. You've lost us both."

A small gasp had Kate and Jack turning together. Sarah and Tim stood transfixed at the open bedroom door. How much had they heard?

Jack picked up his bag and pushed past his children. "Sorry, guys. I have to get out of here."

Kate heard the Tahoe start up. He had left her to pick up the pieces of their children's fractured lives. Alone.

"What's happening, Mom?"

"What was Dad talking about?"

"Do you have another child somewhere?"

The barrage of questions ripped into her like rapid-fire bullets.

Kate crossed to them. "Come in and sit. I'll tell you everything." Truth was powerful. It had the capacity to heal—and to tear her family apart.

She led them to the window seat in the master bedroom. The window faced east, framing what the kids used to call "the good morning mountain." When they were little, they sat there each day to watch for the first sign of the sun peeking over the evergreens.

Kate watched them now, looking confused and so young. What she would say in the next minutes would set the course for the rest of their lives. She sat opposite them. Leaning in, she took each of their hands and sought wisdom, and the words that eluded her.

"First of all, your Dad and I love you both very much and we always will. Nothing can ever change that. What we're going through right now, none of it is your fault. None of it."

"What's going on, Mom?" Sarah met her mother's eyes straight on. "What was all that about?"

"How much did you hear?"

"Enough," Sarah said and pulled her hand away.

"Do you have another kid?" Tim asked.

"No. There's no other child." Her chest grew tight. She swallowed the knot in her throat.

"Does this have something to do with Hutch? Dad wouldn't even talk to him," Sarah said.

Kate looked at her wise and observant daughter. This capable young woman she had raised was not going to give her an inch.

"Okay." Kate straightened her shoulders and took a deep breath. "Dad and I have had our problems. Every marriage does. You got an inkling of some of them earlier, and more in what you overheard just now.

"Dad had responsibilities at work. He had to go home. I did my best to hold it together here. Sometimes it wasn't easy." She didn't elaborate. They knew nothing of the vigil.

She looked at Tim. "I wanted so badly just to get you out of that place. When I saw you Friday, I was frantic. You had been attacked. The evidence had cleared you. And you still weren't free to go!" She tightened her fists.

"I called Dad so many times. Finally, he answered. But he was with someone and couldn't talk. Said he couldn't get home until the hearing."

"Was it a woman?" Sarah turned her face and stared out the window.

How could she tell them about the sultry voice in the background? "Let's just say I was upset. I needed your Dad and he wasn't available."

"So what did you do?" Tim asked.

"I cried. I was numb. Then I took a long hot shower. I was on the deck when Hutch stopped by with take-out for dinner. He wanted to update Dad and me on the upcoming hearing and Grady's unsuccessful attempts to have you moved for your safety. Hutch knew how upset I was and assumed Dad was back.

"After we ate and talked, I was exhausted and fell asleep on the couch. Hutch did too. Dad came in around four a.m. and went ballistic, jumped to all the wrong conclusions. *Nothing* happened. But he wouldn't believe me."

Guilt over what could have happened seized her. She

and Hutch had come so close to acting on old feelings. She struggled not to let her face betray her.

"I can understand why Dad would be upset if he found you and Hutch asleep on the couch. He knew you'd been together in college," Sarah challenged her.

"That was before I even met your Dad." Kate sat back, weary.

"Shut up, Sarah," Tim said. "You know Mom would never do anything. And Dad should too."

Kate allowed herself to relax a little.

Then he sucked in a big breath. "I want to know about the baby."

Tim's words hung in the air. No one spoke.

While Kate searched for words, she realized that Sarah held her brother's hand. She looked at her children and braced herself. *How am I going to do this? It will destroy everything.*

Her children sat together on the window seat like they were five and two years old again. "This is the part I never wanted you to know, either of you. I'll tell you the truth. Just remember that I love you both, more than anything in the world."

"Just tell us," Sarah said in a monotone voice.

"When you were almost three, Sarah, we rented a house on Martha's Vineyard. I don't know if you remember. We planned to go with Hutch and Constance, but they got divorced that winter. We convinced him to come with us.

"Dad and I were fighting a lot back then. One night he stormed out and was gone for two days. I was a mess. I had a two-and-a-half-year-old and didn't know where my husband was or if he was coming back. Hutch found him. They got into a fist fight and Hutch came back alone."

Kate couldn't look at her children. She knew what her

next words would do to them, to their family.

"No!" Sarah was shaking her head. "I don't want to hear this."

Tim said nothing.

"Marriage is a sacred vow," Kate said. "I broke that vow one time. But even one time is unforgivable. There is no excuse."

"You fucked him!" Sarah was on her feet, her voice accusing.

"Sarah, please." Her daughter's words rammed into her with more force than Jack's ever could.

"Did Dad find out?" Sarah asked.

Kate shook her head. "No. Not then."

"I can't listen to anymore of this. You act like you're so perfect—the perfect mother, the perfect wife. It's all a lie!"

"I made a mistake, a big mistake. I can't change that. But I have spent my life since then trying to be the best mother, the best wife I can." She reached for Sarah.

Her daughter recoiled and backed away. "Don't touch me."

"You said Sarah was almost three when that happened?" Tim's voice trembled.

Kate pushed her hands through her hair and prayed to anyone who would listen to get them through these next few minutes.

"Is that when you got pregnant?" The words were barely audible. "With me?" The shock and disbelief in his eyes gave way to anger.

She sat down next to him. "I love you, Tim," she said and prayed he could hear that love.

He pushed her away and stood up. "You lied to me my whole life!" He looked out the window and then leveled his eyes on her. "Now it makes sense. Why I was never good at sports, why I never measured up to Dad's expectations." He was screaming. "He hates me. *I'm* the bastard child!"

"No. It's not like that." She went to him but he turned away. "Dad and I both love you. We've always loved you. We've given you the best we have to give. You are an extraordinary person and we are very proud of you." She promised them the truth and had to say it all. "You also have the best of Hutch in you—the caring, the sensitivity, the steadiness."

He pivoted and looked at her hard, the child in him gone. "Yeah, real caring and sensitive. He didn't want me either."

"He didn't know. And neither did Dad. Not until this weekend. You were the secret I treasured and kept locked in my heart." He was slipping away from her. "I have always loved you." She reached for him.

"NO." He stepped away. "You lied to everyone. Who are you?" Face streaked with tears, Tim turned to his sister.. "Are you leaving? Wait for me."

Kate followed them out of the room. "Wait. Please." She begged from the upstairs landing.

Tim looked up and spoke in a cold voice that hurt her more than if he had screamed. "I need to get out of here. Now. Away from you." He closed the door.

Feeling hollowed out like a shell that's been tossed onto the sand, she collapsed on the top step. She had no more tears. It was so much worse than she could have imagined.

Everything was gone.

42

February

Soft, sugary snow drifted down, covering the frozen lake. Ice
fishing shanties dotted the wide expanse. Off to the right,
someone had cleared an area of snow, an invitation to local
kids for a pick-up hockey game.

Wrapped in an Irish knit cardigan, Kate stood looking
out the French doors. A foot of new snow covered the deck.
Tiny figures with sleds darted up and down the steep hill on
the far shore. Bare trees exposed in sharp relief the old
abandoned shack, stripped now of all cover, much like her
long-hidden secrets.

Kate shivered as the winter chill penetrated the glass
panes and seeped into her bones.

She turned away and surveyed the mostly empty
space. This once magical place now depleted, abandoned. The
family had come separately to take what they wanted, each of
them traveling now in individual orbits.

Kate wrapped the last of her personal keepsakes—the piece of slate painted "I love you Mom" by Sarah at age eight, the beaded bracelet Tim made at six—and taped the box. She closed her eyes and in her mind, she heard the sounds of children laughing and running through the house. She hoped the new owners would fill it with love, their children with squeals of joy. Maybe one day they too would find a turtle, paint their initials on its back with Bubble Gum Pink nail polish, and spend the rest of the summer looking for it.

Wiping a tear, for the good times and for all that might have been, Kate wished for the hundredth time she'd had the money to buy Jack out. She hadn't seen or talked to him since the divorce. It had been bitter and contentious. No surprise there. Connecticut's "equitable distribution of property" was meaningless in the end. By the time Jack's debts were paid off, there wasn't much left to distribute, equitably or otherwise. They'd lost the business as well as the Fairfield house. But having to sell the lake house—that was the worst.

Kate walked through the silent house. She saw the outline on the bedroom wall where Sarah's poster of Nick Lachey and "98 Degrees" had hung. She fingered the hook in Tim's room that had held his basketball hoop laundry bag and smiled at the marks on the floor where a seven-year-old Tim had tried out new hockey skates. She opened the linen closet and touched the carved lines on the doorjamb where they had marked the children's height each Memorial Day.

Upstairs she entered the void that had been the master bedroom. Nothing of them remained, all destroyed that July day when everything imploded.

Downstairs she buttoned her coat, wound the wool scarf around her neck and hefted the last box. She locked the door and took a long, last look at the lake. Everything loaded, she drove down the driveway and didn't look back.

Ahead of schedule, Kate drove into town and parked in front of Jenny's. She stepped out and looked around, despite the sub-zero temperature. She would miss Willow Bend.

The warmth of the wood burning stove felt good as Kate entered the store. Rubbing her gloved hands together, she was struck by the sensation of going back in time—the worn pine floors, the smell of fresh pies and rich coffee, the antique cash register and huge wheel of Vermont cheddar on the polished oak counter. So much was the same; yet, everything was different.

"Is the closing today, Kate?" Jenny came around the counter to hug her. "We're going to miss you."

"Thanks, Jenny. I'm going to miss you too."

"Keep in touch, okay?"

Kate nodded but knew she would never return to Willow Bend.

The cowbell over the door clanged and a cold blast of air blew in. Norm Johnson and Hannah Ward came in and stamped snow off their boots. They laughed and warmed their hands by the stove. Ms. Ward looked thinner and wore fashionable jeans. She shook the snow off the hood of her parka and revealed auburn highlighted hair cut in stylish layers.

"How was the graduation ceremony at the police academy last night?" Jenny asked.

"Very nice," Constable Johnson said. "Travis will make a good law enforcement officer. Willow Bend is lucky to get him."

"Do you think you'll miss it, Norm?" Jenny placed two raspberry corn muffins and coffees on a tray.

"Nope. Getting too old for that game." The constable

turned and saw Kate. "Mrs. Rourke, it's good to see you."
They shook hands and he picked up the tray.

Hannah Ward stepped forward. "I want to thank you,
Mrs. Rourke. I should have done this a long time ago. Without
your call to Norm that night, no one but me would have been
looking for Mel." She extended her hand.

"You're welcome." Kate shook her hand and watched
them walk to a table in the corner. She smiled as Constable
Johnson put his free arm around the small woman's shoulders.
She hoped Mel's mother would find happiness.

As she was leaving, Kate noticed a display of beautiful
handmade wooden bowls, richly crafted pepper mills and pens
on a shelf by the door. She studied the excellent workmanship
and wondered who the artist was. She picked up the cream
colored embossed card—Norm Johnson: Woodworker and
Designer.

The sun was shining a half hour later when Kate
stepped out of the lawyer's office. She drove north past the
wrought iron gates of Ethan Allen College. Tim was no longer
a student there. She knew from Sarah that Tim liked his job
working with inner-city teens in Rutland's drug and alcohol
program. Seven months and her son still refused to speak to
her. But Kate hadn't given up. She wouldn't.

It had taken time for Sarah to talk to her and accept her
calls. Thanks to Joe, mother and daughter were finding their
way back to each other.

She chose to believe a new beginning was possible for
all of them.

She had one more thing to do.

~~

The scenic drive to Woodstock, Vermont, nestled on the banks of the Ottauquechee River, wound through small towns and villages. Kate passed picturesque covered bridges as she approached the town center, resembling a Currier and Ives print. The Woodstock Inn, a grand old building set back from the road, dominated one side of the town green.

Kate drove to the main entrance where a valet took her keys and a porter retrieved her suitcase. Entering the lobby, Kate was wrapped in warmth and elegance. Heavy comfortable-looking chairs and side tables with muted lamp light sat grouped around a crackling fire. Guests milled about in the adjourning public rooms and bar.

A bellman accompanied Kate to her suite, an extravagance she allowed herself this one time. The sitting room had large windows that overlooked the expansive grounds she knew came alive with color in the spring and summer. She went into one of the bedrooms and sat on the edge of the king-size bed. Doubt and self-recrimination flooded her. *What am I doing here? What was I thinking?* She thought about the call she had made earlier that day.

She'd had no contact with him since he'd walked out that horrific morning. She had hurt him deeper than she'd thought possible, upended everyone's life, destroyed her marriage and her family. She had caused more pain than she'd ever thought herself capable.

She would have a glass of wine in the lobby and then check out. She'd stay in a small motel somewhere off the highway and head back to Connecticut first thing in the morning.

Downstairs, Kate sipped a glass of cabernet by the fireplace, then wandered over to the floor-to-ceiling windows that fronted the Inn. She leaned against the wall and watched

303

as snowflakes fell softly in the early evening dusk.

Black wrought iron lamps, meant to resemble old-time gas lanterns, lined the semi-circular drive and cast pools of soft yellow light on the snow. She tried not to notice the couples, bundled up to ward off the cold as they strolled the grounds.

Then she saw it. The white Beamer drove in and parked at the valet.

She straightened. A small, unbelieving smile lit her face.

Acknowledgments

Many people helped to make this dream of writing a
book a reality.
To them I owe my utmost thanks.

My late parents, Pat and Buddy (Daniel) Sheehan, who taught
me to believe in myself and to believe I could do anything I set
my mind to.

My teachers who gave me the tools I needed to accomplish
this.

Present and past members of the Wethersfield Writers' Circle:
Cristina, Gloria, Jon, Liz, Martha, Robyn, Sara, Annie,
Bobbie, Elizabeth, Karen, and Sandra. These women
encouraged me throughout the process and critiqued more
versions of this novel than they probably ever wanted to read!

My editor, Eileen Albrizio, who worked with me to make this
book the best it could be.

Sara Strecker for her expertise in helping me format and
publish this book, and for her artistic creativity in helping to
design the cover.

Kathy Maxey Scarcello for her amazing photograph of the lake
for the cover.

My countless friends whose encouragement kept me going. You know who you are! And to my lake friends, Ellen is all of you.

Special thanks to my family who never gave up on me.

My husband Rich who patiently afforded me as much uninterrupted time to write as I needed, even when other things were pressing. He willingly read numerous drafts of this book, and sometimes knew just the perfect turn of phrase when I was stuck. A retired police captain, he was my in-house resource for all things police related. Any errors are mine.

My daughter Kristen, always my first reader and champion since she was a little girl, also read countless drafts of the novel and gave invaluable suggestions regarding the plot and characters, as well as the reactions, interactions, and speech patterns of the teen characters. A photographer, Kristen shot the author picture and helped with cover design.

My son Michael, my go-to-guy for all things technical, helped me solve computer problems and glitches, showed me how to back-up all my work, and "found" the manuscript more than once when I called him in tears to say "I lost it all!"

My love and thanks to each of you.

About the Author

Diane Sheehan Shovak was born and raised in Boston, Massachusetts. She moved to Connecticut in 1970 to pursue graduate study and a career in Speech-Language Pathology.

Diane has always loved writing for her own enjoyment and to chronicle family events, especially their summers spent on Lake Saint Catherine in Wells, Vermont. Since retiring, she joined a writing group, the Writers' Circle, and published personal essays, a short story, and a poem in two books published by the Circle: Spilled Ink in 2013 and Here Joseph, You Take the Baby: A Christmas Anthology in 2016. She posts regularly on the blog site ctwriterscircle.wordpress.com

Deceit is her first novel.

Diane lives with her husband of forty-two years in Wethersfield, Connecticut. They have two grown children and two handsome, remarkable grandsons.

Contact Diane at dianeshovak@yahoo.com

Follow her on Facebook at Diane Sheehan Shovak and at Connecticut Writers Circle